Branded Wives
Erin Wade

© 2017 Erin Wade
ISBN-13:978-1981406395
ISBN-10:1981406395
www.erinwade.us

DEDICATION:

To the one that has always supported me in everything I have ever undertaken. You have encouraged me and have always been my biggest fan. Life is sweeter with you. Erin

* * * * * * * *

A Special Thank You to my wonderful and witty beta, **Julie Versoi**. She makes me a better storyteller.

Contents

Chapter 1

Ash Denton smiled as she checked the amount of her royalty payment for the month. Her new murder mystery was already the number one best-selling book on *The New York Times* list.

She closed her laptop as her partner placed a steaming cup of hot coffee on her desk.

"Denton, Layne, in my office, now," Captain Ames yelled from his doorway.

"We got a slice and dice in Westover Hills. Here's the address." Ames didn't waste time with pleasantries.

"Good Morning to you too, Captain," Colten Layne, grinned at his boss.

"Did you hear me say Westover Hills, Layne," Ames grimaced. "A quick resolution on this will allow me to keep all the Richie Riches in this town happy and my ass intact. Move it."

"Male or female?" Denton asked.

"Woman. May be Laura Trent. Thirty-nine. Very wealthy." Ames barked.

"Your ride or mine," Ash asked as they strode from the office.

"I'll drive," Colt said. "That way you can take notes, just in case you find anything book worthy in this case."

"Probably a domestic dispute," Ash wrinkled her brow. "In my ten years on the force, we've had only one homicide call to Westover Hills and it was a domestic."

"The captain will be happy if we close this one before the press grabs it," Colt nodded.

"Laura Trent," Ash dug into her memory, "isn't she married to Jeb Trent? They support that orphanage in Ecuador."

"Yeah," Colt agreed. "She was Miss Texas several years ago, first runner-up to Miss America. Her last name was London. Old family money on both her parent's sides. Her ancestors came over on the Mayflower or something like that."

The Trent estate sat on five perfectly manicured acres. Heavy wrought iron gates stood open to allow the authorities to come and go.

Ash examined the crime scene as Colt took information from the first officer to arrive at the home.

The dead woman was Laura Trent, the wife of second-generation oil magnate Jeb Trent. According to the housekeeper, who had found the body, Jeb Trent was in Argentina on an oil deal.

Laura Trent's body had been propped up in bed to look like she was reading a book. She was dressed in a blue, silk gown. Her hair and makeup were perfect as if she were expecting a visitor. The only thing out of place in the bedroom was the inordinate amount of blood that stained the downy comforter. Her throat was sliced from ear to ear. There was a deep stab wound in her abdomen,

A red rose was tucked behind the woman's ear. A single word was branded into her forehead, "Whore."

"Branded," Ash snorted. "Who would cowboy up and brand someone?"

"I'd say death has a brand," Colt commented. "How'd you like to meet your maker with the word *whore* branded on your forehead?"

There was no sign of struggle. A large amount of blood on the bed told Ash she had been in the bed when the killer slashed her throat. The officers found no murder weapon in the house.

Ash knew she would have to wait for the medical examiner's report to find out if the killer had molested Laura.

Colt looked over the scene. "I never get used to seeing a beautiful woman murdered," he said quietly. "What a waste."

"Anyone see anything?" Ash asked.

"Nothing," Colt said. "Once one enters the gates, the estate is surrounded by an eight-foot fence with high hedges on both sides of it. Very private.

"Whoever was here knew the gate code. It was accessed at nine last night. They disarmed the house alarm system at the same time. The gate opened automatically at two this morning, allowing a car to leave. I am betting the time of death was between nine last night and two this morning."

"Let's turn CSI loose in this room." Ash closed her notepad. "Hopefully they can lift some prints, hair or semen. A nice DNA match would be great." She knew she was dreaming. That would be too easy.

"I demand to see my daughter," an authoritative voice rose above the din of onlookers and police officers in front of the house.

Ash braced herself for the first encounter with the family. She always hated to tell a family member their loved one was dead. It was even harder when the victim had been as viciously murdered as Laura Trent had.

Vivian London was a beautiful, older version of her daughter. She wore old money well. Apprehension was already clouding her green eyes.

"Please," she spoke to Ash as if she knew the answer to her question. "May I speak to my daughter?"

Ash took her elbow and led her to a room away from the entryway. She didn't want her to see Laura's body being wheeled to the coroner's waiting van.

"Mrs. London is there someone I can call to be with you?" she asked gently.

"Why would I want…?" the words died on her lips as she realized Ash was about to confirm what she already suspected.

"Laura is dead," Ash ducked her head and repeated the words that always sounded so hollow, "I am so sorry for your loss."

"No! No!" Vivian London's knees buckled. Ash caught her and supported her weight until she could get her to the sofa. Tears ran down her face, leaving tracks on her makeup. "How?"

Now for the even harder part, Ash thought. "She was murdered, Mrs. London. It happened sometime last night."

"Who would want to kill Laura?" Vivian whimpered.

"I don't know, but we will find out," Ash promised.

A broad smile broke across Ash's face as her wife greeted her at the door with an ardent kiss and a glass of wine.

"According to the news, you've had the day from hell, Sergeant Denton," she frowned as she helped Ash slip out of her jacket.

"It suddenly just got better," Ash smiled as she pulled her wife into her arms for another soul-soothing kiss. The buzzing of the oven pulled them from their enjoyment of each other.

She released Lana and picked up both their glasses to follow her to the kitchen. "Something smells wonderful," she said.

"Your favorite," Lana smiled, "Beef Wellington. Sit at the bar so we can visit while I put the finishing touches on dinner."

Ash watched Lana as she moved about the kitchen. She was her world. They had been married four years, and she still couldn't believe Lana had agreed to marry her.

Dr. Lana Denton was gorgeous by anyone's standards. Tall and slim, with thick, black hair that danced around her shoulders, framing the most beautiful face Ash had ever seen. Her dark brown eyes always sparkled when she saw Ash. Ash loved her so much it hurt.

Ash pulled Lana into her arms. Lana smiled at her almost shyly as she gazed into her eyes. "You have to eat first," she murmured against her lips. "Then mama will make it all better."

They lay on the sofa, curled into each other. Dinner had been wonderful. What followed later had been pure magic. Lana always left her breathless.

"I knew Laura Trent," Lana said softly, as she traced circles on Ash's chest. "We worked together on the fund drive for the library. I can't believe anyone would kill her. She was extremely nice. Very down to earth."

"We've ruled out the husband," Ash told her. "He's in Argentina. They're trying to get in touch with him. He's in some god-forsaken area where there's no cell phone service. I hope he doesn't see it on a newscast before we notify him."

"They seemed very much in love," Lana said. "He was crazy about her. He was always dropping by to see her. Much the same way you drop by to see me."

"I feel for the poor guy," Ash said. "If he loved her as much as I love you, he will be living in hell for the rest of his life."

"The ME's doing the autopsy on Laura Trent at nine," Colt said. "Want to join me?"

"Not really," Ash wrinkled her nose, "but I know I have to."

"I heard Doc Mercer broke up with her boyfriend," Colt waggled his eyebrows. "I may take a shot at her. What do you think of her?"

"She's way out of your league," Ash teased.

"Oh! Look who is talking," Colt laughed. "The woman who married one of the top criminal psychiatrists in the county. She is so out of your league. I still don't know what she sees in you."

Colt was teasing, of course. He knew what Lana saw in his partner. At five-nine, and one-hundred-forty pounds, Ash was lean and shapely. The hour a day she spent in the gym honed her already perfect body. With her long, wavy blonde hair and piercing blue eyes, she was a woman that drove men and women crazy. Her damn dimples were just icing on the cake. Ash grinned, showing them to Colt.

"Why don't we double date?" Ash suggested. "Lana and Mercer are good friends. Mercer might even agree to go out with you just to spend time with my wife."

"That's why I keep you for a partner," Colt laughed. "You keep me humble."

"Not an easy task," Ash joked.

Both detectives dodged a rookie as he ran out the double doors of the morgue. They knew he was headed for the men's room to throw up.

"Hey, Doc," Colt grinned at Mercer, "We thought we'd come cut up with you."

Mercer's assistant snorted, trying not to laugh at Colt's morgue humor. The doctor rolled her eyes.

Risa Mercer was one of those Swedish beauties with fathomless blue eyes and full, red lips. Although she was always very cool and professional, Ash suspected she was just as fiery and passionate as Lana. She hoped Colt would find someone like Lana.

Mercer smiled briefly at the two detectives she and her staff referred to as Pretty and Prettier. She led them to the steel table that was now the resting place for Laura Trent.

"Obvious cause of death is the deep laceration across the throat." Mercer started in the no-nonsense voice she used to explain autopsies. "Single deep stab wound to the abdomen."

The ME pulled the sheet down Laura's body as she showed them the damage the perp had done. "What you may not have seen is that he cut off her nipples, and she was pregnant."

Ash glanced at Colt, as an excuse to look away from the dead woman's desecrated body.

"The inscription on her forehead is made with a branding iron." Mercer continued. "She had consensual intercourse with a male about two hours before she died. There was no semen."

"How do you know it was a male?" Colt interrupted her dialogue. "Could have been another woman."

"Depth of penetration," Mercer glared at him.

"Could have used a dildo," Colt countered.

"Lack of abrasions on soft tissue. There are several differences between a male penis and a dildo or fingers. Even you should understand, hard and smooth, Detective Layne."

"A dildo covered with a condom would produce the same results," Colt argued.

"There was also pubic hair present. Unfortunately, nothing from which we could extract DNA." Risa finished.

"I'm not hearing anything that would convince me the killer could only be male. I think we should keep an open mind." Colt shrugged, "You're the forensic pathologist, Doc. I was just asking for my information. It is good to know these things."

"Because you do a large number of autopsies," Mercer glared at him.

Ash gave her partner a "shut up" look and asked a question. "Can you give us a time of death?"

"Between eleven and one," Risa answered. "Based on the progression of digestion, I would say she had a glass of wine, sex, more wine with cheese, and then death. My guess is they had sex, imbibed and fell asleep. The killer slashed her throat while she was sleeping. She never saw it coming."

"I'm certain you are DNA testing the baby?" Ash said.

"Yes, I'll have those results this afternoon."

"Do me a favor, please?" Ash frowned, "don't release the DNA info on the fetus until I get a DNA sample from Jeb Trent? I want to make certain he is the father before we destroy his world."

##

Chapter 2

"Looks like an affair that went bad," Ash made notes in her book, as Colt drove toward Lana's office. "If Trent was in Ecuador, it's a safe bet he wasn't the guy having sex with her the night she died."

Colt nodded his agreement. "Can we agree we don't have anything conclusive to indicate the perp is a man?"

"I have to agree with you," Ash said.

"It is amazing how many women cheat on their spouses. What would you do if Lana cheated on you?" Colt asked.

"I hope I never find myself in that situation," Ash growled. "I don't even want to think about it."

"I doubt you ever will," Colt grinned. "Your lady is crazy about you. For the life of me, I can't figure out why."

Colt pulled the car to the curb and dropped Ash off at Lana's office.

"Thanks, buddy," Ash smiled. "See you in the morning."

Colt watched as Ash disappeared from his rear-view mirror. They had been friends all their lives. They had always had each other's back, even in elementary school.

Colt recalled how crushed he was when Ash had confided in him—at 16—that she was gay. Her admission that she liked girls had destroyed his dream of them marrying and raising a family. *Damn, our kids would have been gorgeous*, he thought.

Ash turned out to be the best wingman a fellow could ever want. She steered him away from the girls that preferred her and introduced him to the girls that really liked him.

Their senior year of high school, the male population was crazy for Mary Lou Arnold. Ash told him not to waste his time. Mary Lou was going to the prom with her.

He smiled. He was glad his best friend had found Lana. She was the perfect woman.

The department frowned on officers moonlighting, but Colt had run his private investigation service long before joining the Fort Worth Police Department. He specialized in catching cheating spouses in compromising positions. Colt's photos had won more high-priced divorce settlements than any other factor in the Dallas-Fort Worth area.

He read the address of his next stakeout as he waited for his Super-Sonic Meal to make its way out the drive-through window.

He parked fifty feet from the gated community of the city's newest council member and waited. He washed down the last of his burger as the gates to the upscale private homes opened. He tailgated on the car entering the community and easily located the address he needed.

He wasn't going to take photos tonight. He always observed for several days to get a feel for his subject's routine. Establishing a pattern in these situations was important.

Around eight, Councilman Manny Martinez backed his silver Mercedes convertible from the garage. Colt made a note of his license plate and followed him.

Martinez had the reputation of being a lady's man. He had skated on accusations ranging from sexual harassment to rape.

Colt suspected that Martinez was the money scrubber for a local drug cartel. The man owned a couple of run down, fast-food chicken places and always seemed to have plenty of money.

The Seventh Street Gang had deemed Martinez the token Hispanic for the City Council. The Seventh Street Gang was a group of influential business leaders that ran Fort Worth. Their endorsement had guaranteed Manny's seat on the council. Colt snorted as he wondered who was using whom in their little arrangement.

Martina Martinez's family had left her a very successful chain of Mexican food restaurants and large land holdings. She was a hard worker and took care of business. Mrs. Martinez was positive her husband was cheating on her. She wanted a divorce that would remove Manny from her life and leave him penniless.

Colt wanted to put Manny Martinez away for running drugs in his town.

Martinez entered the Reata, one of Fort Worth's top restaurants. A valet whisked away the silver Mercedes. Colt parked on a meter across the street and waited.

After an hour, Martinez walked out of the restaurant with a blonde beauty on his arm. They walked next door to the Long Weekend Comedy Club. Colt followed.

The comedy club had theater seating around a stage. Dim lights lit the audience, and the stage had a single spotlight shining on it. Colt let his eyes adjust to the low lighting and looked around for Martinez. He spotted him and his blonde mistress on the sixth row. Bleached blondes always stood out in low lighting. He walked up the far side of the seats then made his way across until he was sitting two rows behind the couple.

The couple snuggled and kissed like two teenagers. Colt detested cheating spouses.

The lights went out in the audience, and the stage lights brightened. Colt could tell from the way Martinez had shifted to his side that his hand was now up the blonde's skirt. She giggled and pushed him away.

Colt slipped out the back of the club. He had seen enough to know his job would be easy. Martinez wasn't very smart.

##

Chapter 3

Dr. Lana Denton reviewed the file of her next patient. There was no doubt the woman had a mental disorder. Lana hoped she had stayed on her meds this week.

Jessica Barton was beautiful. A computer software genius, she owned the state's largest private software security firm. Jessica made seven figures a year. She owned a lake estate with no mortgage and drove a new Lexus. She never revealed this information to Dr. Denton. I wouldn't be good if anyone found out she was under the care of a psychiatrist.

Jessica had one major problem in her life. Women loved her. Tall and shapely, she emanated sex appeal. Women followed her home from the grocery store. Her next-door neighbor was always bringing her dishes she had cooked just for her. The young woman at the dry cleaners insisted on carrying Jessica's clothes to her car, touching her on the way. Waitresses always rubbed all over her, when serving her. At least, that was the way Jessica saw things.

The truth was women paid little attention to Jessica. She hadn't had a real date since high school, and she had trouble maintaining any long-term relationship. Apparently, good looks also needed a personality to attract and hold women. Jessica was very shy. She communicated much better with computers than people.

"You lucky, devil," Jessica said to herself. She straightened her collar as she entered Dr. Denton's office. Lana's brilliant smile told Jessica she had missed her. She wondered how much longer Lana could resist the urge to touch her.

"Have a seat, Jessica," Dr. Denton nodded to the chair in front of her desk.

Jessica ignored her and took a seat on the sofa across the room, forcing Dr. Denton to move from behind her desk to sit in the armchair across from Jessica. She liked looking at Lana's legs. She wished she would wear shorter skirts.

Dr. Denton opened her notebook. Unlike many doctors who had moved to the iPad, Dr. Denton still took her notes on a yellow legal pad.

"How was your week?" Dr. Denton asked. "Any special events you want to share with me?"

Jessica knew that Dr. Denton wanted to hear about her latest escapades with the ladies. She loved it when Jessica described the hot sex she had with her next-door neighbor or the waitress she had spent the weekend shagging.

No doubt, about it Jessica had a delusional disorder. The delusion that was front and center in her life was her raging affair with Dr. Lana Denton. She knew Lana would refer her to another psychiatrist if she ever realized the things Jessica fantasized doing to her.

"Jessica, how have you been?" Lana's question dragged her back to reality.

"Good," Jessica said. "Better than good. Best week of my life. I have a new lover."

That answers that question, Lana thought. *She's off her meds.*

"Anyone I know?" Lana asked.

"Probably," Jessica grinned. "She is a high-society lady, like you."

Lana smiled as she jotted down notes.

"I spent the entire weekend with her," Jessica continued. "Her husband is out of the country. He left her all alone. Someone had to take care of her needs."

"I read in the paper that the firm you work for landed a large contract," Lana said. "That is quite an accomplishment."

"Yes," Jessica shrugged; irritated that she had changed the subject.

She didn't tell Dr. Denton her firm had won the intranet security contract for the city. As far as Dr. Denton knew, Jessica was just a low-level programmer. Lana had no idea Jessica owned the company.

"The article said you and your team spent all weekend installing firewalls and setting up the proper protocols for the city's computers, so they can all talk to one another and share information on a single server maintained by your firm."

"That's why I am taking off the next two days," Jessica nodded. "We worked around the clock transferring their data into our system. We did it on the weekend, so nothing would be interrupted.

"This is a real coup for my firm. We'll be hiring several new software programmers to help with the workload."

"So, you worked all weekend? You didn't spend it with a girlfriend?" Lana clarified. "Have you been taking your meds?"

"Off and on," Jessica grimaced. She hated it when Lana caught her in a lie. "They make me feel funny like my head's in a fog. I didn't take them this weekend. I needed to be clear headed for the move."

Lana shifted in the chair and crossed her legs. Jessica watched her skirt move up her beautiful thigh. She licked her lips as she stared at Lana's legs. She realized there had been a long silence. She slowly raised her eyes from Lana's legs to her eyes. Jessica blushed when she realized Lana knew she was coveting her. She pulled a sofa pillow across her bosom and hugged it.

"Jessica, you must stay on your meds. If you stay on them, they will level out in your system, and you will always feel normal. The head-in-a-fog sensation will go away, and you will be able to function without these hallucinations."

"I'll try," Jessica promised. She didn't want to tell Dr. Denton she preferred the hallucinations to the reality of her life.

##

Ash knocked on the open door then entered the ME's office. "Hey, Risa, give me some good news."

"Not today pretty girl," Risa laughed. "I've got nothing but bad news for you."

Ash groaned. "Lay it on me."

"I lucked out. We had Jeb Trent's DNA in the database from the shooting during that break-in at his office last year. Remember we took DNA from him

20

and all of his employees to disqualify them as suspects?"

"And…" Ash prodded her.

"…and the baby Mrs. Trent was carrying doesn't belong to Mr. Trent."

"Infidelity at its finest," Ash mumbled.

"Yeah," Risa huffed. "Did CSI come up with anything for you?"

"Nada," Ash grunted. "I've hit a dead end on finding anyone who makes branding irons too."

"I am running the baby's DNA through CODIS," Risa continued. "I'll let you know if I get a hit."

"Thanks, Risa."

The doors to the morgue swung open, and Colt escorted a dark-haired man into the room.

"Mr. Trent, this is Dr. Risa Mercer and my partner Ash Denton. Risa, Mr. Trent would like to see his wife's body."

Risa nodded and led Trent to the refrigerator. She pulled out the drawer, marked L. Trent.

Trent stared at is wife's face, and then looked up at the ceiling. He seemed to be fighting to gain control of his emotions.

"The officer informed me of her mutilation," Trent choked.

"Yes, sir. Her nipples were cut from her body," Risa said.

He nodded and turned away. "Is there anything else I should know?"

"Dr. Mercer is waiting on information from the pathologist to complete her report," Ash said gently.

The detective guided Trent from the morgue. "Are you up to filling in a few blanks for us?"

"Thank God for Ash Denton," Risa said as Ash led the grieving man from the room.

"I guess you are now an official member of the Ash Denton fan club, too" Colt commented as he slid the drawer back into the refrigerator.

"Yes," Risa smiled weakly, "I had no words to tell that man his wife was pregnant with another man's baby."

"Another man's baby!" Colt repeated incredulously. "I am betting that's our motive."

Ash leaned back in her chair. She had hit the wall on her new book and the Trent murder case. She had agonized over whether to tell Trent his wife was pregnant with another man's baby.

Lana had helped her with the decision by pointing out that the information would become known eventually. The sooner she told Trent, the better.

Colt had been researching information on a cold case, so Ash had driven to the Trent home and given Jeb the bad news alone. Colt hated doing death notifications. He hated infidelity notifications even more.

Ash could still see the look of utter disbelief in Trent's eyes. The man refused to believe his wife had been cheating on him.

The sound of her cell phone pulled Ash from her thoughts. The ringtone told her it was her beautiful wife.

"Hi, honey," she said.

"Sweetheart," her soft, sultry voice always stirred deep emotions in Ash, "I am leaving the office. See you in half an hour."

"Can't wait. Love you," Ash whispered into the phone.

"Love you, too."

Ash had lived alone until she met Lana, so she had learned to cook, clean and do all the things that make a home. She slid the meatloaf into the preheated oven and made iced tea. She would wait a few minutes before starting the vegetables.

Her home had always been her sanctuary. Lana had made it even more so. They both delighted in having a place that was serene and safe, where they relaxed and worked thru situations thrown at them by the outside world.

##

It had been thirty-five minutes since Lana called. She was probably in heavy traffic. She placed everything in the warming oven and returned to her office.

She smiled at the thirty-six books perfectly lined up on the bookshelf. They represented six years of her life. All had eventually become best-sellers, making her a multi-millionaire.

She wrote under the pseudonym, Adrian Austin. Only Lana and Colt were aware of her literary accomplishments. She loved police work and enhanced all her stories using her day-to-day law enforcement experiences.

The sound of the garage door told her Lana was home. She moved quickly to put dinner on the table.

##

"Dinner was incredible," Lana tiptoed to kiss her wife. She took Ash's hand and led her to the office. She pulled Ash down to sit beside her on the sofa.

"I know we agreed not to bring our work home with us," Lana smiled sheepishly, "but I am dying to know Trent's reaction."

"He was devastated," Ash said. "I can't imagine anything that would hurt more than losing one's wife and then finding out she was unfaithful. I'm certain he isn't involved in his wife's murder."

"I'm having a hard time wrapping my mind around it myself," Lana frowned. "Laura Trent was crazy about Jeb. She talked about him all the time.

"Of course, it is entirely possible to be madly in love with someone and still have sex with someone else," Lana said. "Our Christian ethics have led us to form a society demanding monogamy. The truth is men and women are often tempted to have sex with someone other than their legal partner."

"Wow, Dr. Denton, could you make cheating sound any more clinical." Ash pulled her wife into her arms and kissed her, a deep, satisfying kiss.

"I don't think I could survive if you ever cheated on me," Ash murmured against her lips. "I don't know what I would do."

"There's no danger of that, darling," Lana reassured her. "It's all I can do to keep up with my homework. You'll never find me seeking extracurricular activity."

##

Later Lana pulled on Ash's shirt. "Damn, you are so sexy in that," Ash grinned. Her heart was still beating frantically from their love making.

"That was most enjoyable, darling," Lana said sensuously. "Now I need to work on a couple of cases before we go to bed and continue our evening."

Ash was not surprised to find that Lana had dissolved her writer's block and happily spent the next two hours turning out several new chapters of the book.

Ash was writing a psychological thriller and needed some technical information from her wife. Lana always closed her door when she worked. She was watching videos of clients she had seen earlier in the day. Ash tapped on her door, giving her an opportunity to turn off the player.

"Come in."

"I apologize for interrupting you, but I'm at a crossroad in my story."

"I welcome the break, darling. How can I help?" She laid down her pen and removed her glasses.

"How do you determine when a patient is so dangerous you should notify the authorities?" she asked.

"You mean at what point does the safety of others outweigh doctor-patient privilege?"

Lana furrowed her brow, thinking how to answer her wife's question. "If I feel a patient has harmed or will harm someone, I inform the proper authorities."

"Have you ever had such a patient?"

"Oh, yes, several," she said. "I can't discuss the cases with you. Confidential information!"

"If you ever had a patient that made you feel unsafe, would you tell me?"

'I promise you will be the first to know," she smiled. "Are you at a stopping point?"

"I am," Ash grinned.

"Then, perhaps you would like to shower with me."

It crossed Lana's mind that she should have her wife check out Jessica Barton, but she brushed the idea aside as Ash caught her hand and led her to their bedroom.

##

Chapter 4

Colt slowly crawled through downtown traffic, staying two or three cars behind Manny Martinez's silver Mercedes.

The man finally made his way to the section of West Seventh Street that went out of town toward the city park. He crossed the Trinity River Bridge then turned into Forest Park. He pulled his car into a turnout across from the duck pond.

Colt drove past the Mercedes, parked and walked back to where he could get a clear shot of Martinez. He wondered if the man was meeting the blonde bimbo from Saturday night.

Two men approached Martinez and joined him on the park bench. One man carried a brown leather briefcase. The other carried a sack of bread for the ducks.

Colt shot photos of the three men.

After a brief exchange, both men left, leaving the briefcase. Martinez made a phone call. Colt could hear him laughing. He put the briefcase into the trunk of his car. Colt made photos of all his actions. He took a picture of Martinez's license plate.

Martinez put the top down and drove to gated apartments in the most elite section of Fort Worth. He tapped the keypad and drove in. Colt followed and turned left when Martinez turned right.

Colt pulled his car into the first empty parking space he saw and sprinted around the apartments in time to see Martinez park his car. Colt pulled the visor of his cap down lower.

Martinez walked five doors down to apartment 129. The briefcase was in the trunk. He knew it would be safe for a couple of hours, and that was all he needed.

Colt attached a GPS tracking device to the Mercedes, then walked to the walkway across from the apartment. Suddenly the door burst open, and the blonde charged out, yelling at Martinez. Colt stepped into the tall shrubs beside the apartment window.

"I am not just some booty call you can stick it to anytime you feel like it," the blonde yelled.

"No. No, baby." Martinez tried to soothe her. "That is not why I came here. I came to take you to an early dinner at a nice place. Then maybe later, if you want to thank me…"

He kissed her. Colt was capturing it all on camera.

"Oh, Manny, I'm sorry. I thought you just came by to fuc…" Martinez put his hand over her mouth.

"Get in the car," he hissed. "I'm hungry."

Colt didn't hurry. With the GPS, he could easily find Martinez's car. He pulled up at Eddie V's Prime Seafood as the valet drove away with the Mercedes.

Colt followed the Mercedes into the parking garage and parked one story above where the valet parked the Mercedes. Even though the valet had set the alarms on the convertible, it took Colt less than one minute to pop the trunk and grab the briefcase. He closed the trunk and sprinted to his car, careful to avoid security cameras.

By the time he drove past the Mercedes, the valets had silenced Martinez's alarm and ascertained that no harm had befallen the convertible. No need to alert the owner. "Bird probably flew through here," one of them yelled.

Later that night, Martinez was getting his "Thank you," from the blonde when Colt set off the convertible's burglar alarm. He ran from the apartment in nothing but his underwear, the half-naked blonde was behind him.

From the shadows of the apartment across the walkway, Colt captured some of his best shots.

##

Colt was waiting for Mrs. Martinez when she opened the restaurant at seven the next morning.

"I have some very scenic shots for you," he grinned, as he followed her to her office.

"These will guarantee I won't have to pay spousal support to the little worm." Mrs. Martinez was gleeful as she handed Colt the large manila envelope full of money.

"I don't think you will need to worry about divorcing him," Colt said. "I believe the drug cartel is after him. Remember, you know absolutely nothing about his drug dealings."

"I truly don't," she frowned. "Until you told me, I had no idea of his true business."

##

Colt hid the briefcase behind the false wall in his home. He would turn it into the department later.

He was certain of Martinez's fate when the cartel found out he had lost their money.

##

Chapter 5

"I need some damn results, and I need them quick," Captain Ames growled at his two best detectives. "We have another dead wife. Get over there and let me know what is going on. If this starts to look serial, I want your wife on this, Denton."

"Brandt, Collins," Ames followed them into the bullpen, "we've got a floater in the Trinity. Find out who he is."

"I'll drive," Colt said.

Ash nodded and holstered her Glock. "Where is this one?"

"The Towers," Colt smirked. "With all that money and all that security, how did anyone get to her?"

Ash pushed a button on her phone, calling Risa. "How is the prettiest ME in Texas?" she teased.

"Anxious, McPretty," Risa laughed. "You only call me when someone is dead. You headed to The Towers?"

"Yes, we should be there in ten. How about you?"

"I'm already here. I do wish you two would keep up with me." Risa teased.

"I suspect that would take more than the two of us," Ash laughed.

"Um, I suspect one of you could do it," Risa continued to flirt with the stunning, young detective. "You never know until you try."

"Are we still talking about the crime scene," Ash chuckled uneasily.

"Did I scare you?" Risa laughed as she disconnected the call.

"Damn, Ash, all the women want to sleep with you," Colt laughed. "Wait until I tell Lana."

"Just good-natured teasing," Ash grinned. "Please don't stir up my wife. Risa is Lana's best friend."

"I know," Colt frowned. "Sometimes we just have to find ways to lighten the situation. Risa cuts up with me, too."

"Have you given any more thought to double dating with Lana and me?"

"I don't know," Colt shrugged his shoulders. "Risa is about the most gorgeous woman I have ever met. What chance do I have with her?"

"Okay, now you are just fishing for compliments," Ash grinned. "You know you're movie star handsome."

"Yeah, then why did my wife leave me for another man? I was good to her, Ash. I worked around the clock to give her everything she wanted. I loved her. I still do."

"Losing the baby in the first trimester had to be hard for her," Ash frowned. "I know it devastated you."

Colt nodded and looked away. He still couldn't discuss the loss of their unborn son.

"Maybe Linda just wanted time with you," Ash surmised. "I know Lana gets very cranky when I'm away for extended periods of time."

"Unfortunately, it's the nature of our job," Colt huffed. "Honestly, I'm pretty sure Lee Dawson's multi-million-dollar bank account attracted her more than anything."

Colt didn't tell Ash that his ex-wife still called him for booty calls when her wealthy husband left town. He didn't want his friend to know how weak he was when it came to Linda. After two years, he still couldn't live without her. Apparently, she needed him too.

Ash's phone announced a call from Captain Ames. She put it on speakerphone so Colt could hear.

"Are you there yet?" Ames' tone was accusatory as if his detectives were taking their sweet time getting to the crime scene.

"Just pulled up," Ash said.

"Risa called me," Ames continued. "She said it looks like a serial to her. Risa has been without sleep for the last twenty-four hours. She worked all night trying to identify the bodies from that club fire on West Seventh St. Give her all the help you can. Call me. Let me know what you think."

The entry to The Towers was as serene and placid as ever. The epitome of secure money. The delivery dock told a different story. Risa's van was backed up to the loading dock, and cruisers blocked access to the building.

Colt pushed the button on the service elevator taking them to the penthouse.

Ash and Colt gathered information from the first responder and talked with the maid who had found the dead woman. Risa's boys were putting the body into a body bag when Ash entered the room.

Just before the man pulled the zipper over her face, Ash saw "Whore" burned into her forehead.

She walked to the ME and leaned down to listen to her discretely delivered information.

"Elizabeth Trask," Risa spoke softly into her ear, "wife of Evan Trask. He's the youngest of the Trask brothers and the owner of this Tower."

"Are you doing okay?" Ash noted the dark circles under her friend's eyes. Risa simply nodded.

The ME and detective's blonde heads bobbed as they asked and answered each other's questions.

"So, bottom line," Ash exhaled slowly, "same MO. No breaking and entering. She seemed to know her killer. Let me know as soon as you complete the vaginal examine."

Dr. Lana Denton quietly slipped into the penthouse, observing the activity.

"I'm looking for Detective Denton," she informed a uniformed officer as she showed him her badge.

The officer pointed toward Risa and Ash. "Oh, the Barbie Twins. They're over there, with their heads together."

"Yes, well, one of them just happens to belong to me." Lana huffed as she realized her wife and best friend were real-life Barbie dolls. Both were tall and slender. Their incredibly perfect, blonde, good looks were storybook beautiful. She suppressed a flash of jealousy.

As Lana approached, Ash straightened to her full height and Risa placed a hand on her forearm. "I will call you as soon as I know something," she said.

Ash nodded and turned, almost walking into her wife. "Honey, I'm so glad you're here. We could use a new perspective on this case."

She led her wife to a quiet study where they could talk. "I am so glad, Ames called you in on this," Ash said, as they sat down beside each other on the sofa.

"I try not to bring my crazy cases home, but Ames insisted on you. Frankly I have been dying to ask your opinion on a few things that bother me about this case."

"Why would he call me in on a murder that is obviously a domestic situation?" Lana studied her wife's face. "This place is a fortress. Only someone with all the security codes and pass cards could get in here. I'd guess the husband did it."

"Mumm," Ash hummed, "Except that it was the exact MO as the Laura Trent murder last week."

Lana furrowed her brow. "Since I have clearance for the case, give me the gruesome details."

"Both women were propped in bed as if reading. Both women had their throat cut from ear to ear. Both had a single stab wound to the stomach, and both had their nipples cut from their bodies. Each of them had a red rose tucked behind her ear.

"The word "Whore" was branded into each woman's forehead."

"Oh my God!" Lana looked away briefly.

"Laura was pregnant, but not with Trent's child," Ash concluded. "Risa is checking to see if Elizabeth had relations before she died. If so, the murders will be identical.

"I don't expect Elizabeth to be pregnant," Ash added. "I do expect to find she had sex before dying."

Lana pinched the bridge of her nose, a move Ash always found endearing. She knew her wife was cataloging the information she had provided her.

"There is one more piece of evidence, only Risa, Colt and I know," Ash continued. "Laura consumed cheese, crackers, and wine before her death. An empty bottle of Peter Michael Cabernet Sauvignon Oakville au Paradis 2012 was at the murder scene. The same wine bottle is here.

"According to the internet, there were only 1,785 cases made. I have contacted the vineyard and am waiting for a list of all their clients who purchased that particular wine."

"There you are," Colt burst into the room. "I could use a little help out there. I can't contact..." He trailed off as he realized Lana was with his partner.

"Sorry, bro," Ash stood. "I was bringing Lana up to date on both cases. Ames sent her to see the crime scene for herself."

"Good," Colt smiled. "We could use a fresh pair of eyes on this one."

"I can't contact Trask," Colt said. "It seems he has been somewhere in Canada for the past week. Any chance the three of us could go somewhere and brainstorm?"

"As long as we're downtown. I have a client meeting in two hours," Lana smiled at her wife, "why don't you take us to Reata for lunch?"

"It would be my pleasure," Ash nodded. "Maybe we can find some connection between Laura Trent and Elizabeth Trask."

"You mean besides the fact that both their last names begin with T and both are filthy rich," Colt said.

##

Lana sipped her wine and turned to Colt. "Ash tells me you would like to date Risa."

Colt sputtered and blushed. "Do you share everything with her?" He asked his partner.

"Just the good stuff," Ash grinned. "You and Risa together would truly be a good thing."

"I just seem to get all tongue tied and goofy around her," Colt admitted. "What if she shoots me down?"

"Why don't we invite you and Risa to dinner at our home, Friday night," Lana suggested. "I'll invite her and tell her you'll be there. If she says no, you can give up the chase, with no damage to your working relationship or your ego."

"Yeah. Yeah, that works for me," Colt agreed.

"Call Pretty and Prettier. I am ready to go over the autopsy results," Risa instructed her assistant.

Ash and Colt put on the usual shoe covers and gowns required to enter Risa's domain.

"Officers," Risa greeted the two, "I'm not finished, but I'm exhausted, so listen carefully.

"Exact, same MO as Laura Trent. Slashed throat, a stab wound to the abdomen and nipples removed. Apparently, the nipples are the perp's trophies. He meticulously cuts them off right against the breast. For your info Colt, there was consensual male on female sexual activity before death. Just like Laura Trent, Elizabeth Trask was in her first trimester. Same wine and cheese were at the party.

"You both know Jamie, my assistant. She will complete the autopsy. I am going home, for some much needed, sleep. I wanted to answer all your questions before I left for the day, so you can catch the son-of-a-bitch that's butchering women in our town.

"I'm turning off my phone, so don't call me."

Lana looked over the crime board the two detectives had assembled. The heading simply said, "Wives." Beneath each woman's photo was a list of similarities in their murders. A few facts were new to Lana.

Both had been members of the same sorority in college. Both had graduated in the same graduating class, and both were very wealthy—old family money.

Both women had worked on the same library fund drive as Lana. That had been a happier time—before Linda cheated on Colt.

Lana noticed the information about the nipples and fetuses were left off the board. Also missing were the facts that "Whore" had been burned into each woman's forehead and that wine and cheese had been present.

Risa joined Lana in front of the board. "I will never understand cheaters," the ME said as she read the new information. "They had everything one could want, yet they still cheated on their husbands."

"Whore," Risa snorted. "I guess death has a brand."

"Makes a powerful motive," Lana nodded thoughtfully. "If the husbands hadn't been out of town, I'd put my money on them."

"Yeah, pretty convenient," Risa frowned. "Where are Denton and Layne? I've got some more bad news for them."

"They are in the captain's office." Lana tilted her head toward Ames' office as her wife and Colt opened the door.

"Wow! Must be our lucky day, Colt," Ash bent to brush her wife's lips with hers. "The two most beautiful women in the world in our bullpen."

"Why don't you buy us a cup of coffee and let Risa give us her news?" Lana ran the tip of her tongue between her lips and winked at her wife.

"Across the street, okay?" Ash asked.

All three nodded and followed her out the door.

They waited as the waitress poured their coffee.

"Good or bad news," Ash asked.

"I haven't even told Ames yet," Risa frowned. "It is going to hit the fan when I do."

"What?" The three chorused in unison.

"When I went to complete the autopsy on the fetus, this morning," Risa frowned, "it was gone."

All three looked at her as if toads were jumping from her lips.

"Gone?" Ash gasped.

"How? When?" Lana said.

"I don't know."

"Let's pull security footage and see who was in the morgue last night," Colt said.

"Did that first thing," Risa shook her head. "Someone shut it down after midnight. It was off when I came in this morning. They entered through the back door, using my passcode. I swear I had nothing to do with it. I have no idea how someone got my code."

"So, we can't match the DNA of this baby with the DNA of Laura's baby?" Ash inhaled deeply, trying to figure out what to do.

"Whoever took the fetus knew little about DNA," Risa grinned. "I still have the umbilical cord. I was able to pull DNA from it, and yes, the babies had the same father. Still, I feel violated that someone was able to enter my domain and steal a fetus."

"Obviously, both women were seeing the same man," Lana said. "Surely people saw them together. We just need to narrow it down to the men they had in common. Right now, we have to face Ames."

"My lab, my problem," Risa huffed. "I'll tell him."

The four returned to the precinct prepared to inform Ames. They were surprised to find that someone had added two words to their crime board. Left of Wives was Branded and to the right was the word Club. The board now read Branded Wives Club.

"All of you, in my office now," Ames bellowed.

"Oh, shit, not another one," Colt mumbled.

Ames gave them a quick rundown. A man had tried to enter one of the upscale loft apartments of the Firestone Building. Fortunately, a security guard had spotted him and given chase. The perp had gotten away.

Stacy Vanguard, the young woman who lived in the lavish apartment, was frantic. Her husband was out of town on business and wouldn't be back for a week.

Ash and Lana went to interview her. Ames sent Colt to pick up Martina Martinez. She had reported her husband missing. His description fit the floater they had fished from the Trinity.

##

"Mrs. Vanguard, do you have friends or relatives you can visit until your husband returns," Ash asked.

"Yes, but I don't see why..."

"A murderer is targeting young women when their husbands are out of town," Ash said. "You'll be safer somewhere else."

"Stacy. May I call you Stacy?" Lana's disarming smile put the woman at ease.

"Yes," Stacy Vanguard nodded.

"Obviously, you and your husband are very wealthy," Lana let her gaze travel around the room filled with antiques and priceless artwork.

Stacy nodded again.

"Tell me, with whom are you having an affair?" Lana's direct question took the woman by surprise.

"How do you…? What?" Stacy gasped. "No! I'm not having an affair with anyone!"

"Are you pregnant?" Lana didn't pull any punches.

"I want both of you to leave, now!" Stacy stood and walked to the door. "I don't want to talk to you anymore. You're insulting."

"Mrs. Vanguard," Ash said smoothly, "Dr. Denton is not trying to insult you. She's trying to save your life. Please pack an overnight bag and stay with friends until your husband returns or have a friend stay with you. Will you do that?"

Stacy nodded. "Yes, of course, Detective."

Ash tried one more time. "Mrs. Vanguard, if you are having an affair, please give us the name of the man?"

"Out! Both of you get out," Stacy screamed.

"That went well," Lana huffed as she buckled her seatbelt.

"You think?" Ash leaned over and kissed her wife. "Do you have to go to work today?"

"Yes, I have two appointments I have to keep. One will get off her meds if I don't monitor her every week, and the other is suicidal."

##

Lana finished her notes in Jessica Barton's files just as she heard her announcing her arrival to the secretary. Lana flipped on the video camera in her office.

"Dr. Denton is ready for you, ma'am," Jackie showed Jessica into the office.

"Good afternoon, Jessica," Lana smiled. "Please sit down." She motioned toward the chair in front of her desk. Jessica walked across the room and plopped down on the sofa.

Lana knew they played the same game every week. She let it play out because it gave Jessica a sense of having control of her life.

She picked up her notepad and pen and walked to the chair in front of Jessica. She was inwardly gleeful as she noticed the scowl on Jessica's face when she realized Lana was wearing slacks today.

"How is your love life, Jessica?" She smiled as she set down.

"Dr. Denton, you know I have no love life," Jessica chided her.

Good, she has stayed on her meds, Lana thought.

"Anything important happen in your life this week," she engaged her in conversation.

She took a long time to answer. She seemed to be trying to decide if she should confide in her. "Someone murdered my lover," she frowned.

41

Lana nodded cautiously. "I am so sorry for your loss," she said. "What was her name?"

"Whose name?" Jessica frowned.

"Your lover," Lana said. "What was your lover's name?"

She chuckled. "Dr. Denton, you are playing with me. You know I have no lover."

"Is there anything you would like to talk about today?" Lana asked.

"I have a new young woman at the company," Jessica screwed up her face as if she were in pain. "She is incredibly brilliant; the best programmer I have ever met. She is almost as good as I."

"That's wonderful," Lana encouraged her.

"There's one problem," Jessica continued. "Every time she walks into my office, she walks around my desk and sits on my lap."

"How do you react to that?" Lana narrowed her eyes, watching Jessica's reactions.

"I just sit there," she smiled slyly. "I would never touch her. She might file a sexual harassment suit against me. Since I am her boss and all."

"That is very smart on your part," Lana reinforced her fear of being sued. "You could lose everything in a suit like that."

Jessica nodded. "I just sit there, but she won't leave me alone. She pulls her skirt up to her waist, and she never wears panties. I don't look at her. I look away. She grinds into me. She just wants me so much."

Okay, so totally off the meds, Lana thought.

"She unzips my pants and puts her hand…"

"Jessica," Lana said harshly, "you know you are having flights of fantasy. No young girl is having sex with you in your office."

Jessica glared at her as if she hated her. For the first time, Lana felt uneasy with this patient. *I really should give Ash her name*, she thought.

"You haven't taken your meds all week, have you?"

"I took one or two," Jessica continued to glare. "Why can't you accept the fact that women find me desirable? Is it because you find me repulsive?"

"I don't think you're repulsive, Jessica," Lana tried to keep the disapproval from her voice. "I just want you to be able to control yourself when these women make advances to you."

"Yes, I should," Jessica agreed, "and I do control myself. I never put my hands on them unless they beg me to. Sometimes, I just have to give them what they are begging for."

"Jessica, you must take your meds," Lana said firmly. "If you aren't going to take your meds, I can't help you. I will have to send you to another doctor. Do you understand?"

Jessica pulled the pill bottle from her pocket and shook out two of the tablets. She threw them in her mouth and swallowed them. "There, you happy now?"

Lana nodded. "Promise me you will do that every morning at eight o'clock."

"I will take my pills every day if you promise to wear skirts for our sessions." Jessica raised her head smugly. She had won the battle.

##

Chapter 6

At seven in the evening, two detectives met Evan Trask at the airport baggage claim. They waited until he pulled his suitcase from the carousel, and then flanked him on both sides. He had expected his wife and driver.

"Mr. Trask, I am Detective Ash Denton, and this is my partner Colt Layne," the blonde woman shoved her badge in front of Trask to prove her statement.

"I don't understand," Trask growled. "Why are you picking me up? Where're my wife and driver?"

"Please come with us, sir," the woman insisted. "We will explain in the car."

The female detective sat in the back seat with Trask and destroyed his world. His wife was dead, murdered by some maniac. She had been pregnant. They had wanted a baby so badly.

Then came the gut twister. The baby wasn't his.

The car was speeding along the freeway! Bright lights spun around him. The detective mumbled words of sympathy. Everything was a blur. The scene had to be a nightmare. Evan Trask couldn't stop his head from whirling around. He slumped forward in the seat.

"I think he has passed out," Ash told Colt. "Pull into the first service station you see. I'll get some wet paper towels."

Cold paper towels revived Trask. He straightened up and tried to make sense of where he was. Then it all came crashing back to him.

"Is there someone we can call, sir," Ash asked him.

"Could you please take me to my brother's house," Trask requested. "I don't want to be alone."

Colt keyed the address into his GPS, and they made the trip in silence.

"We will need to talk with you tomorrow, when you feel like it," Ash informed him. "You can come into the station, or we can come to you."

"I'll call you," Trask mumbled as he climbed out of the car. Ash escorted the stunned man to the front door of his brother's home and rang the doorbell.

"He's off my suspect list," Colt said as Ash climbed into the front passenger seat.

"Mine, too."

Ash texted Lana she was on her way home. It was almost nine. "Do you mind dropping me by the house? I'll ride in with Lana in the morning."

Colt nodded. "Remember the floater in the Trinity?"

"Yes."

"Turned out to be our newest city council member. Martinez, the one we suspected of fronting the drug cartel." Colt's expression was gleeful.

"Doesn't say much for the Seventh Street Gang and their choices to run our city," Ash snorted.

"Yeah, makes me wonder if some of the Seventh Street guys may be involved with the cartels, too," Colt said.

Ash shook her head. "You're probably right. You have a nose for these things. Let's make them our top priority after we catch the asshole that is butchering women."

Colt keyed in the access code to allow entry into Monticello Estates. Ash and Lana owned the home at the very top of the hill. The view was spectacular. As they reached the drive, Colt keyed in the number that opened the gate on the driveway leading to Ash's house. Talk about security.

Ash had owned the house for six years. She had paid cash for it when she received her first big royalty check.

Most people thought that Ash had married money, and Lana was the owner of the home.

That was fine with Ash. She didn't want people digging too deeply into her finances and learning of her alias.

Colt pulled into the driveway and drove to the back of the house.

"Tomorrow night at seven," Ash reminded him.

"You sure Risa knows I'll be here," Colt asked. "Does she want to spend an evening with me?"

"She was delighted," Ash reassured her friend. "She likes you. Don't blow it."

Lana was propped up in bed, reading. Ash's heart lurched for a second. She shook her head, trying to rid her mind of the image of the two dead women propped up in bed as if reading.

"Darling, I'm so glad you're home." Lana slipped off her glasses and placed them and her book onto the nightstand.

"What are you reading?" Ash leaned down to kiss her.

"The latest Adrian Austin book," Lana smiled. "I have an in with the author, so I get the first book off the press. It came today."

"The author is anxious to hear your critique," Ash said as she headed for the shower.

"So far, it's spellbinding," Lana called after her.

Lana was still reading when Ash walked back into the bedroom. Her hair was damp. A towel wrapped around her and tucked in at the waist. She walked toward the armoire for her pajamas.

"What are you doing, darling?" Lana said in her sultriest voice.

"Getting pajamas," she grinned.

"I don't believe they're necessary," Lana smiled as she lifted the covers for Ash to slide into bed with her.

"But you're necessary," Ash murmured as she pulled her into her arms and kissed her deeply. "So necessary for my happiness."

##

"Who the hell let her in here?" Captain Ames was ranting at Carter. "Where are Denton and Layne?"

"They're taking a statement from Evan Trask," Carter said.

"Get Denton in here, quick." Ames hissed. "Layne can take a statement by himself."

Ash stopped dead in her tracks as she realized Nora Glade was taking a photo of their Branded Wives Club white board.

"Nora, to what do we owe this honor?" Ash greeted the woman that had been the bane of her existence, with open arms.

47

"Smooth as ever, I see," Nora grinned as she hugged Ash a little longer than she should have.

"And you are lovely as ever," Ash smiled. "What can I do for you?"

"Tell me about the Branded Wives Club," Nora's wicked smile didn't leave her lips. "You have any suspects?"

"None we can name right now, but we have a person of interest," Ash lied. "Listen, Nora, I saw you take a photo of our whiteboard. Please don't use it in any way. It is a little insensitive, but you know how the officers get when they are operating on four hours sleep a night. We have everyone working around the clock on this one. Help us keep it from getting ugly."

Nora surveyed the white board. "Looks like it is already pretty ugly."

"Promise me you won't print anything you got here today, and I promise you I will give you a call the minute we arrest someone."

"I'll hold this info for one week," Nora said. "Or until there is another victim. Women have a right to know some maniac is running loose, killing women."

"Thanks," Ash nodded.

"Branded Wives," Nora huffed. "Branded Wives Club—Death has a Brand. That will be my headline. This story is mine to tell, Ash. Don't you dare screw me over on this!"

"I won't," Ash said as Nora stomped from the room.

"Denton," Captain Ames waved her into his office. "Can you keep a lid on this?"

"I hope so, sir," Ash frowned. "That's why I left the info about the nipples and the fetuses off the board. I was afraid some reporter would get in here."

##

Risa Mercer keyed in the access number. "Hey, Risa," Ash's happy voice welcomed her as the gate to the community opened. "Come in."

Risa drove slowly through the multi-million-dollar houses. *Lana must be one hell of a shrink*, she thought. *I know what McPretty makes. She can't afford this.*

Risa was glad to see Colt was already there. If she had been the first to pick, she would have picked Ash, but since she wasn't available, Colt would do. He was certainly easy on the eyes. She loved his offbeat humor and rugged good looks. Since she swung either way, Risa never lacked for dates.

Risa had joined the Fort Worth crime lab two years ago. Ten years in New York's crime lab made Cowtown look like a walk in the park. She liked her job, and she liked the people around her.

She had met Lana right after college. Lana was a Harvard girl and Risa had graduated from Boston University, the top forensic science school in the nation.

Risa had gone to work for the New York Police Department in the medical examiner's office, and Lana had joined the force as a junior profiler. They had become close friends. If Ash had to be off the market, she was glad Lana was the one to take her. They were perfect together.

Ash and Colt met her as she got out of the car. "Where is Lana," she asked, handing her host a bottle of red wine.

"Keeping an eye on our steaks," Ash grinned. "I'll just open this and let it breathe. Colt will show you to the patio."

"Perfect timing, as usual," Lana hugged her friend and Colt poured her a glass of wine.

"You have a gorgeous home," Risa complimented.

"Thank you. We rarely entertain here," Lana explained. "Ash says it's her sanctuary, and she only wants to share it with me."

"Lucky you," Risa raised her glass as if toasting her friend.

"Yes, indeed," Lana agreed.

"The day is so perfect we thought we'd dine outside," Ash said as she carried a large bowl of salad to the table. Colt followed close behind with baked potatoes.

"Steaks are ready," Lana called. "Bring your plates."

The evening was perfect. Colt and Risa laughed and talked about everything under the sun. They settled into a comfortable relationship.

"Would you mind giving me a tour of your home?" Risa said. "It's lovely. I would like to see it."

"Of course," Lana led the tour through the house. The last room they visited was Ash's study.

"I see you are an Adrian Austin fan," Risa said, running her hands over the books lined up on Ash's bookshelf.

"I am," Ash nodded.

"We both are," Lana added.

"I've read all her books," Risa smiled. "I can't wait for her new book to come out. I pre-ordered it on Amazon. It is her thirty-sixth book and she titled it *Thirty-Six Ways to Die*. I think that is so clever."

"Yeah, she is one clever bastard," Colt snorted.

"Do I detect a bit of envy," Lana asked.

Colt shrugged and took Risa's elbow, leading her toward the foyer.

Lana and Ash said their goodnights and Colt walked Risa to her car.

"I had a wonderful time tonight," Risa said, as she tiptoed to kiss Colt's cheek.

"As did I," Colt smiled. "Maybe we could go out to dinner tomorrow night. Just you and me."

"I'd like that," Risa smiled as she slid into her car. "Until tomorrow night."

For the first time, Colt thought that he might be able to break the addiction called Linda.

##

Stacy Vanguard called her lover. There was no reason she couldn't stay with him while Van was gone. Van shouldn't leave her alone so much.

The knock at her door told her he was here. It was late. She pulled him into the apartment and kissed him hard. The police had scared her with their talk of serial murderers. She felt safe now that he was here.

"I brought wine," he smiled "and some cheese. I love wine and cheese."

"Me too," Stacy led him to the kitchen. "You are very sweet. I love the red rose."

##

"It has been one week," Ash glanced at her partner. "Is Risa still speaking to you?"

"Speaking to me and kissing me," Colt's smile reminded Ash of a small boy who had just received a wonderful present. "We're going dining and dancing tonight. You and Lana should join us."

"You don't need an old married couple tagging along," Ash smiled.

"Yes, we do," Risa approached them. "Call your wife and see if she would like a date night."

"Where are you going?" Ash wasn't aware of too many great dance clubs in Fort Worth.

Risa whipped out her phone and dialed Lana. "Hey, pretty girl, we are trying to talk your stick-in-the-mud wife into going out with us tonight."

Risa listened as Lana talked.

"No," Risa smiled. "Colt is taking me *boot scootin'*. Dinner at Cattleman's and dancing at the White Elephant Saloon."

Risa held her phone out to Ash. "She wants to speak with you."

"Hi honey," Ash smiled. "Sure, if you'd like to, I am fine with it. Okay. You and Risa set the time and where to meet." He handed the phone back to Risa.

"Thanks, Ash," Colt grinned. "You will have a good time."

"Anytime I can hold my wife and dance is a good time," Ash nodded. "We are looking forward to it."

At four o'clock, Colt slid his Glock into his holster and pulled on his suit jacket. He was looking forward to tonight. Food, dancing and a lot to drink, maybe he would get lucky tonight. Risa was a light drinker, and straight-laced, but maybe partying with Ash and Lana would loosen her up a bit.

He looked around the bullpen. He was the only one in the office on a beautiful Friday afternoon. The second shift hadn't arrived yet. The phone lit up on the line indicating a transfer from 911. He was the only one there to answer it.

"Homicide," Colt barked. "Detective Layne speaking."

"My wife, oh God my wife," a man sobbed into the phone. "My wife."

"What's wrong with your wife?" Colt asked.

"She's...she's...it's awful."

"Sir, what is wrong with your wife?"

"She's dead," the man sobbed. "She's dead and oh, God."

"What is your address," Colt pulled a pad toward him.

"The Firestone Apartments," the man choked.

"What's your name," Colt already knew the answer.

"Van Vanguard. Please hurry. It's awful."

Colt called Risa. "No dancing tonight, baby. Just got a death call from the Firestone apartments. Take the van. I'll call Ash. Meet you there."

"Captain," Colt leaned into Ames' office. "Stacy Vanguard has been murdered."

"Son-of-a-bitch," Ames howled as Colt left the room.

Lana and Ash pulled onto the parking lot behind the Firestone. Risa and Colt were already on the scene.

Colt was trying to talk to a man that was so distraught he didn't make sense. Colt cast a pleading glance at Lana.

"I'll handle him," she nodded to Colt. "You and Ash do your thing."

The stench in the apartment told Risa the body was already in decomp. She sprinkled a couple of drops of peppermint essential oil onto three masks. She put on one and handed the other two to Ash and Colt.

"You're a life saver," Colt smiled as he slid the mask over his nose. He headed off to question anyone he could find.

"Stay with me," Risa told Ash. "I am going to do the minimum here, then take the body to the morgue."

"She's been dead about a week," Risa said as she pulled the sheet from the body.

Stacy was staged just as the other two women had been. Propped up as if reading a book. "Whore," was stamped across her forehead. The letters, now purple, were cracked and wrinkled from decomposition. A withered, red rose, rested behind her ear.

"Throat slit," Risa continued. "Stab wound to abdomen and...What the hell?"

Ash leaned over Risa's shoulder to see what had surprised the unflappable doctor. Something was between the dead woman's legs.

Risa nudged it with her gloved finger. "Coffin birth," she grimaced. "Can't be more than five weeks old. Postmortem fetal extrusion, the buildup of gasses caused her body to expel the fetus."

Ash put her arm around her shoulders. She could tell Risa was disturbed. The sight was shocking, even for an ME. Although she had heard of the phenomena, it was extremely rare. It was the first time Ash had witnessed it.

"Bag her, boys," Risa instructed. "Take her straight to a drawer. Keep this with her." She pointed to the fetus.

Risa ordered two uniformed officers stationed at both doors entering the morgue. "I'm not taking any chances on someone stealing anything before I do the autopsy in the morning."

The four returned to the precinct. Captain Ames was waiting for them. It was after nine.

"Do you ever sleep?" Colt asked his captain.

"Not when you two keep bringing in new bodies." Ames said. "Is she a Branded Wife?"

"Yeah," Colt nodded. "According to Risa's estimated time of death, she was killed the same night Ash and Lana tried to get her to leave her apartment."

"If she had just given us a name," Lana sighed. "We'd know who the killer is."

"You want to grab some dinner," Risa smiled shyly at Colt. "I don't want to be alone right now."

"I know how you feel," Colt nodded. "Dinner with you would be great."

"I think we will just go home," Lana murmured. Cases like this one always disturbed her. She honestly didn't know how Risa did her job.

##

Colt dropped his gun and badge on the table in his foyer. He poured a glass of scotch and turned on his laptop. His detective business was more demanding than ever. It seemed like half the married people in Fort Worth were cheating on their spouses. It was obvious Colt's reputation for delivering the goods for a non-contested divorce was spreading among the town's wealthy married couples.

Colt looked at the photo the man had emailed him. The woman was beautiful, with high cheekbones, long auburn hair, and soulful green eyes. He had worked with her on several big cases. She was the assistant district attorney. She was intelligent and dedicated. Her husband, a criminal attorney, had tossed his hat into the political ring and was running for state senator.

"You think she's cheating on you?" Colt emailed the man again.

"I don't know," the attorney answered. "I have to know for certain before I get too far along with my campaign."

He agreed to Colt's fee and payment. "Half now and the balance when I receive the photos, right?"

Colt emailed him the post office box address where he could mail the first payment. He hoped he wouldn't collect the second half of the payment. He liked and respected ADA Christine Canton. He couldn't say the same for her husband. Everyone in town knew Robert Canton was a player.

##

Monday was a perfect example of a crappy first day of the week. Ash shook her head as she read the front-page headlines of the *Star-Telegram*.

Cowboy up and brand a woman, ripped across the page. Nora had spared no one's feelings. Ash wondered where she had gotten so much detailed information. Obviously, she had been a busy girl since the last time Ash saw her.

The paper carried photos of each of the dead women beside their husbands. He was thankful she hadn't learned of the mutilations and the pregnancies.

Ames charged into the room.

"I know," Ash cut him off before he started. "I just finished reading it."

"That woman is a pain in my ass," Ames hissed. "Every politician in town will be crawling up my butt before the day is over.

"Where is your partner? He does still work here, doesn't he?"

"He's following up on the Martinez murder," Ash scowled.

"Well, do something," Ames growled. "Even if it's wrong."

Ash picked up the three files and headed for the morgue. Hopefully, it would be quieter there.

Risa was dictating into her microphone when Ash entered. "The fetal DNA matches the other cases." She turned off the machine and gave Ash a sad look. This case was getting to everyone.

"Want to take me to coffee, McPretty," she smiled.

"Love to," Ash held out her elbow. Risa linked her arm through Ash's and they walked across the street to the coffee shop.

"I am sorry the case ruined our plans Friday night," Ash said as she stirred cream into her coffee.

"Not your fault, sweetie," Risa shook her head. "You have any thoughts on this case?"

"I'm ashamed to admit I don't even have an idea. Whoever this bastard is, he is the father of all the babies. What kind of man kills a woman carrying his child?"

"Maybe that is why they were murdered," Risa said. "He screwed around with them then murdered them when he got them pregnant."

"It would have been a whole lot easier to use a damn condom," Ash huffed. "I think he planned on getting them pregnant. I think he has staged every move of his little game."

Risa nodded. "What are you going to do?"

"Start over. Somewhere I am missing something."

"I like you, Ash Denton," Risa smiled slightly. "You're a good cop."

"Thank you, Risa. That means a lot to me, coming from you. Speaking of good cops, have you heard from my partner this morning?"

"No, I haven't talked to him since Friday. We had dinner, and then went our separate ways."

"You went home alone," Ash raised her eyebrows in surprise.

"Yes," Risa chuckled. "I like Colt a lot, but we aren't that far along yet. His ex-wife called him, and he ran out of the restaurant as if his tail were on fire."

"Her husband must be out of town, again," Ash frowned. She knew Colt thought she was unaware of his continued affair with Linda.

"So that's the way it works," Risa said thoughtfully. "Her husband leaves town, and Colt fills in for him while he's gone."

"Something, like that," Ash nodded. "He just can't seem to get Linda out of his system."

"Until he does," Risa said, "I don't see any future with him. I don't do bed hoppers."

"I completely understand," Ash said.

Ash entered the Trent Oil building. Jeb Trent's office was on the tenth floor. Ash's appointment was for ten a.m. She had written several questions on the outside of Laura Trent's file. She quickly read them to make certain she had left out nothing.

"Detective Denton," a secretary greeted her and led her into Trent's office. "Mr. Trent will be right with you. His meeting is running longer than he expected. Please make yourself at home. There is coffee on the sidebar and magazines on the table."

Ash made certain the office door was closed and made a quick search of Trent's drawers, which yielded nothing.

She smiled when she saw that Trent's bookshelf contained hardback copies of all her Adrian Austin books. She ran her hand across the spines, then noticed a manila envelope stuck between two of the books. She pulled out the envelope and examined its contents. She quickly placed the envelope inside Laura Trent's folder. She was comfortably seated, thumbing through a magazine when Jeb Trent entered his office.

"Detective Denton," Trent shook her hand then sat down across from her. "I apologize for keeping you waiting. I know how busy you are. What can I do to help?"

"Nothing, Mr. Trent. I just wanted to touch base with you and see how you are doing."

"As well as can be expected," Trent grimaced. "Are you any closer to catching the killer?"

"No," Ash faked a pained look. "We have hit a dead end. Have you thought of anything that might help us?"

Trent shook his head. "I don't know why anyone would kill my wife, except for the obvious. I'd rather not dwell on that."

"I understand. Well, I won't take up any more of your time," Ash stood to leave. "Here is my card. Please call me if anything occurs to you or if you just need a sympathetic soul to talk to."

Trent nodded silently.

Ash called Lana from her car phone. "Honey, can you get away for lunch? I can be there in fifteen minutes."

"I'd love to," she giggled.

God, I love her.

They went to a quiet little restaurant outside of town. She didn't want anyone interrupting them. They placed their order and waited as the server sat their drinks in front of them.

Ash pulled the envelope from the file. "Look at these."

Lana studied the photos for a long time. "Obviously, they are of Laura Trent and her lover. While it is clearly her, he is never identifiable."

"Do they appear to be photoshopped?" Ash asked.

She studied each photo for a long time. "No, they are original."

"That is what I thought, too. Clearly these photos were taken before Laura's murder, so Jeb Trent was aware of his wife's infidelities."

"What are you going to do now?" Lana asked.

"Visit Trask and Vanguard," Ash said, "and try to locate the photographer who took these pictures. He will know who the lover is."

##

Chapter 7

As he had done many times, Lee Dawson shuffled through the photos of his wife and Detective Colt Layne. He knew Layne warmed his wife's bed every time he left town.

Linda hadn't been able to stay away from Layne for even a month. The week after they had returned from their honeymoon, Lee had overheard her talking on the phone to the handsome detective, begging him to see her.

Lee examined the manila envelope again, searching for some clue as to who had mailed him the photos. There was nothing. He had received the envelope on the date of their first anniversary.

The picture that hurt him the most was the one of Linda completely naked, straddling Layne, her head thrown back in ecstasy. He had seen that same look on her face when she was with him. He had been so proud he could make her look like that. Obviously, anyone could!

He shoved the photos back into the envelope and dropped it in his desk drawer. He had been stupid. He had married the bitch without a prenuptial. His father had warned him. He had been so certain she was the love of his life. She had rocked his world from the first time he laid eyes on her at the library fundraiser. Her long blonde hair and pale blue eyes had captivated him. She was tall and slender. She always wore dresses that showed just enough cleavage and leg to drive a man crazy.

It hadn't mattered that she was another man's wife. Some insignificant cop wasn't going to stop him from having the woman of his dreams. He snorted as he thought of how quickly she had turned into his worst nightmare.

He never gave her any indication he knew about her frequent liaisons with Layne. She continued to play the part of the loving wife, and he continued to fuck her. That was all he wanted from her now. He would use her for sex until he found a way to be rid of her. A way that wouldn't cost him a fortune.

Jessica Barton sat in the office of Christine Canton. The assistant district attorney had requested her help in solving a rash of crimes that originated from the internet.

"Ms. Barton," Christine smiled broadly, as she entered her office. "I'm so sorry I kept you waiting. I was waiting for this printout. I wanted to go over it with you."

Jessica stood and extended her hand to shake Christine's. She wanted to touch the beautiful auburn-haired ADA. "No problem, Mrs. Canton. I'm just glad to be of some assistance to you."

Christine placed the printout on the table and pulled two chairs close together so they could see the information.

Jessica wondered if Christine was aware of how tightly their thighs pressed together.

"We have had a series of attacks on teenagers, both boys and girls. The threat seems to come from this chatroom, but we can't pinpoint the location of the server. The signal disappears somewhere in Syria, but it must be here in the states because the predators are here."

Jessica nodded and then scanned the information she placed in front of her.

"Are you able to share with me the details of the cases," she asked.

"With your security clearance, I can share all information with you," Christine informed her.

"Tell me about the first case. Don't leave out any details. Jessica felt revulsion as she listened to Christine go into detail about the rape of a fourteen-year-old who had invited into her home, a boyfriend she had met in the chatroom."

The name of the chatroom was *Parents Don't Understand Me*. There were thousands of chats about how unfair parents were.

The girl had entered the chatroom after being grounded by her parents for skipping school. After midnight, she aired her complaints against her parents. Knight Rider had responded to her, and they quickly became chatroom friends.

Knight Rider gave her his email address and suggested they leave the chatroom and just chat with one another, via email.

He confided in her that he was sixteen and having trouble keeping his grades up because his parents were going through a divorce. He was glad he could talk with her, and she understood him.

Over a three-month period, she told him where she went to school, emailed him her photo and gave him her cell phone number. She told him she was always home alone on Saturday mornings when her parents did the grocery shopping.

Using her phone information, he got her address. One Saturday, he had watched her parents leave and then knocked on her door.

Her parents had returned home to find her in shock and bleeding. They took her to the hospital, and she agreed to a sexual assault forensic exam. They found no matches to the rapist's DNA in the national database.

"I can't believe she was that stupid," Jessica frowned. "She sent a photo and all that information to a total stranger."

Christine nodded. "From the descriptions, there are three men, in their mid to late thirties, preying on these young people.

"We get a case a month that traces back to this chatroom. Can you locate it?"

"I can try," Jessica nodded. "I'll need to use the computers in my office. They're a little more sophisticated than your laptops."

Christine laughed. "I'm sure."

"Do you want to come with me, or do you want me to get the location and relay it to you?"

Christine checked her calendar. Her husband had a meeting that would run late. She decided to see Jessica's set up.

"How long do you think it will take you," Christine asked as they rode down in the elevator.

"An hour, max" Jessica smiled shyly. "We're located in the old Flatiron Building. It's just a few blocks away. We can walk."

"I've always loved that building," Christine said as they approached the Flatiron Building. "I never knew what was in it."

"I love it, too," Jessica smiled. "That is why I purchased it several years ago. It houses the heart of our operations. We take up every floor."

"There are no signs or anything," Christine noted. "How would anyone know you were here?"

"Exactly," Jessica laughed. "We are in the security business. We don't advertise our location because we don't want some nut trying to test our abilities."

"That makes sense," Christine nodded as Jessica opened the door to the lobby.

Jessica felt her better half taking over. She knew it would just be a matter of time before Christine Canton would become her lover.

As promised, Jessica located the server in less than an hour. It was in a home in the West Ridglea area. Christine called, but couldn't get a search warrant until the morning.

"I can't believe you did that so quickly," Christine smiled. "The tech guys in my division have been working on that for months. You're outstanding."

Jessica ducked her head as if embarrassed by her praise. "I'm glad I could help you," she said.

"Have you had dinner?" Christine picked up her purse. "Let me buy you an appreciation dinner."

"I'd like that," Jessica blushed again.

Christine found the computer genius to be very entertaining, she was funny and brilliant. Jessica had traveled all over the world, something she hoped to do someday. She was surprised to find the restaurant closing around them.

"Oh, my," Christine whispered, "We have talked until closing time."

Jessica insisted on paying the check. They had dined at a very expensive restaurant and drank quite a bit of wine.

"This was supposed to be my thank you to you," Christine linked her arm through Jessica's and leaned against her heavily. She felt solid. Good and solid. The wine was getting to her.

Colt watched as ADA Christine Canton clung to the woman as they left the restaurant. He photographed them from across the street. They laughed and talked all the way back to Christine's car.

Jessica enjoyed the feel of Christine clinging to her arm and the pressure of her body leaning against her as they walked. She was beautiful.

"Are you certain you can drive home," Jessica asked as she pulled her keys from her purse. "I fear you've had too much wine."

"I'm fine," Christine giggled as she dropped her car keys.

They both bent down to pick up the keys and only managed to bang their heads together. Jessica straightened up and gently pulled Christine up to lean against the car. "Now, you stay put, while I bend over and pick up your keys," she laughed.

Christine wasn't certain how it happened. Jessica straightened up and placed the keys in her hand. Her back was against the car. She turned her face up to Jessica. "Thank you," she whispered as Jessica's lips captured hers.

"I'm driving you home," Jessica said as she guided her to the passenger side of her car.

Christine didn't argue as she slid into the passenger's seat. It was nice to have someone take care of her. She dozed.

"What is your address," Jessica asked gently.

Christine mumbled numbers Jessica couldn't understand but did catch the street name. She pushed *home* on the in-dash GPS and saw the street. She let the device guide her to Christine's house.

"Christine," she shook her shoulder, "what's your gate code?"

"1812," she muttered.

Jessica opened the gate and drove the car into the garage. She shook Christine awake.

"You're home. I'm leaving." She brushed her lips lightly against Christine's. She tasted sweet, like fine wine.

Jessica called a taxi to pick her up on the corner, three blocks from Christine's house.

##

Colt felt a sickening feeling in his stomach as he watched Christine kiss the stranger. He hated taking the photo. He watched them leave in Christine's car. The detective hated that she was cheating, even more. Sometimes his private investigating business was worse than police work.

Colt walked to his car. He was tired. All he wanted was a good night's sleep. His cell phone played the sound reserved for Linda. He didn't answer. He couldn't deal with her tonight.

The detective drove the short distance to his home. He had purchased an older home in the TCU area and had spent every free minute and dollar, restoring it to its original glory.

The house was a large, two-story, with dormer windows, a real front porch, and a large, perfectly manicured yard. It was in the city's historic district, and it was close to work.

He pulled his car into the detached garage and leaned his head forward, resting his forehead on the steering wheel. His thoughts went to Risa Mercer. He wondered if Risa was the kind of woman who would cheat on a husband.

The faces of the three members of the Branded Wives Club danced across his mind. He shook his head to dislodge the images. They had paid a high price to sleep in a stranger's bed.

Colt's cell phone pulled him from his thoughts. Robert Canton's name appeared on the screen. "Hello, Robert."

"Well, did she see anyone tonight?" Robert was demanding, overbearing and obnoxious. He would make a perfect politician.

"No," Colt lied. "All she did was work."

"Keep me posted." Two beeps signaled Robert had ended the call.

Sometimes Colt thought about closing his detective business, but he made three times the money the city paid him. Occasionally, he received a huge tip, like the one from Martinez. He was still trying to decide what to do with the million dollars in the briefcase. Not whether to keep it or turn it over to the department, but how to invest it.

Colt locked the door behind him. He disarmed and rearmed his alarm. He placed his Glock and badge on the entryway table. He looked around his home. It was tastefully furnished and meticulous. He had completely renovated it. It was as beautiful as Ash and Lana's home.

He showered, dressed for bed, poured himself a glass of Chivas Regal and settled on the sofa in his living room. The portrait of Linda in her wedding gown still dominated the space over his fireplace. Maybe, by the time it was cold enough to build a fire in the fireplace, he would be man enough to burn it. His hopes of sanity hinged on Risa Mercer.

He sipped his scotch and wondered if Risa would be receptive to spending a week in the Caymans with him. He could kill two birds with one stone, court Risa and deposit the drug money into his Cayman account.

Captain Andrew Ames watched his two top detectives. They were deep into a serious conversation. The two were the model for other homicide officers. They were dedicated and tenacious in their pursuit of criminals.

He had been their commanding officer throughout their entire career. They had made a name for themselves as rookie patrol officers. When Ames was named Sergeant over CID, he had requested the pair. His promotion to captain had meant a move up for them. They had truly found their niche in homicide. During their ten years under his command, they had never failed to close a case. He was certain no one else could claim a record like that.

Unlike most, who chose law enforcement as a career, Ash and Colt were extremely camera shy. Both refused publicity. They were adamant that their photos never appear in the news. Consequently, Ames was always the face of the department. The publicity was good for his career in many ways.

Ash's discovery of the photos in Trent's office had given the case an entirely new twist. While the men had joked about the Branded Wives Club, it did seem the women *were* targeted because of their infidelities.

At Ames' insistence, Ash had made copies of the photos and then returned them to Trent's office. They couldn't be used as evidence if Ash stole them from the man. Ames had forbidden Ash discussing the photos with anyone else, even Colt. He knew they would eventually find a reason to get a search warrant for Trent's office and legally find the photos. He didn't want to take any chances on the bastard walking free on a technicality.

Colt's phone rang. A hysterical Martina Martinez was sobbing in Spanish. Colt walked out of the squad room to a quiet corner in the hall.

"Mrs. Martinez, please calm down. My Spanish is not good enough to keep up with you."

"I…I didn't know who to call. They told me they would kill me if I called the police."

"Who told you that?" Colt spoke slowly, trying to calm the distraught woman.

"Two men. They came to my restaurant. They are looking for money Manny had. I know nothing about money. The little worm was always broke; always stealing from my cash registers."

"Stay where you are. I will be right there," Colt promised.

Ash was in Ames' office when Colt returned to the bullpen. He stuck his head into the office. "Can I take an hour for personal business Captain," he asked.

"I guess," Ames frowned, "I was just telling Ash about ADA Canton."

The bottom fell out of Colt's stomach. "Oh, God, please don't tell me something has happened to her?"

"No," Ames hurriedly explained. "She has a location for the Chatroom Killer. She requested you two on the arrest since you have been working the case with her."

Ash saw the look in her partner's eyes. Whatever his personal business was, it was important to him. "Go, take care of your personal business, I'll take care of Christine. Catch up when you can."

Colt nodded and left the room.

"Is he okay?" Ames asked.

"Oh, you know, Linda," Ash grimaced. "I think she is still bothering him."

"Maybe we can give her name to whoever is initiating these women into the Branded Wives Club," Ames said sarcastically.

"That is karma at its finest," Ash agreed.

Ash met the ADA in the lobby of the criminal building. "You have a search and arrest warrant," she asked.

"Right here," Christine patted her purse. "His name is Tyree Fisher."

"How do you want to run this," Ash said.

"A SWAT team is meeting us at the corner down from the house. Once they surround the place, so the creep doesn't get out the back door, you and I will politely knock on the front door."

"Stand in front of me until the door starts to open," Ash reminded her, "then step out of the way. I'll burst through the door and handcuff him. Does anyone else live in the house?"

"According to our records, he lives alone," she said.

Ash pulled her car into the perp's driveway and escorted Christine to the door. "Put on your best insurance sales face," she suggested. "Try not to kill this guy. We're pretty certain there are two or three others involved. We need him to turn on them."

Ash nodded and rang the doorbell. She stepped back, so only Christine was visible through the door peephole. She waited as the deadbolt clicked and the door opened a crack. Like a bolt of lightning, the detective kicked open the door, had the man face down on the floor, and cuffed. She Mirandized him as she pulled him to his feet. The man hadn't been difficult to take down. He was a mere husk of a man.

"Wow!" Christine exhaled. "I heard you were fast, but...," Both laughed as the tension of the takedown slipped from their bodies.

Tyree Fisher made Ash rethink her theory on the zombie apocalypse. The man looked as if he had risen from the dead. The stench of urine-laced body odor and stale tobacco made the detective grit her teeth and wish for one of Risa's essential-oil masks.

Fisher's eyes almost disappeared into recessed sockets and hollow cheeks inverted beneath sharp cheekbones. The emaciated man looked as if someone had shrink-wrapped his bones in skin. Ash was certain the man had AIDS. Needle-tracked arms confirmed Ash's suspicion Fisher was an addict.

"Keep him away from the general population until we rule out AIDS," Ash instructed an officer who placed the handcuffed man into a black and white.

"Here," Christine held out a small bottle of hand sanitizer. "I am only sorry I don't have enough for you to bathe in."

"So am I." Ash gave her a lop-sided smile and coated her hands in the sanitizing liquid.

Christine and Ash began a methodical search of the house. One room was a high-tech computer bank. Computer screens provided the only light in the room. Each computer was on a different chatroom. One computer seemed to be accepting orders from the internet. Ash flipped the light switch and stared at the many photos of teenage boys and girls taped to the walls around the room.

There seemed to be a reason for the placement of the photos, but Ash wasn't certain what it was. "Bring him back in here," she instructed an officer.

Tyree stared straight ahead, as Ash spoke to him. "Why are these photos divided into three different groups?" Ash asked.

Tyree blinked but said nothing. Ash walked to the wall that contained only girls. "Whom do you place on this wall?"

"I want my attorney," Tyree yelled suddenly.

"Give me five minutes alone with him and he'll only need a doctor," Colt growled as he joined the team.

Tyree swallowed nervously and eyed Colt.

"Yeah," Ash nodded. "Let's leave Tyree in officer Layne's custody while we search the rest of the house." She pulled Christine's arm to lead her from the room.

"Close the door behind you," Colt smiled maniacally at Tyree and removed his knife from the pocket of his jeans. "Tyree and I want to get real, up close and personal.

As Christine pulled the door closed, she heard Colt say, "Where I come from, we castrate animals with undesirable characteristics."

"Wait! Wait!" Tyree screamed. "I can tell you what you want to know."

Christine raised a questioning eyebrow at Ash. "Works every time," the beautiful detective grinned as she re-entered the room.

"That wall," Tyree point to the girl's only wall, "is for the little fools who asked to be raped."

"That wall," he pointed to the boy's only wall, "is boys that may have died during the…ah…transaction."

He gulped as he turned to the wall containing boys and girls. "They were sold to the highest bidder. I don't know what happened to them."

Christine's beautiful face seemed to crumble. "Oh, my God. I have a special place in our version of hell for you," She hissed in Tyree's face.

"Take him to the precinct," Colt shoved Tyree toward the door. "And give him his phone call to his lawyer. Don't bathe him until after his lawyer's visitation. Whoever is representing this sack of shit should have the opportunity to share the full essence of the man."

Christine shook her head. "Good job. You two are very good." She had heard the two detectives were very skilled at playing hardball without ever crossing the line.

"There must be over a hundred pictures here," Christine frowned as she walked around the room. "Far more victims than we have complaints."

She looked closely at each computer. "This one seems to be accepting orders for their victims."

She read one of the orders. "WU12. WTB."

"What does that mean," Colt stared at the screen.

"White, under twelve. Want to buy," Christine translated.

"How are you ever going to identify all these kids," Ash scowled. "This is a living nightmare. There aren't just two or three scum suckers involved. It's a sophisticated ring. These kids are sold to the highest bidder."

"We have a new cyber security firm on board," Christine said. "If anyone can help us they can."

"Leave everything just as it is," she instructed the SWAT team. "Cyber-crimes will be here in a few minutes."

"We're going to leave it with you," Colt said. "You know the drill, when you turn up the first body, we can get involved full force."

"Thanks," Christina squeezed Colt's arm. "You have already been a tremendous help."

As Colt and Ash drove away in Colt's car, the ADA called Jessica Barton.

"You okay," Ash asked her partner. "Get your emergency taken care of?"

"Yeah," Colt nodded. "You know they fished Martinez out of the Trinity last week?"

Ash nodded.

"The drug cartel he was involved with is threatening his wife. They're trying to force her into taking his place in their drug distribution business.

"I'm certain these are the same people who killed Manny. She could be their next victim. She knew nothing about her husband's business. She is scared to death.

"I'm going to set up surveillance on her home for the rest of the week. Just in case, they try to convince her."

"Want some help?" Ash volunteered.

"That would be great." Colt nodded. "We'd better let Ames know what we are doing. We never know when something like this will blow up in our faces."

Ash called Ames, then her wife.

Ash took the nine p.m. to one a.m. shift and Colt watched Martina's home from one until she went to the restaurant in the morning.

The public's reaction to the news coverage of the Branded Wives Club was unbelievable. The ever-insatiable public wanted every detail about the murders.

Requests poured in from news shows and TV personalities wanting to interview the investigators on the case.

Ames spent more time appeasing the press than supervising his squad. Twelve-hour days were the norm instead of the exception. His star detectives refused to be interviewed or photographed.

Colt didn't want his private detective clients to know he was a cop.

Ash didn't want anyone to see her photo and connect her face with Adrian Austin. As Austin, she traveled outside of Texas, for book releases and autograph parties.

The attention from the news media had also turned up the heat from the top brass.

Risa had confirmed that the death of Stacy Vanguard was identical to the prior two, right down to the DNA of the baby.

Ash's phone dinged a text from Colt. "Pulling up behind you."

After a few minutes, her partner slipped into the passenger side of Ash's car.

"Everything's quiet on the Western front," Ash joked. "Not even so much as a stray cat."

"I'll take over now," Colt said. "You get some sleep."

"Nah, Lana has gone to her parents for the weekend," Ash frowned. "Not much to go home to right now. The house is empty without her."

"Yeah," Colt huffed. "I know the feeling."

"I'm sorry, Bro," Ash apologized. "That was totally insensitive on my part."

"No, forget about it. You can't walk around on eggshells for the rest of our lives. I was just having a mini pity party."

"Did you see Risa's final report on Stacy Vanguard?" Ash asked

"Yeah," Colt sighed. "I think these women were targeted because they were cheating wives. I hate infidelity, but I wouldn't kill someone over it. God knows I would have killed Linda years ago."

"Any word from Mrs. Martinez?" Ash asked. "Have those men tried to contact her again?"

"No," Colt said. "Hopefully, they have gone away. Let's continue this stake out until Friday, and then give it up."

"I got a call from Christine this afternoon," Ash said. "She has…"

Both stiffened as a black sedan parked down the block from Martina's home. After five minutes, two men emerged from the vehicle and moved toward the woman's house. The glint of moonlight off a barrel told Ash, at least one man had a gun.

"They're armed," she whispered.

Colt whispered, "Our, now you see me now you don't move?"

Ash nodded.

The two detectives silently slid from Ash's car and flattened against the fence that ran along the sidewalk to Martina's drive.

They had run their maneuver many times. They had no need for communications. Ash went around one side of Martina's house, and Colt took the other. They trapped the two drug dealers between them.

As they reached the corners of the house, they could see the men trying to pick the lock on Martina's back door. Suddenly the back yard lit up like a park, and the men whirled around, their guns drawn.

"Police," Ash barked. The gunmen swung around and started firing in her direction. Ash jumped back behind the house, as two quick shots snapped through the night.

The faces of both men burst open as Colt's Glock drove a bullet into the back of each one's head. In the throes of death, one of them fired a wild shot that lodged in the roof overhang.

The wail of sirens told Ash, someone had already called the police.

When it all went down, Colt was glad they had looped in Captain Ames. Christine had gotten them a search warrant in a short amount of time. A thorough search of the two-drug dealer's apartments had yielded names and details of drug transactions. Armed with the information, Christine had obtained every warrant they had requested.

Just as Colt had suspected several of the powerful players in the Seventh Street Gang were involved with the drug cartel. Their arrests and subsequent indictments had broken the back of the drug cartel in Fort Worth. National News picked up the story and requested an interview with the person responsible for the operation.

"That would be you, Captain," Ash and Colt had insisted. "No way are we getting in front of a camera."

##

Jessica tried to keep the spring from her step as she walked into Dr. Denton's office. She didn't want her to know she was falling in love with someone else. She had been on her meds for over a month. Dr. Denton was right. She didn't feel foggy headed, and she wasn't having fantasies about every woman she met. She was only fantasizing about ADA Christine Canton. She wondered if she would be adequate for her.

"Jessica, right on time, as usual, I see." Lana started to pick up her pad when her patient sat down in the chair in front of her desk.

No power games today, Lana thought.

"What would you like to talk about today?" Lana watched her closely. She was different.

"First, I want to say that you were right. The medicine does level out, and the fogginess goes away." Jessica beamed as if she had discovered a miracle. "I have been on my meds for over a month, and I feel…normal."

Lana studied her patient for several minutes. She wanted her to continue talking, to dive into her lurid fantasies.

"I visited a friend and his family Sunday," Jessica said. "It was my godson's birthday. I enjoyed it."

Lana waited to hear how her godson's mother had pushed her into the utility room and kissed her. The fantasy never came.

"Are you seeing someone?" Lana asked casually, rearranging the items on her desk.

"Maybe," Jessica smiled. "I don't want to discuss it. I don't want to jinx it."

"Is everything okay at work?" Lana smiled.

Jessica nodded.

"No more unwanted advances from the young woman at work?"

"We both know that was just my imagination running wild," Jessica chuckled. "Real love is always so much better than anything imaginary."

Lana wondered if Jessica had gotten laid.

Chapter 8

Christine read the list of twenty names. Twenty out of one hundred and fifty-nine. It had taken Jessica and her team over a month to track down the identity of the twenty teenagers. Now for the hard part: notifying the families and finding the teens.

She looked up and smiled as Jessica entered the restaurant. They had formed the habit of lunching together daily, to discuss the case. Today, she wanted to go over the list with Jessica.

Christine continued to be impressed with Jessica's abilities with a computer. She had used facial recognition software to match the photos on Tyree's wall with people in the national missing person's database.

Now she was in the process of writing a program to match email addresses with the owners of those they had discovered on Tyree's computers. They still had a long way to go before this case was over.

Tyree Fisher had plea bargained for a twenty-five-year sentence and had given them lists of his clients. All transactions had taken place over the internet, so Fisher had never met most of the pedophiles.

Fortunately, all the men had paid with their credit cards or PayPal. It hadn't been too difficult to track them down.

"ADA Canton," Jessica shyly smiled as she sat down beside her in the circular booth.

"Ms. Barton," she giggled as she addressed Jessica as formally as she had greeted her. "Look, we have addresses and parent's names on all twenty of these kids."

"Now you begin the hard part," Jessica grimaced as she thought about notifying parents. She moved as closely to her as possible, so she could see the list. Christine was soft and warm.

"Your next step isn't an easy one either," Christine noted. "Are you having any luck matching the missing teens with the buyers?"

"I have matched three dead John Doe's in the morgue, with the photos. We can give those parents definite resolution to the horror of the unknown; they have been living with."

"Want your usual, beautiful?" the waitress flirted with Jessica.

Christine smiled as she noticed how Jessica blushed and nodded her head. "Same for my lady, too," she said.

Christine found it endearing that she seemed to be embarrassed by the attention women sometimes paid her. For one so brilliant, she was extremely shy and sweet.

"As soon as you provide me with the names of the men who paid with their credit cards, I'll issue warrants for their arrests," Christine said.

"How will you charge them?" Jessica asked.

"I will throw the book at them. Murder, solicitation, indecency with a minor. The list goes on and on." Christine scowled. "I want the bastards that harmed these children to die in prison. They are the worst of the worst, preying on naive children."

"I love your passion for what you do," Jessica smiled.

"And I love your passion for computers," Christine smiled back. "We make a good team."

"Yes, we do," Jessica nodded.

"How will you prove the credit card holder is a criminal?" Jessica asked. "Can't they simply say they lost their card or that someone else used their card?"

"You have a good point." Christine said. "I'll set up a special task force to run a sting operation on them."

##

The first body rolled into the morgue at eight a.m. Sunday morning. Risa had just set down her cup of coffee and slipped into her lab coat. Detective Colt Layne accompanied the body. The sight of the handsome detective almost made Risa forget how upset she was about being called in on her day off.

"Morning pretty lady," Colt smile didn't hide the exhaustion in his eyes. He had been up all night. "I hate to start your day off like this, but it's only going to get worse."

"What is it?" Risa wryly eyed the body bag.

"Body," Colt grimaced. "Good news is decomposition is complete, so no smell."

"Bad news is I'll have a hard time determining the time of death." Risa helped Colt transfer the body bag onto the stainless-steel lab table. It was light. "Tell me what's going on."

"We think this is one of the teens trafficked by Tyree. There are three more where this one came from."

Risa closed her eyes briefly. "The way you and Ash have been working this case, like pit bulls with a bone, I knew it was just a matter of time until the bodies would start materializing on my table."

"Yeah," Colt nodded. "It's a damn shame. Dumbass kids. They leave themselves wide open to these freaks."

"When did you sleep last," Risa eyed the disheveled man. "You look like hell."

"Compliments are all I ever get from you," Colt grinned. "I'm going home to sleep as soon as Ash relieves me."

"Why didn't you call me when they found the body," Ash asked Colt, as she draped her suit jacket over the back of the chair.

"And interrupt the first decent date you've had with Lana in a month. No way. Obviously, I managed without you." Colt chuckled. "Now you owe me one."

Colt tossed a file onto Ash's desk. "Here's what we have on the body I just delivered to Risa. Carter called me on my way here. It looks like we have three more bodies in the perp's back yard."

Ash nodded. "Now, go home and get some sleep. I'll see you tomorrow morning."

Ash watched her friend stagger slightly from exhaustion as he walked from the bullpen. She opened the file and began to read.

The pervert had gone by the names of *The Lawman and The Enforcer* in all his dealings with Tyree. Christine's computer genius had traced his payments through his PayPal account. Christie had gotten a court order to force PayPal to turn over the information she needed.

The man's real name was Phillip Solomon. He was single, wealthy, a pedophile and a killer. He was in interrogation room four.

Ash decided to visit with Risa before she spoke with Solomon. She walked to the break room for coffee. It was lukewarm and strong enough to hold up the wall by itself.

"Good morning, Doc," Ash greeted.

"I'm glad you think so," Risa huffed. "What the hell is wrong with kids nowadays?"

"Spoiled, coddled, uninformed, entitled, naïve; should I go on?" Ash poured her coffee into the morgue sink and pitched the cup in the trash.

"I bet this one wished he had listened to his parents by the time he died," Risa frowned. "This is pretty gruesome, Ash. I'm glad I'm just dealing with a skeleton. Makes it less realistic."

"Do you have a cause of death?"

"Yeah, broken neck," Risa said. "Looks like someone just snapped his neck. I only hope he died before they did this to him."

Risa pulled the sheet down to the skeleton's knees.

"What the hell is that sticking through his stomach cavity," Ash scowled.

"A nightstick," Risa almost whispered. "It was inserted here." She turned the skeleton to its side so Ash could see the baton protruding from the sacrum.

"That is where the rectum would have been," Risa painted her a clear picture of the cruelty of the abusers. "In here and out through the stomach wall."

"I get the picture," Ash exhaled sharply.

"I have the bastard in interrogation, but I've got to get control before I question him, or I might just stick a nightstick up his…"

"I'm ready for a break," Risa smiled. "Buy me a cup of coffee?"

"Gladly," Ash helped her slip off her lab coat.

Ash and Risa waited until the waitress poured their coffee and placed a Danish in front of them.

"We have three more coming in from the same place," Ash warned her. "Carter is sending them in as soon as they finish digging them up. Do you need to be there?"

"No, I'll be of more service here," Risa stirred her coffee. "I sent my team out there."

"Risa, I'm sorry you're getting this dumped on you," Ash grimaced.

"Believe it or not," Risa frowned, "I've seen worse. I left New York because the animals kept finding new and horrific ways to kill and maim each other. I'd hoped Texas would be different."

Ash's phone dinged a text message. "Just wanted to thank you for a wonderful night. I miss you." Lana had included a selfie of herself in the negligee she had worn to bed last night. A copy of *Thirty-Six Ways to Die* was opened and lying flat across her breasts, showing just enough cleavage to make Ash wish she were with her.

"Groan," Ash text back. "I see you're reading my favorite author."

"I have the hots for your favorite author," Lana text back. "Call me when you have time. Love you."

"Love you, too."

"I can tell by that goofy grin on your face; that was Lana," Risa laughed. "You two are wonderful together."

##

Captain Ames was sitting at his desk when Ash returned. "Sorry you had to come in on your day off," he said. "Brandt is sick. I'm not sure Carter can handle this alone."

"It's okay, Captain. I just had to get my head on straight before I questioned Solomon. I would like to rip out his throat. So, I had to get control."

Ames nodded. "Any new leads on the BWC case?" The Branded Wives Club had been reduced to the BWC acronym by the news media. Ash thought they gave everything initials because they were too lazy to spell or speak the entire words. Acronyms always made things seem less heinous.

"Nothing new. I want to visit Trask," Ash said. "Things have been so crazy with the drug bust and the pedophile case; I haven't had time."

"At least, the BWC killer has been quiet for over a month," Ames frowned. "I fear it is just the picnic before the fireworks."

"I think I will let Solomon stew for a while, and see Trask," Ash said. "A brisk walk to The Towers will be good for me. A Sunday visit might catch him off guard."

Ames nodded. "For my part, you can leave Solomon shackled there for the entire forty-eight hours we can hold him. It is Sunday. Easy to forget a fellow locked in a room out of sight."

"Yeah, but overnight should do the trick," Ash grinned. "I'll probably be in a better frame of mind tomorrow, and Colt will be back. He is the very best bad cop in the world."

Evan Trask was dressed to go out to dinner. He wondered who would be ringing his doorbell at this hour and why the doorman had allowed anyone up without notifying him.

"Detective Denton," Trask opened the door and stepped back to allow Ash to enter. "It is good to see you. I never had the opportunity to thank you for your kindness after my wife's death."

"No thanks necessary, sir. Just one human to another. I wanted to do all I could to help." Ash looked Trask up and down. "I see I am interrupting your evening. I just wanted to check on you and see if you need anything."

"Only my wife's killer captured and brought to justice," Trask smirked.

"As do I," Mr. Trask. "Well, I'll let you get back to your evening.

Trask closed the door and waited until he heard the elevator ding and the doors close. He did not want to ride down with the detective.

Ash stepped into the elevator, punched the button, and got off one floor below Trask's apartment. She waited until she heard Trask ride the elevator to the lobby then she climbed the stairs to the penthouse floor.

She tried the door, and it was locked. One look at the state-of-the-art lock told her she couldn't pick it. She followed the hall around the suite looking for another entrance. She found the service entrance.

"Come on, hurry up." A woman's voice with a strong Spanish accent called. "We will miss the show."

"I have to set the alarm," another Spanish voice answered her. "Oh, hell! What is the new code?"

"3481 and pound sign. Hurry."

Ash pressed herself into the alcove at the end of the hall. *3481*, she memorized the code. She waited until she was certain the elevator was gone and then let herself into the penthouse.

She searched the bedroom first. She wondered how Trask could sleep in a bed that had been covered with his wife's blood.

She found nothing in the bedroom and moved around the spacious suite looking for Trask's study or an office.

The first two doors she had opened were extra bedrooms. "Let's see what is behind door number three," she said aloud. "Bingo!"

She checked Trask's desk drawers, under his desk blotter and found nothing. She checked the bookshelves and was a bit disappointed that not a single copy of Adrian Austin's novels was present. She looked behind pictures and furniture for a safe. Behind a painting of Trask looking very self-important, she found the safe. She had no idea of the combination.

She returned to Trask's desk, flipped to the back of his day calendar and found nothing. His personal phone book yielded no information either. She slumped down in Trask's chair trying to think. She lifted the calendar that fit into the desk blotter. She felt as if she had won the lottery. A combination was on the blotter. She wrote it on one of Trask's sticky notes and went to the safe.

"Left, right, left," Ash said aloud as she turned the dial to the designated number. The final number clicked into place, and an electric whirring sound slid the lock bar back. Ash pulled the safe door open and surveyed the contents. On the bottom shelf, beneath several insurance policies and stock certificates, was a manila envelope like the one she'd found in Jeb Trent's office.

Ash pulled the photos from the envelope and shuffled through a dozen photos of Elizabeth Trask in very compromising positions. She briefly wondered how Elizabeth could get her legs that high.

She spread the photos on Trask's desk and copied them with her iPhone. Ames would be so proud of her. Ash returned the photos to the envelope and carefully placed it back exactly as she had found it.

Ash had just finished setting the alarm and closed the door when she heard the elevator open.

"I'm glad you opted for dinner here," Trask laughed. "I will call the kitchen and have them cook whatever you would like."

"Evan, you are too good to me," a female voice cooed.

Ash froze. She knew that voice. She'd heard that voice almost every day for four years. Ash pushed aside the raging anger she felt and quickly ran down the fire exit. Her legs were shaking when she reached the bottom floor and exited through the service entrance.

##

Ames and Ash printed the photos from Ash's cell phone. As with the Laura Trent photos, Elizabeth was easily identifiable, but her lover was not.

"It's almost as if he is posing her for the photos," Ash commented.

"He certainly keeps any image of himself out of sight," Ames nodded. "Take a run at Vanguard and see if he has the same type photos."

"I'm seeing a pattern developing," Ash said. "I'm pretty sure the lover and the murderer are the same, but who is the damn photographer?"

"Or the husbands could have done it," Ames suggested.

"They all have iron-clad alibis. They were all out of the country when their wives died," Ash said.

"Remember that show where two strangers met on a train and decided to kill each other's wife." Ames frowned. "Each husband had the perfect alibi because a perfect stranger killed his wife."

"You may be right, Captain. How do we prove it?"

"I don't know, but let's keep this to ourselves. I don't even want Colt to know. You know how impatient he gets. I would like to have all the pieces to this puzzle in place before I put it out there."

"I'll re-interview each husband and see if they all have alibis for the nights the other wives died." Ash volunteered. "If you are right, at least, one of the three should be without an alibi the night of each murder."

"See what you can find out about Vanguard." Ames nodded. "As soon as we have enough proof for a warrant, we'll contact ADA Canton."

##

"Jessica! Jessica! Wake up sweetheart," Christine gently shook her cyber genius.

Jessica jumped, and then looked around trying to ascertain her location.

"I didn't mean to startle you," Christine said, "I...your door was unlocked, and I wanted to give you the news."

Christine watched her as she ran her fingers through her long, dark hair. She looked like a little girl that had just awakened from a nap. She fisted the sleep from her eyes and smiled sweetly at the ADA.

"Did you just call me sweetheart?" she grinned.

"It just slipped out," Christine frowned slightly, "I was trying not to startle you."

"Yes, of course," her grin spread even broader. "I'm sorry. I worked all night to get more names for you. I fell asleep with the door unlocked."

"You must be more careful," Christine teased. "How would it look if someone robbed the city's security specialist or worse?"

Jessica inhaled deeply. Christine smelled of bath soap, perfume, and hairspray. She was the most beautiful woman Jessica had ever met.

"They couldn't get past the reception area," she said. "I...I have at least fifty names for you. I have names and addresses."

"Why don't you go home and shower?" Christine eyed her jeans and pullover. She looked young. It was the first time she had seen Jessica in anything but a tailored pantsuit. "I will meet you for breakfast in an hour."

"I have an apartment at the top of the building," Jessica shrugged. "I live here during the week and go to the lake on weekends to regenerate."

Christine nodded and licked her lips, moistening them. "I'll just wait here for you."

"Fifteen minutes," Jessica grinned as she stepped into the elevator.

As promised, Jessica returned fifteen minutes later, impeccably dressed. Her employees began arriving and greeted Christine as Jessica folded the printouts she had worked on all night. "We can go over these at breakfast," she said. Her brown eyes sparkled as she followed Christine out the door.

"Colt," Ash smiled, "you are just in time to assist me in interviewing Phillip Solomon."

"He's been here all night?" Colt grinned as he nonchalantly made his way to the coffee bar. "No need to hurry."

"I wanted to wait for you," Ash nodded. "You know bad cop and psycho cop."

"It would be easy to go psycho on this slime bucket," Colt said. "Risa just filled me in on some of the things he did to those kids. What a sick bastard!"

"ADA Canton wants to bury him, so the more we can get out of him the better, but by the book. Her words, not mine," Ash led the way to interrogation room four.

"Whoa," Ash backed out of the room. "It smells like our pedophile has soiled himself."

"I demand my attorney," Solomon screamed. "Now!"

Colt ignored the man's insistent demands for an attorney. "I'm going to have someone clean you up first," he said.

An hour later, Solomon sat in interrogation room two. "Here," Colt shoved a cell phone toward him. "Call your attorney."

Colt looked through the file Ash had assembled the day before. She had the photo of the boy that had been on Tyree's wall. He was a sweet, cherubic-looking young man. According to the missing person's report his name was Brady Thomas, thirteen.

Along with the picture, were the morgue photos of Brady's skeleton showing the placement of the nightstick. Colt clutched his fist and glared at Solomon. If he had a nightstick in his hands, he'd beat the pompous bastard to death.

"My attorney is on his way," Solomon smirked. "He said I didn't have to talk to you without him."

"We're going to Mirandize you, just to save time," Colt turned on a video camera and read Solomon his rights.

"We don't need to talk to you," Ash said as she spread the photos of Brady Thomas out in front of Solomon. We have these.

"This is a PayPal receipt showing your credit card was used to purchase this young man from an online website.

"This photo shows Brady's body being dug up from your back yard," Ash continued.

"Someone stole my wallet and all my credit cards," Solomon said smugly.

"And yet they were still in your wallet along with your personal belongings you placed in your bag when we booked you yesterday."

Solomon's eyes darted around the room and finally rested on the photos. "I don't know how that got in my back yard," he sneered.

"We do," Colt snorted. "After you tortured and abused this poor kid, you snapped his neck. Then you dug a hole in your expansive back yard and buried him."

"You can't prove that," Solomon screeched. "You are just making that up."

"I probably couldn't prove it alone," Colt smiled sinisterly, "but we have one of the finest forensic pathologists in the country, and she can prove it beyond a doubt."

"She has collected your DNA from Brady's body," Ash said disgustedly.

"The real clincher is your fingerprints all over that nightstick," Colt hissed.

"Of course, my fingerprints are on the stick," Solomon grasped at straws. "That doesn't mean I killed him."

Colt slowly slid all the evidence back into the file. He placed himself between Solomon and the camera, then leaned down and whispered into the pedophile's ear. "If I don't start hearing the truth, as soon as that camera is turned off, I am going to ram my fist down your throat all the way to your dick, grab it and pull it up through you lying teeth."

The door opened, and Solomon's attorney stepped into the room.

"I told you not to talk to them," the lawyer barked.

"I didn't tell them anything," Solomon squealed.

"I'd like to hear the evidence against my client," the attorney said as he snapped open his briefcase and removed a legal pad and pen.

Ash spread out the photos again and walked the lawyer through the evidence. "We have three more bodies like this one," she finished.

The attorney silently slid his pad and pen back into his briefcase. He snapped shut the clasps and stood. "You need to call someone else. I refuse to accept this case." He couldn't leave the evil in the room fast enough.

"Wow!" Colt said gleefully. "Look at that. You've had your one phone call, a visit from your attorney, and now you're all ours. Detective Denton, why don't you get a cup of coffee or maybe lunch? Take your time." Colt pretended to turn off the camera.

"No! No! Don't leave me alone with him," Solomon begged. "I'll talk. I'll answer any questions you have."

"That's more like it," Colt said.

Solomon provided names and dates, other burial places and other men who had participated in his "little soirees"—as he called them. ADA Christine Canton and Jessica Barton were in the viewing room listening to the confession.

"Look," Solomon shrugged, "we didn't mean to kill them. We were just looking for a little action."

Christine wasted no time filing every charge she could conjure against Solomon. A public defender was appointed to defend Solomon after two other criminal attorneys refused his case.

Jessica was in court every day, observing Christine fighting for a guilty verdict against Solomon.

Phillip Solomon was convicted and sentenced to life in prison at the Gatesville, Texas facility.

Tyree Fisher had succumbed to AIDS before Phillip Solomon went to trial. Christine had hours of video statements from Tyree to use against other pedophiles who had participated in the nationwide trafficking ring.

Colt tossed the newspaper on Ash's desk, "She put the bastard away," he said. "Gatesville."

"Ooh," Ash shrugged. "Couldn't happen to a nicer guy."

"What's Gatesville," Risa asked.

"The prison with the highest incident of prisoner rape in the nation. In law enforcement circles, we call it Rapesville." Colt cocked his head to the side. "I suspect Phillip Solomon will get all the action he can handle and then some."

"Okay everyone," Captain Ames stood at the front of the bullpen for roll call. He went over the cases the department was working and asked for reports.

"I want to thank all of you for the way you handled the Internet Pedophile case. Your cooperation with the DA's office and your attention to detail have led to the recovery of ninety-eight live teenagers who were being trafficked by the pedophiles.

"We located the bodies of fifty-nine others. We have recovered all but two of the young people who were taken by the ring. Carter and Brandt will continue to work on the case. Keep your eyes and ears open and report anything suspicious to them.

"Now for the fun stuff," Ames held up a handful of tickets. "Time to purchase your tickets for the Policeman's Awards Banquet. I have a feeling several of the officers in this room will be receiving trophies this year. I want our squad to bring home the Detective of the Year honor."

"And, folks, we need to solve the BWC case."

##

Chapter 9

Dr. Lana Denton pulled her file on Jessica Barton from the drawer. Jessica was one of her biggest success stories. Once she had convinced the woman she had to stay on her meds, she had become a different person.

She never discussed her cases with Ash, not even her success stories. Doctor-patient confidentiality was something Lana adhered to religiously. If a patient sought help from Dr. Lana Denton, they could be confident no one would ever know their name was on the beautiful physiatrist's patient list.

Watching Jessica's transformation from a timid, delusional recluse to a happy, confident woman had been like watching a caterpillar morph into a beautiful Monarch butterfly. *Butterflies don't live very long*, Lana thought.

She looked up as her secretary ushered Jessica into her office. "How are you today, Jessica?"

"I'm great," Jessica said enthusiastically, as she sat down in front of her desk. "And you?"

Ash's gorgeous face flashed into her mind. "I am excellent," Lana smiled.

"How are things going at work?" she asked.

"Couldn't be better. Everything is running smoothly. No problems."

"And women have stopped coming on to you?" Lana raised a quizzical eyebrow.

Jessica laughed. "It is amazing how your medications have made me unattractive to the other women, Dr. Denton."

"Yet you are attractive to someone special, aren't you?" Lana pushed. She wanted to know who her special someone was. "She likes you as much as you like her?"

"I think so," Jessica grinned.

Jessica brushed an imaginary bit of lint from her jacket sleeve. She wasn't certain how to approach the next subject.

"I am doing very well," she smiled shyly, "aren't I?"

"Miraculously," Lana laughed.

"I thought that perhaps I could cut my sessions back to once a month instead of every week."

"I think that's an excellent idea," Lana nodded. She always let her patients tell her when they no longer needed her as a crutch.

"Let's set your next meeting four weeks from today," she added. She scribbled Jessica's thirty-day prescription on her pad and handed the sheet to her.

"Excellent, excellent," Jessica's dark eyes danced as she stood to leave. "Thank you, Dr. Denton. Thank you so much."

##

"Darling, please zip me up," Lana backed up to her wife.

"I will," Ash bent to kiss the nape of her neck, "but it goes against everything I am feeling right now."

"Humm," Lana hummed as she turned to pull her close for one last soul-searing kiss before they left for the awards banquet.

"Is Colt bringing Risa tonight?" she asked as she settled into the chair Ash pulled out for her.

Ash nodded. "What would you like to drink? I'll fight my way to the bar."

"Wine." She looked around the table to see who was sitting with them. Captain Ames and his wife, Debbie; Colt and Risa; ADA Christine Canton and her husband. *Should be a fun night*, she thought.

Ash returned to the table with Risa and Colt in tow. "Wine for my lady," she bowed ceremoniously and winked at her.

Colt pulled out Risa's chair and wandered off to the bar.

"You look radiant," Risa complimented her friend. "Although I've had no reason to wear it, I'm pretty sure I recognize that look."

Lana blushed slightly and sipped her wine. She spotted Christine across the dance floor. The ADA was laughing and holding onto a friend for dear life. It was obvious she was enjoying herself.

Lana could see Captain Ames and his wife dancing a slow dance. Everyone was enjoying the party.

"Shall we," Ash stood and held out her hand to her wife. Lana slipped into her arms, loving the feel of Ash's firm body against hers.

When the dance ended, Lana was beside Christine and her friend.

"Lana, Ash," Christine smiled a brilliant smile, "Have you met our Chief of Cyber Crime, Jessica Barton?"

Jessica moved so Lana could see her. "Jessica, this is Dr. Lana Denton and her wife Detective Ash Denton." Christine made the introductions.

Ash couldn't help noticing the look that passed over her wife's face at seeing Jessica. *She knows her*, Ash thought.

A slow smile spread across Jessica's face as she held out her hand to shake hands with Ash. "Detective Denton, it's a pleasure to meet you. I read your name almost daily in the newspaper. It's good to put a face with the name."

She turned to Lana and nodded her head slightly. "And you're married to Dr. Denton. Lucky woman."

"Yes," Ash smiled. "Lucky me."

"I requested seating with your party," Christine smiled. "Jessica and I have worked so closely with homicide lately; I feel like I am a part of your team."

"A very welcome part," Ash grinned. "Honey, Christine and Jessica broke open the Internet Pedophile case or as the news media dubbed it, the IP case. I worked it from the office, so I never met Jessica."

"I have been following that case closely," Lana said. "I never saw your name associated with it," Lana addressed Jessica.

"She insisted we keep her name out of the paper," Christine looked admiringly at Jessica. "She's very modest. Much like Ash and Colt."

The rest of the evening was delightful. The couples danced, dined, and exchanged stories. Jessica was charming and entertaining. She kept the table in stitches with her internet failures and successes stories.

"Jessica holds the copyright to several popular iPhone apps and games," Christine discreetly informed Lana. "She truly is a computer genius."

"Jessica was invaluable to us," Colt added. "There's no way we would have ever rooted out the sleazeballs in the IP case without her."

Jessica bowed her head self-consciously. "Getting me involved was Christine's idea."

"May I borrow the three of you for a minute," Captain Ames addressed Colt, Ash and Jessica. The four walked to a quieter end of the room.

"Where's Robert?" Lana asked Christine.

"I wish I knew," the ADA answered. "At the last minute, he said he had urgent business and told me to use his ticket to take a friend. I invited Jessica."

"Nothing serious, I hope?" Lana said.

"Probably has to do with the campaign. I try not to get involved with it," Christine shrugged. "Excuse me. I think I'll powder my nose."

"I'll join you," Risa, followed the ADA from the room.

Jessica returned to the table as the three law enforcement officers continued talking.

"Is everything okay?" Lana asked

"Yes," Jessica said. "Just some loose ends in the IP case. Would you like to dance?"

Lana had no good reason to turn her down, so she joined her patient on the dance floor.

"Thank you for not outing me," Jessica whispered in her ear as she smoothly moved her around the dance floor.

"I would never do that, Jessica," Lana smiled. "I take doctor-patient confidentiality very seriously."

"I was a little frightened when I saw you," Jessica added. "I thought my world was about to come tumbling down."

"Why would you think that? You are doing wonderfully. It has been a joy to watch you tonight. You are so different from the woman I see in my office."

"I was afraid you would tell Christine I was a delusional schizophrenic. I love her," Jessica whispered. "This isn't one of my delusions. I truly love her. I stay on my meds for her."

"When a patient has improved as much as you, I would never do anything to jeopardize their chances for a normal life." *I never diagnosed her as schizophrenic*, Lana thought.

"You know she's married." Lana watched Jessica's eyes as she gave her the information she had obviously chosen to ignore.

"I know. It's okay," Jessica's eyes darkened. "I don't have to be with her. I only want to be around her. I'd never ask her to cheat on her husband. I could never trust a woman who'd cheat on her husband. If she cheated on him, she'd cheat on me."

"Jessica, have you been treated by other psychiatrists who have diagnosed you as schizophrenic?"

"No," Jessica's mouth twisted into an eerie smile. "I diagnosed myself."

The song ended, and Jessica guided Lana back to the table.

"There you are," Christine smiled at Jessica.

"With my wife," Ash frowned as she pulled Lana possessively into her arms for the next dance.

"So, how do you know Jessica?" Ash whispered in her wife's ear. A slight tremor ran through Lana's body, and she clutched Ash tighter.

"She's a professional acquaintance," she looked up at her wife. Ash knew her so well.

Ash knew it would do no good to question her further. She never discussed her clients.

The mayor tapped the microphone. "May I have everyone's attention? As you know, we are gathered here tonight to honor those law enforcement officers who have been outstanding in their field."

After an hour of acknowledging officers, the mayor reached the highest award given by the city.

"This was a tough decision," the mayor said. "It came down to two officers. Two detectives who have made a big difference in law and order in our town.

"Together they broke the largest drug cartel in our city and took down some pretty high ups in the process. They helped cybercrimes apprehend and successfully prosecute some of the most degenerate of criminals, a gang of internet pedophiles preying on our teenagers.

"They still have one case I would like to see closed," the mayor frowned. "I trust that will happen soon."

A slight titter ran through the crowd.

"I said it was difficult. I misspoke," the mayor grinned. "It was impossible. So, for the first time in our history, we are awarding the Officer of the Year Award to two detectives you all know well: Ash Denton and Colt Layne."

Lana and Risa walked to the front of the room. Lana leaned into the microphone. "I'm Ash's wife Lana, and this is Dr. Risa Mercer, we are accepting the awards for Ash and Colt tonight. I leave you with the words I am certain anyone married to a law enforcement officer has heard a thousand times. They had to leave. There was a break in the case."

Everyone laughed and gave the absent detectives a standing ovation.

As the two women walked back to their table, Risa's phone went off. She answered, spoke for about a minute, and then looked at Lana. "Sorry, I have to go, too. Can you get home okay?"

Lana suddenly realized she was without a car. Ash and Colt had taken theirs, and Risa was taking her own.

"I need to call a cab," she pulled her cell phone from her purse.

"Nonsense," Christine said. "Jessica and I will take you home."

"What address did you say," Colt asked as Ash gunned the sedan forward.

"I didn't," Ash said.

"You going to share it with me or do I have to guess where we're going?"

"Lee Dawson's place," Ash growled.

Colt jerked upright. He couldn't speak. "Linda?" he finally rasped.

"I don't know," Ash said. "Dispatch did say something about the BWC."

Colt choked on the bile that rose in his throat. He couldn't get Linda's beautiful face out of his mind. All the times he had held her. All the times he had made love to her. He loved her. Dear God, he loved her. He knew he shouldn't. Maybe he had gotten a break. Maybe fate had taken care of his cheating ex-wife for him. He would be free of his addiction to her. How could this be possible?

"How do you want to handle this?" Ash frowned as they pulled in front of the Dawson estate.

"Same as always," Colt shook his head as if clearing away memories.

"Do you want to see the body?"

"No, I'll see her in the lab," Colt shrugged. "You handle it just like you always do. I'll see what the responding officer has to say. If we are not careful, I will be taken off the case. I want to catch this bastard."

Risa met an ambulance as she drove up the road to the Dawson estate. *Maybe this one lived. Maybe we can catch this killer,* she thought.

The van from the coroner's office was in front of the house when Risa arrived. She parked her car next to Ash's car. A distraught Colt was sitting in Ash's car, his head in his hands. Her assistant was pushing the gurney carrying a body bag containing the latest victim.

She found Ash in the bedroom. The scene was like the other three: wine, cheese, a single red rose and copious amounts of blood on the bed.

"I met an ambulance," Risa frowned, "Did you get a shot at the perp?"

"No," Ash grimaced. "His wife shot him."

"What," Risa barked.

"Apparently, Dawson is our BWC killer," Ash said. "I'm not sure what happened. Linda had been stabbed and was hysterical. I sent her to the hospital. Have you seen Colt? I need to let him know the person in the body bag isn't Linda."

"He's still in your car."

Ash's phone dinged a message from Lana. "Home safe and sound. Missing you."

She texted back, "Love you."

##

Colt Layne paced the waiting room. Linda had been in surgery a little over an hour. He couldn't believe she was alive. His emotions had taken a roller coaster ride as he thought she was dead and then found out she was alive. From the scene, they had ascertained that Dawson had tried to kill her, but she had gotten to the gun she kept in her nightstand and shot him through the heart. Colt smiled. He had taught her to use a gun.

"Any word?" Captain Ames and his wife joined Colt in the waiting room.

"None yet," Colt shook his head. "Where's Ash?"

"She and Risa are still working the crime scene," Ames said. "We don't want to get sloppy just because it's one of our own, so to speak."

"Thanks, Captain," Colt nodded. "I appreciate you being here."

A tall, thin doctor entered the waiting room. "Mrs. Dawson is doing fine. Fortunately, the blade didn't hit any vital organs, and we were able to repair the damage done. The nurse will let you know when she's in her room."

"May I see her now?" Colt asked.

"Just for a minute. She may not know you. She is still heavily sedated. I will send a nurse for you when Mrs. Dawson is moved to recovery."

Colt ran his hand through his thick brown hair. *How could this happen?* He thought.

"Hey, Babe," Colt leaned over and kissed Linda's forehead as he clasped her hand in his.

"Colt, stay with me." Her voice was barely a whisper.

"I will, baby. Don't worry."

She slipped into unconsciousness as the nurse motioned Colt to leave.

"I hate to ask this of you, but I need you and Ash to question Linda together," Ames met Colt as he returned to the waiting room. "I just spoke to the doctor. He said she would be much better tomorrow after the drugs wear off. I want you, Ash and Lana to question her in the morning."

"Of course," Colt frowned.

"I don't want you to have any contact with her until then," Ames said sternly. "I want you to go home."

"But Captain..." Colt growled.

"That's not a request," Ames scowled. "It's an order. If we don't handle this case carefully, it'll bite us in the butt."

##

Lana answered her phone when the face of her beautiful wife appeared on the screen. "Hi honey," she breathed. "How much longer will you be?"

"We are wrapping up this mess. One more report to fill out and I'll be on my way to you. I'm sorry you were left without a vehicle tonight. I didn't realize Risa and Colt came in Risa's car."

"No problem. Christine and Jessica brought me home. Love you."

"Love you, too," Ash said.

Lana smiled as she thought of her ride home with Christine and Jessica. They had been funny and a little flirty with one another.

Lana had met Christine when they worked on the library fundraiser. She had been impressed with the tenacity of the assistant district attorney and her quick intelligence.

She had been surprised to learn that Christine was married to attorney Robert Canton. Robert had the reputation for being a ladies' man. He had made advances to Lana more than once, even though she was married. After she had told Ash about the man's forwardness, Canton's advances had stopped.

The Jessica Barton she now knew seemed much more fitted for Christine. However, she didn't figure Christine for a cheater and suspected the woman would ask for a divorce if she became serious about Jessica.

"Wow, great security," Jessica had said as they pulled up to the gated community. "You have a gate opener?"

"They're programmed into our cars." She had hesitated only briefly before giving Jessica the code to key into the gate keypad.

Ash met Risa at seven a.m. in the coffee shop across from the station. She wanted to get information on Lee Dawson's autopsy from the ME before she got Linda's story on the shooting. She had met with CSI at six to get their take on what had gone down.

Dawson's body had been found face down in the bed, indicating he was standing over Linda when she shot him. The blood spatters from the gunshot had a definite blank space where Linda's body would have been reclining on the bed.

Blood from Linda's stab wound had pooled on the bed. Every element of the BWC murders was present: the wine and cheese, and a knife for removal of nipples. It looked like Dawson was their BWC killer. The only thing missing was the branding iron.

Risa Mercer had gone in at five a.m. to do all the tests Ash had requested. She had been surprised when she had insisted on the testing of Linda's blood. Lord knows there was plenty of it. Both Dawson's had bled all over their bed.

"Did you get what you wanted from CSI," Risa smiled as she slid into the seat beside Ash.

"Yes," Ash nodded. "It looks like Linda was flat on her back when she shot Dawson, and his body fell across her onto the bed."

"The angle of the gunshot wound is consistent with that," Risa agreed. "The bullet entered the chest and exited through the back. A perfect heart shot."

"Anything else?" Ash said.

"I suspect you already knew this," Risa shrugged slightly. "She was pregnant. Less than a month, judging from the amount of human chorionic gonadotropin in her blood."

Ash raised an eyebrow, "English, please."

Risa laughed softly. "Human chorionic gonadotropin or hCG is the hormone produced by the placenta shortly after an embryo attaches to the uterine lining and builds up rapidly in the mother's body in the first few days of pregnancy.

"Does the baby's DNA match the father in the other three cases," Ash asked.

"The DNA fragments in the blood don't match the male DNA we have on the other fetuses." Risa bent her head. "It is also not a match for Lee Dawson."

"Jesus, Christ," Ash huffed. "With how many men was Linda sleeping?"

"Yeah, she is a piece of work." Risa snorted. "I guess the baby's Colt's."

"Listen," Colt said as they approached Linda's room, "don't be all hardass on her, okay?"

"All we need are the details on what happened," Ash nodded. "All the evidence we have collected looks pretty much like self-defense."

"Colt, I have been wondering when you would get here," Linda exclaimed as they entered the hospital room.

Her greeting to Ash was less than enthusiastic. "Hello, Ash."

"Linda," Ash nodded and took a seat in the chair at the foot of her bed.

Colt pulled a chair close to the side of her bed. "Honey, are you up to answering some questions?"

She nodded tentatively.

"Why don't you start with what led up to the shooting?" Colt encouraged her.

"Lee was supposed to be out of town, but he returned early." Linda watched Colt's face as she told her story. "I was watching a reality show on the TV in the bedroom. Lee opened a bottle of wine and set out some cheese and crackers. I changed into my pajamas and got into bed. We made love.

"After we watched a TV show, Lee went to the bathroom to get ready for bed. When he returned, he walked to my side of the bed with his hand behind his back. Before I knew what was happening, he stabbed me in the stomach. The pain was intense. I must have passed out.

"When I came to, Lee was gone. I got the gun from my nightstand. I was trying to stop the bleeding when Lee returned. He was carrying a red rose. I hid the gun under the covers.

"He said my death would look like one more of the serial killer's murders because I was a whore.

"He screamed and ranted like a madman. He told me he knew I was screwing Colt and that I hadn't even waited until the ink dried on our marriage license before I had crawled back into your bed.

"I tried to reason with him, but he was insane. He started toward me with the knife. I knew he'd slit my throat. I shot him." Linda broke down and burst into tears. "Colt, it was horrible. I've made such a mess of everything."

Colt consoled her. "It's okay, baby. It's over now. I'm here. No one is going to hurt you."

"Did Lee buy the wine, or was it some you had in the house," Ash asked casually.

"I'm sure it was wine we had in the house," Linda sobbed softly. "Lee never bought groceries or anything. The housekeeper took care of things like that."

##

Chapter 10

It seemed Nora Glade had a direct line to the precinct. She had landed the headlines of the *Telegram* with her in-depth story of the police department's resolution of the Branded Wives Club murders. Lee Dawson was tried and convicted by her article. From reading her quotes of Linda, it was evident she had somehow interviewed Linda Dawson. Glade hadn't even bothered to call the police department to verify her information. As far as she and her readers were concerned, Dawson was the BWC killer.

##

Ash flashed her badge and introduced herself to Van Vanguard's receptionist. "I need to speak with Mr. Vanguard."

"Do you have an appointment?" she asked guardedly.

"This badge says I don't need an appointment," Ash smiled. "Just show me which office is his. I'll announce myself."

The receptionist looked undecided.

"Of course, you don't have to, if you prefer I arrest you for obstructing justice," Ash added.

"First door on your right," the woman pointed down the hall.

Ash nodded and headed for the door. She could hear her on the intercom, warning Vanguard.

Van Vanguard was the youngest of the three recent widowers. A trust fund heir, he was remarkably down to earth and easy going. He was watching the door for Ash's entrance. He didn't rise from his chair.

"Detective Denton, what a pleasant surprise," Vanguard motioned toward a chair, "Please, have a seat." A copy of the *Star-Telegram* was on his desk.

"I see by this morning's paper, you have solved the murders of my wife and those other unfortunate women," Vanguard said.

"We are wrapping up a few loose ends," Ash nodded as she settled back in the chair.

"What can I do to help?" Vanguard moved things on his desk as if they required his attention.

"Both Jeb Trent and Evan Trask have admitted to having their wives followed and photographed because they were certain they were cheating on them. Do you also have such photos?"

"What if I do?" Vanguard asked.

"We believe Dawson had an accomplice," Ash said. "We believe the man who took the photographs also aided Dawson in the murders of the women. We need to catch him."

"I didn't exactly hire someone," Vanguard volunteered. "I don't know who he was. I received a lurid photo of my wife and another man in the mail. A note said to contact the email address if I needed additional photos.

"His photos saved Donald Morton a fortune when he divorced his wife for infidelity.

"He was damned expensive, but he was worth it. His photos were very explicit. I don't know how he managed to get the angles he did."

"How did you pay him?"

"I received the photos in the mail. Instructions accompanied them: where to leave the money and what would happen if I didn't. I left twenty thousand in an envelope in the rare-books section of the library."

Ash raised her eyebrows. "Twenty thousand is expensive for a photo shoot. That amount of money sounds more like a hit contract."

"I had already contacted my attorney to get my ducks in order, to divorce Stacy. Here's his name and phone number. You can check with him."

"You left twenty thousand dollars for someone you had never met," Ash asked incredulously. "How'd he know you would pay him?"

"He said the money had to be in the right place at a certain time, or he would post the photos on Facebook and all over the internet.

"The photos were gold to me. They proved infidelity, which made my prenuptial come into play. I didn't have to pay her any support at all if she was unfaithful to me. Obviously, I didn't want to look like a complete fool, so I didn't want the photos smeared all over the internet."

"May I see the photos?" Ash asked.

"You can have them if they will help." Vanguard opened his desk drawer and tossed the familiar envelope to Ash. "Detective, I wanted a divorce from Stacy, but I didn't want her murdered. I'll do anything I can to help."

"Do you have the original note giving you the email address," Ash asked.

Vanguard dug around in the lap drawer of his desk and pulled out several pieces of paper. "This is the original note I received and a copy of the emails. As you can see photos are all we ever discussed."

##

"Captain, I am going to lock myself in interrogation room one," Ash informed her supervisor. "I need to spread out all the photos and go over them with a fine-tooth comb. If anyone asks, I'm not here."

Ames nodded. He knew Ash was still not satisfied with the resolution of the BWC murders.

Ash went over each photo with a magnifying glass, looking for anything that would give her some idea where the pictures were taken, or who the man was with the women. She was certain the same man had been having an affair with all three women.

A high-definition video camera was used to take the shots. She had originally assumed the photos came from a single-lens-reflex camera. A video camera made more sense than an SLR. Using a video camera allowed the man to maneuver the women into positions easily recorded. Later, he pulled only the photos showing clear shots of the women.

A video camera would not require two men. The lover could set up the camera in advance and have it video as he made love to the women.

She confronted Trask and Trent with her knowledge of the photos. Each man finally admitted to having such photos. They voluntarily turned them over to Ash when she informed them they would be persons of interest if they didn't cooperate. They both told the same story Vanguard had told.

120

A close examination of the original photos confirmed her suspicions. She was positive the lover, and photographer were the same person

She called Christine Canton. Maybe she and Jessica could help her track down the email.

Colt awoke to the smell of coffee and bacon. He couldn't stop the smile that spread across his face as he recalled falling asleep beside Linda. She had been out of the hospital and living with him for over a month.

"Hey sleepy head," she smiled as she carried a cup of coffee to him. "Are you going to spend all day in bed?"

"If you'll stay with me," he grinned. She leaned over and kissed him, and then placed the cup in his hands.

"Your phone has been ringing off the hook this morning. It's the precinct."

"This is the last day of my leave. They probably want to make sure I am coming back. Would you…"

"Bring it to you," she smiled. "Of course."

Colt leaned back against the pillows and headboard. *God, she makes great coffee.*

He sat the cup on the nightstand and took his phone. She sat down on the side of the bed. She was gorgeous. She always made his heart skip a beat. Unfortunately, she affected other men the same way.

"Hurry," she grinned, "breakfast will be on the table in two seconds."

He watched her leave the room. He loved everything about her. Well, almost everything. The fact that she had cheated on him was always in the back of his mind. She *had* come running back to him admitting that she had made a horrible mistake. Now he was getting a second chance at love. He didn't want to screw it up.

He recalled a movie, *Of Human Bondage*, starring Kim Novak and Lawrence Harvey. It was about a tortured man who could not stop loving a woman, no matter how despicable she was. The story hadn't ended well.

He jumped when the phone in his hand rang. "Layne," he barked.

"Hey Buddy, just checking to make certain I'm getting my partner back tomorrow." Ash's voice sounded happy.

"I'll be there, rearing to go," Colt laughed. "Anything special going on, I should know about?"

"Same old, same old," Ash sighed, "murder and mayhem."

"How's Linda," Ash asked.

"She's doing very well," Colt said. "We'll talk when I see you."

##

"Hmm, something smells good," Colt slipped his arms around Linda from behind. He inhaled deeply, enjoying the scent of her hair. "I think it's you."

She turned in his arms and kissed him. "I bet it is the bacon," she laughed. "Now, eat."

"I'm supposed to be taking care of you," he grinned as he cut into his eggs."

"After the last few days, you should know I feel fine," she smiled seductively.

122

"You sure do feel fine." His smile was infectious. "I don't want you to overdo it."

"I'm fine, honey," she said. "You get back in the saddle. I'm sure they have missed you the past month. I truly do appreciate you taking your vacation to care for me."

"That's what one does when one loves someone as much as I love you." Colt carried his plate to the sink, rinsed it and placed it in the dishwasher.

"I have to meet with my attorney today," she glanced up at him as she wiped the breakfast counter.

"Oh, for what?"

"It seems I'm Lee's sole heir. He left everything to me," she shrugged. "He probably did that, so no one would suspect him when I joined the Branded Wives Club."

"We don't need his money," Colt scowled. "Let someone else have it. We have enough money to live comfortably."

"Silly rabbit, one can never have enough money," Linda laughed. "After what he did to me, I deserve whatever I get."

"Would you like me to go with you?" Colt asked.

"No, I'll be fine. Mr. Phillips will just be going over the will and the estate with me. I can handle it."

##

ADA Christine Canton closed the file she had reread twice. She still didn't know what was in it. She couldn't concentrate. She hadn't spoken to Jessica for almost a week, and she was going crazy. She missed her. She tried to think of some excuse to call her.

Why hadn't Jessica called her?

She was reaching for the phone when it rang. "ADA Canton. Oh, hello Ash, what can I do for you?"

"I need some help from your cyber chief," Ash said. "Could you and she meet Lana and me for lunch today?"

"Yes, of course. Just tell me when and where." Christine jumped at an excuse to see Jessica.

"I also need a search warrant for Dawson Pharmaceuticals," Ash added. "Specifically, I want to search Lee Dawson's office for photos."

Christine had the search warrant delivered to Ash. Then she called Jessica.

Jessica's secretary told Christine she was in her apartment. She had worked all night on a new tracking software and had stayed with it until she had worked out all the glitches. "Ms. Barton is very dedicated. She's probably asleep."

"Please put me through to her apartment," Christine insisted.

Jessica's voice was husky with sleep when she answered the phone. Christine felt a pang of guilt. "Jessica, I'm sorry. Did I wake you?"

"Oh, no. I was just lying here thinking of you." She bit her lip. "I'm sorry, Christine that was way out of line."

"No, it wasn't. I've been thinking about you, too." Christine's voice was soft and sweet. "I have a legitimate reason for calling you. Ash and Lana Denton want to meet us for lunch. Ash needs your help on a case."

"What time?" Jessica was already moving toward the shower. "I'll be there.

"Christine, you never need a reason to call me," she added. "Just, please call me."

##

Christine arrived at the restaurant early, but Jessica was already there. She shyly smiled at Christine as she met her at the door. She led her to a booth in the back of the room.

"I know it has only been four days since we spoke last," Jessica said hesitantly, "but it feels like a lifetime."

"I know," Christine nodded.

Ash and Lana joined them in the booth. After the waiter had placed their drinks on the table, Ash pulled out her photo envelopes.

"These are obscene," the detective said. "If either of you find them too offensive, I'll put them away. I wanted you to see where I am coming from on this.

"This is regarding the Branded Wives case. Each husband received a photo showing his wife in an extremely intimate position with another man.

"The photo was accompanied by a note containing an email address to contact the photographer. Every email address is different. The photographer offers to supply further evidence of their cheating wife for twenty thousand dollars.

"Each husband bought the package. Their wives died soon afterward. I believe the photographer, lover, and murderer are all the same man. I do not believe that man is Lee Dawson."

"Lee Dawson admitted he did it," Christine noted.

"No," Ash said, "His wife said he admitted it just before she shot him."

125

The four sat quietly for a moment. Ash pulled the photos from the envelopes.

"Oh, my," Christine inhaled deeply.

Jessica's face turned red as she blushed. "I've seen enough," she pushed the explicit photos back to Ash. "May I see the email addresses?"

"These are free email addresses," Jessica frowned. "If he was smart enough to use the computers provided in the library or some of the downtown coffee shops, we won't be able to trace it to him. It will trace to the location. We have a time on the emails; maybe we will find a place that has security cameras. We can see who was at that computer at that time."

"Since Colt's ex-wife is involved in this now," Ash grimaced, "I'd like to keep him out of the loop until I find some answers. If I'm wrong, it could cost me his friendship. If I am right, it could cost him the woman he loves."

The couples discussed the case over lunch.

"I can have this information for you by this evening," Jessica said. "Why don't we have dinner at my place at six-thirty? We can see what we have and go from there."

"Sounds great," Ash said. "Where is your place?"

Jessica's place turned out to be one of the most beautifully appointed penthouses Lana had ever seen. The tasteful decorations highlighted priceless statues and artwork. There was an air of luxury and impeccable taste about it.

A maid and butler took care of everything. Dinner was perfect. The four retired to Jessica's study where she sat down behind her desk.

"As I feared," Jessica started, "our suspect was smart enough to use several computers in public places. I have the location of each computer. Let's hope there are security cameras watching them."

The four visited and discussed other cases Ash and Christine had worked on together. It was easy to see they each had tremendous respect for the other.

At nine, Ash and Lana went home.

Jessica closed the door and turned to find Christine staring at her. "What?" She wasn't certain what that look meant.

Christine walked slowly to her and tiptoed to press her lips against hers. Jessica pulled her into her arms and kissed her as she had never kissed anyone in her life. Christine was soft and warm. Her fragrance engulfed Jessica. She filled her senses and shredded her resolve.

She gasped for air as she pulled away from her lips. "Christine, I won't cheat with another man's wife," she croaked. Her voice had deserted her.

Christine didn't pull from her arms but laid her head on Jessica's chest. "What if I weren't another man's wife?" she murmured. "What if I divorced Robert? Ours has been a marriage of convenience for years."

"Then I would be your slave," Jessica whispered as she tilted her chin, and pulled her lips back to hers. "I would spend the rest of my life making you happy."

"I'm afraid I have fallen hopelessly in love with you, Jessica."

"I love you, Christine," she murmured. "You make my life worth living."

Colt hummed a catchy tune as he walked into the bullpen.

"Someone is happy," Ash grinned at her partner. "It's good to have you back."

"It's good to be back," Colt placed his gun in his desk drawer. "Catch me up."

"Vice busted a prostitution ring last night," Ash pitched Colt two photos. "They think they have the last two kids from our internet pedophile case. I'm going to the hospital to identify them."

"I haven't picked up a take home unit yet," Colt slipped his gun back into his holster. "You got one?"

"Yeah, but you can drive," Ash tossed the keys to her partner.

"How's Linda," Ash inquired as Colt pulled into traffic.

"She's great," Colt smiled. "It's great to have her back."

"Hum," Ash snorted.

Colt glanced at his friend. "She's changed, Ash. You'll see. I think this entire ordeal has made her see there is more to life than money."

"For your sake, I hope so, buddy," Ash said.

"Linda wants me to take her back," Colt smiled. "I'm going to ask her to marry me, again. These last weeks with her have been pure heaven."

"Take it slow, Colt," Ash frowned. "I don't want to see you go through her leaving you again. You almost came unhinged."

"Is that you or Dr. Lana Denton talking," Colt asked.

"Just me," Ash said. "You're my best friend. I don't want to see you hurt again."

"It'll be different this time," Colt glanced at Ash. "I will spend more time with her. Do things she enjoys. I was selfish and absorbed in my work. I have a better handle on how to balance my work and my personal life. You'll see."

##

Chapter 11

Dr. Lana Denton checked her watch. She had ten minutes before her next patient. She called her wife. "How is the love of my life doing?" she purred into the phone when Ash answered.

"Much better now that she has heard your lovely voice," Ash chuckled. "What are you doing?"

"I had a few minutes before my next patient and wanted to hear your voice."

"I am glad you did. Colt and I are at the county jail. I think we have found our last two IP victims."

"You can tell me about it tonight," Lana said. "I will let you go for now. It sounds like you are busy. Love you."

"Love you, too."

Lana hung up as her secretary ushered Jessica into her office.

"Hello, Dr. Denton," she smiled. She almost floated on air. Lana had never seen her as happy.

"My, aren't you jovial today," Lana grinned. "Your life must be going great."

"It is wonderful," Jessica set down in the chair in front of her desk. "I told Christine I love her, and she didn't run screaming from the room."

Lana laughed. Jessica could be entertaining when she tried. "What did she say?"

"She said she was falling in love with me." Jessica beamed.

"Have you told her about your problem?" Lana asked.

"That's what I wanted to discuss with you today," Jessica frowned slightly. "Do I have to tell her? I mean, I can control my delusions with medication. If I stay on my meds, I am perfectly normal."

"Yes," Lana nodded slowly. "You are the most normal person I know, but do you want to enter into a relationship keeping secrets from the one you love?"

Jessica held her gaze for a long time. "No," she said. "What if I lose her? I couldn't bear losing her. She gives meaning to my life."

"What about her husband?"

Jessica hung her head. "She is going to ask him for a divorce. He cheats on her, has for a long time. She has always just ignored it. They have stayed together for professional reasons."

"Have you and Christine had relations?" Lana asked.

"No, that would be cheating. You know how I hate cheaters," Jessica started to get agitated.

"Jessica, have you ever had relations with a woman," Lana asked.

"No," she shook her head.

"Don't you think you should tell Christine all there is to know about you," Lana said. "If she loves you, it won't matter. If she is thinking about upending her entire life to be with you, don't you think she should have the whole truth?"

Jessica dragged her hand down her face as if trying to wipe away her thoughts. She pinched the bridge of her nose. "I…I…can't lose her," she reiterated.

"Ash and I enjoyed our evening with you and Christine," Lana decided to move the conversation to a more pleasant subject. "You have a beautiful home."

"You didn't expect that, did you?" Lana's praise made Jessica smile like a little girl.

"I was surprised and impressed," Lana nodded. "You aren't at all who you led me to believe you were."

"I wasn't trying to mislead you," Jessica explained. "I knew I needed help. I didn't know how much I could trust you, so I didn't tell you everything about me."

"Do you trust me now?" Lana asked.

"Very much," Jessica exclaimed.

"Then let's start over. Tell me about your childhood."

"I had a normal upbringing. My dad was a computer programmer for Electronic Data Systems. I'm a computer savant. As far back as I can remember computers just seemed to communicate with me. I can do anything with computers, anything. I can hack any system and program. More importantly, I can build security systems others can't hack.

"I started writing security programs at a very young age. When I was fourteen, I designed a firewall for banking that is still in use today. No one has ever been able to hack it.

"We built our company into one of the top security firms in the world."

"Does your father work with you?" Lana asked.

"No, he died when I was seventeen." A pained expression crossed Jessica's face. "I don't like to talk about it."

"What about your mother?"

"She also died when I was seventeen. My grandparents raised me." Jessica began to fidget in her chair. "I don't like to discuss their deaths."

"Okay," Lana smiled, as she wrote out her prescription. "I am very pleased with your progress. "Do seriously consider telling Christine about your problem."

"I will, Dr. Denton. Thank you for being my friend and confidant."

After Jessica had left, Lana made additional notes in her file. She had been seeing her for almost two years, and she had never mentioned her parents. Intuition and training told her that was something she needed to pursue. Losing both parents in an accident would be traumatic for a seventeen-year-old girl.

"Christine," Ash greeted her favorite ADA when she answered the phone. "We have the last two IP victims. They are in the hospital. They were scooped up in a prostitution raid. They are practically catatonic. The girl is in terrible shape, and the boy is seriously traumatized. I suspect they were praying that death would find them before their parents did."

"Thanks, Ash. Now for the hard part, letting their parents see them."

"Yeah," Ash sighed, "Honestly, I am glad to turn that over to you."

"I have the security footage from the various public computer stops our BWC perp made," Christine said. "I'll send them to you."

"No, I'll pick them up," Ash insisted.

"Colt back on the job?"

"Yes," Ash answered. "Like I said, I don't want him to know I'm investigating Linda. I'll stop by this afternoon."

"Give me time to talk with Jessica," Christine said. "I think she has the capability to run all the security data at once and match anyone that is on all the different footage. I'll call you back."

True to her word, Christine called back in less than thirty minutes. "Ash, I will drop the security footage off to Jessica. She'll call you when she finishes."

"Thanks, Christine. You know you two make a terrific team."

"She's very talented," Christine agreed. "I don't know how we managed without her."

Christine kicked off her heels and walked barefoot to the refrigerator. She poured a glass of wine and took a long sip before walking into her home office. She had decided to talk to Robert if he came home tonight.

She pulled the familiar manila envelope from her bottom desk drawer. She sipped her wine then spilled the photos from the envelope. There were dozens of them. Robert didn't have affairs. He had one-night stands. Any willing woman was fair game for her husband. She had been amazed at how many women were willing to sleep with a married man. *Morality in this town is virtually non-existent*, she thought. She put the photos back into her drawer. She hoped she wouldn't have to use them.

She was glad she was on a first name basis with the female private detective she had hired to photograph her husband's many illicit affairs. Her mind went briefly to the three widowers who had hired the mystery photographer to procure explicit sexual photos of their wives.

She knew that being married to her gave Robert a modicum of respectability. Criminals often hired him thinking she would pull strings for them. She always refused to prosecute a case Robert was handling. She turned them over to one of the other ADAs.

Looking back, she wondered why she had ever married Robert. He was handsome and fairly, successful. At the time, she thought she loved him. Three months after their marriage, she had started hearing rumors about him and other women. By the time their first anniversary arrived, he blatantly flaunted his little *indiscretions,* as he called them.

She lived on her side of the house, and he lived on his side. They rarely interfered in one another's lives. Theirs was truly a marriage of convenience.

She had thrown herself into her work and had gained the reputation of being a fair but tough district attorney. She rarely lost a case, because she refused to prosecute a case if the police work on it was shoddy. Law enforcement agents considered it a coup if she agreed to prosecute one of their cases.

She heard Robert's key in the door. She walked to the living room to meet him.

"Oh, you're still up," Robert frowned. "I thought you'd be in bed by now."

"I waited up for you," Christine said. "We need to talk."

"Why does, *we need to talk* always sound like the beginning of goodbye?" Robert flopped down in an armchair. He had been drinking, and she could smell the perfume on him.

"You aren't going to start ragging me about my cheating ways, are you?" Robert propped his feet on the coffee table. "We both know it's too late for that. Can't teach an old dog new tricks, you know."

"No," Christine grimaced. "I know you'll never change."

"Well good, we've got that settled," he leaned his head back and closed his eyes.

"I think we should divorce," Christine said slowly.

He didn't move for a long time. She thought he was asleep.

"Who're you shagging?" he finally said.

"I'm not intimately involved with anyone, Robert." Her voice was low and easy much like the one she used in the courtroom to lull a witness into a false sense of security. "I'm just tired of being the laughing stock of the legal world in this town."

"I suppose you want everything," Robert growled, raising his head to look her in the eye.

"No. Just my belongings and car. You can have the house. I just want out." Christine said. We can have a nice quiet, non-contested divorce and get on with our lives."

"What if I don't want a divorce?" His eyes darkened. "What if I like things just the way they are?"

"Then I'll see you in court," Christine said.

"That could hurt my bid for the Senate," Robert said. "Voters don't like divorced men."

"It didn't hurt our new president," she pointed out. "He carried Texas by double digits."

"I want to be the one to file," he nodded. "I'll file for irreconcilable differences. That could mean anything, so neither of us comes off looking like the bad guy."

"So, you are agreeable to divorcing?" she smiled slightly.

"Let me sleep on it." He left the room.

The next morning Robert was waiting for her in her home office. "Good morning,' he smiled. "I've given your request some thought, and I can't just walk away from our marriage with nothing but this house. You know we still owe a lot of money on it?"

"This is all we own," Christine huffed. "You squandered everything you made on liquor and women."

"Still, I'm pleased with our current arrangement," he smirked. "I would need some incentive to give up you. Like you pay off the house, so I have it free and clear."

"Robert, do you know the definition of promiscuity?" Christine's eyes narrowed as she sat down at her desk.

"Of course, I do," he snorted.

"I'm not certain you know just how lurid the definition of promiscuity is," Christine continued as she opened a dictionary on her desk. "Let me read you the definition, and then you reconsider your answer."

She started to read. "Promiscuity is the practice of having casual sex frequently with different partners or being indiscriminate in the choice of sexual partners."

"That will be the main impetus of my reason for filing for a divorce if I file it." She held his gaze.

Christine Canton wasn't a woman easily intimidated, and she knew she had her house in order.

"You make it sound extremely lewd," Robert grinned evilly. "You have no proof."

"But I do," Christine tossed him the manila envelope.

Robert paled beneath his golf tan as he shuffled through the photos.

"You can keep those," Christine smirked. "I have the negatives. Now, about that divorce?"

"I'll have the papers drawn up today," Robert said.

##

Ash met Christine in Jessica's office.

"I found the same guy on all the computers," Jessica said excitedly. "Obviously, he knew he was being recorded. He has on sunglasses and a hoodie in every photo. I can't even make out the color of his hair."

"Is it okay if I take these home tonight and let Lana watch them?" Ash asked Christine. "Sometimes she sees things I miss."

"Of course," the ADA nodded.

Ash collected the DVDs and left.

Jessica walked around her desk and slowly pulled Christine into her arms. Her kiss was soft and tentative. Christine kissed her back; she ran her tongue along Jessica's lips, requesting admittance. She pulled her closer and freely granted her the admission she had requested.

When she could no longer breathe, Christine pushed her away slightly. "I love you," the vibration of her lips against Jessica's drove her crazy.

"I love you, too, Christine." Jessica stepped away from her. "We need to talk."

Christine recalled Robert's musing on the statement the night before. He was right. *We need to talk,* always preceded bad news. She had a feeling this was no different.

"Why don't we sit down," Jessica caught her hand and led her to the sofa. "I'm not certain how to tell you this."

Christine watched Jessica's eyes. They darted around the room as if seeking something to provide her courage.

"I love you very much, but..." Christine interrupted her.

"There's always, a 'but,' isn't there," Christine frowned.

Jessica nodded. "...but, I have a problem of which I want you to be aware. For the past two years, I've been a patient of Dr. Lana Denton."

"Lana, the psychiatrist?" Christine's voice was low and cautious.

Jessica gave a short nod. "I can be delusional."

Christine stared at her. "Delusional? In what way?"

"If I get off my meds, I have delusions that women are after me. That they want to have sex with me."

"If you get off your meds?" Christine repeated. She wanted to be certain she fully comprehended the full extent of the problem.

"If I stay on my meds, I am completely normal," Jessica rushed to reassure her. "I don't know what causes the delusions. Dr. Denton is trying to help me find the root of my need to fantasize such things.

"I want to marry you, Christine, but I will understand if you don't see me in your future.

"I don't expect you to respond right now," Jessica hurried on, "It's important you know where I want to take our relationship, so I wanted to be totally truthful with you."

Christine pinched the bridge of her nose. "I…"

"Please," Jessica smiled slightly, "Don't answer me now. I want you to give some thought to what I've told you."

Christine's phone rang. It was the district attorney. "I have to take this."

"ADA Canton," she answered. "Yes. Yes, sir. I'll be there right away."

"I have to go, Jessica," she stood. "We'll talk later." She tiptoed and kissed her lips. "I love you too. That's all that matters."

##

Chapter 12

"How did things go with your attorney," Colt asked as he kissed Linda hello.

"Superb," she smiled. "You are looking at one extremely wealthy woman."

"I take it things are working out the way you wanted," Colt said.

Linda slipped her arms around her ex-husband's neck. "Things are working out just fine, baby."

"You want to tell me about it?" He kissed her neck.

"Right now, I'd rather make love to you," she murmured.

"Right now," he smiled, "that's all that matters."

##

Colt had grown accustomed to waking to the smell of coffee brewing and bacon cooking. He slipped on his jeans and padded into the kitchen.

Linda poured his coffee and kissed him good morning. "Breakfast is almost ready."

"I love you," he kissed her again. "Thank you for last night."

"Umm, my pleasure," she cooed.

He set on a stool at the breakfast bar and watched her move about the kitchen. *Life doesn't get any better than this,* he thought

He couldn't get over how happy she made him. She seemed to be trying to make up for the misery she had caused him. One night with her had done that.

He had ordered a new wedding ring for her. It was beautiful and very expensive. He wanted them to have a fresh start. Besides, he had thrown the original one he gave her into the Trinity River, the night she had returned it and left him.

After breakfast, he entered the bedroom to find her getting dressed. He slipped his arms around her. "You look beautiful," he grinned.

"Thank you, kind sir," she brushed his lips with hers. "You'd better get dressed, or you'll be late for work."

"What are you doing today?" He casually asked as he tucked in his shirt and pulled on a vest.

"My attorney said the Dawson Estate is mine. I thought I would move my things back there today."

Her words were like a kick in the stomach. Colt had to fight to keep from doubling over.

"What do you mean?" He croaked.

"I mean I am moving back to my estate, darling," she smiled. "You are welcome to come with me."

The pain subsided slightly at her invitation. "I thought we'd live here," Colt grimaced.

"Colt, baby, this is a wonderful home, but it is no palatial estate." She slipped on her heels. "We can discuss it tonight. Okay."

Colt stood dumbfounded a shoe in each hand. Before he could argue, she was gone.

##

"Hey McPretty, buy me a cup of coffee," Risa leaned against Ash's desk. "We need to talk."

"Nothing good has ever come from that lead in" Ash grinned as she holstered her gun and followed the ME from the precinct.

They were sipping their coffee when Risa began. "I know Colt, and you are very close, maybe even closer than siblings."

Ash nodded. She knew she wasn't going to like what Risa had to say.

"You're a damn good cop," Risa inhaled, "You had to see the same things I saw at the Dawson murder scene. Are we going to discuss it or ignore it?"

"Was anything left out of the report?" Ash hedged.

"No, but nothing was added, either," Risa shook her head. "I've done a rape kit on all the victims. When they were pregnant, I ran a DNA on the fetus. I did the same with Linda while she was in the hospital.

"McPretty, you know the wine was the wrong label. The knife to remove the nipples wasn't an X-Acto knife. It was a utility knife. The cheese wasn't the same brand. There were no pictures. Linda is pregnant. Dawson isn't our killer. But his wife may be."

"God, Risa," Ash ran her hand through her long blonde hair. "I've been going crazy trying to locate the photographer. I believe the photographer and the lover in the photos of each victim are the same people.

"As you know, Colt and Linda have never really stopped sleeping together, so I'm sure her baby is his since it isn't Dawson's."

"Guess again, McPretty," Risa grinned an all-knowing grin.

"It's someone else's?" Ash couldn't hide her shock.

Risa nodded her lovely head. "Care to guess whose?"

"Evan Trask," Ash said sadly.

"How'd you know?" Risa was astounded.

"I saw her with Trask. They were going into his penthouse."

"Bottom line," Risa frowned, "it looks to me like Linda murdered her husband in cold blood and tried to make it look like he was the BWC killer and she was one of his victims.

"She had all the details we kept from the public. I'm assuming a little pillow talk with Colt got her that information. Only she wasn't smart enough to get the minute details."

"Risa, this case is driving me crazy," Ash said. "I agree with you that Linda planned the murder of Lee Dawson. I haven't taken the case to Christine because I'm afraid she will throw it back at me. You know how she feels about inconclusive police work. I need hard evidence."

"What about the gun?" Risa asked. "When did she buy it?"

"Colt said he gave it to her for protection right after the BW cases began to materialize."

"Has Colt mentioned any of the discrepancies to you?" Risa said.

"No, he acts like her story is true," Ash shook her head. "If he weren't so crazy about her, he would be investigating her too."

"What about Trask?" Risa said. "Would he be capable of stalking and murdering the women, so his wife's death would look like the work of a serial killer?

"With his wife out of the way and Lee Dawson dead, he and Linda could be together and hold on to all their wealth."

"I don't think so," Ash said. "He fainted when we told him his wife was dead. I'm sure he loved her. I think he started seeing Linda after his wife died."

"Does Colt know Linda's pregnant?" Risa asked.

"I don't think so," Ash said. "I haven't told him, and I'm sure Linda hasn't either."

"Are you going to tell him?"

"No, he's happy," Ash grimaced. "I don't want to be the one to tear his world apart. He's talking about marrying her again."

"That's insane," Risa gasped. "Ash, he's a damn good detective. He knows Dawson's death isn't kosher."

##

Chapter 13

Christine Canton read the arrest warrant for Frank Moncrief. Frank was a friend. They had been friends since law school. He specialized in tort law. He was well known for the class action suits he had won against major corporations. He was a straight arrow and a devoted father and husband. He also received more death threats than most attorneys.

According to the warrant, he'd been arrested for the murder of a young prostitute, Candy Barnes. There had to be some mistake. The DA wanted Christine to handle the case.

Christine called the arresting officer and asked for a rundown on the charge.

Frank had been found at the scene of the murder, trying to resuscitate the young woman. The murder weapon at the scene had only Frank's fingerprints on it, and her blood was all over him.

She asked the detective to keep the crime scene sealed until she released it.

"Did you do a GPR analysis of Moncrief's hands?" Christine asked.

"Didn't have to," the detective answered. "His fingerprints were on the gun barrel."

"I want all the evidence collected at the crime sent to Dr. Risa Mercer immediately." Christine could already tell the collection of evidence had been botched.

Christine called the medical examiner. "Risa, please pay close attention to a prostitute named Candy Barnes. A friend of mine has been charged with her murder. I can tell from talking with the arresting officer that it was sloppy police work."

Christine went to the jail and asked to see Frank. He was haggard and worried about his family. "Christine, thank God you're here," he smiled wryly.

"Frank, what happened?"

"I don't know," Frank said. "It all happened so fast. I'd been looking for Candy for about a month. She had knowledge that would help me nail a corporate criminal. He was one of her Johns and had revealed secrets of wrongdoing to her. Wrongdoing that had cost the lives of several innocent people.

"I had tracked her down to a sleazy motel off I-35 and convinced her to testify for my clients.

"I was talking to her when a man in a ski mask just stepped into the room and shot her. I jumped for his gun, and we struggled. I managed to wrestle it away from him. He knocked me down and fled.

"I called 911 and the police. I tried to resuscitate her but failed. The officers who arrived at the scene cuffed me and let me know they thought I was lying. Next thing I knew, they were Mirandizing me, and here I am. I swear Chris! I didn't kill that girl. I didn't even know her."

"I believe you," Christine nodded. "I'll talk to Millie and get the best defense attorney in town.

"I'll see if I can get two Cracker Jack detectives assigned to your case. If there's a clue to be found, they'll find it.

"First, we need to get you a bail hearing and get you out of here."

Christine pulled her phone from her purse and realized the battery was dead. She made a mental note to recharge it as soon as possible.

Colt checked his phone, again. Linda hadn't returned his phone calls in two days. He'd left dozens of messages. *Maybe she's lost her phone*, he thought. Another little voice said, *Maybe she's through with you.* He was going crazy. He would drive to the Dawson Estate when he got off work.

He wished Ash would get back from the ME's office. Risa was doing an autopsy on a murdered prostitute. Christine had requested they take over the case.

Jessica called Christine's number. Her secretary informed her she was out of the office. She hadn't been in the office for the past two days.

"Is she okay," she'd asked.

"Yes, ma'am, she's extremely busy. I'll tell her you called."

Jessica left word for her to call. She didn't bother calling her cell phone. She'd left half a dozen messages, and now it just went straight to voicemail, which was full.

Jessica poured herself a cup of coffee and walked to the penthouse window that overlooked Houston Street. Downtown traffic was crawling in every direction.

As coffee sloshed onto her shoes, she realized her hands were shaking. She hadn't taken her meds. She walked to her bathroom and pulled her link to sanity from the medicine cabinet.

Why hadn't Christine called her? Had she decided her problem was too much to handle? She opened the prescription bottle. *Dammit, the least she can do is tell me what she's decided.* Didn't she owe her that? Hadn't she told her she loved her? *To hell with it all.* Suddenly she threw the prescription bottle across the room. The bottle hit the wall. The contents scattered across the floor. *Delusions don't hurt nearly as much as reality.*

He answered his phone.

"Where have you been? I'm missing you." Her voice was almost a whisper.

"I've been busy," he said indifferently.

"My husband left town this morning. I'm lonely out here in the middle of nowhere." She giggled. "I was hoping we might get to know each other better."

"Sure, why not," he mumbled. "I can be there in an hour." He had never slept with her. Maybe tonight would be the night.

He arrived at her home in less than an hour. It hadn't taken him long to get things ready.

"Umm, someone is anxious," she laughed when she opened the door.

"I thought we might have a little wine and cheese and get better acquainted." His little-boy smile put her at ease.

"I like a man that takes it slow and easy," she grinned salaciously.

Colt walked into the bullpen. It had been three days since Linda moved back to Dawson Estates. He had drunk himself into oblivion last night and was paying the price this morning. He dug around in his desk for Advil.

He hoped Ash wouldn't notice his condition. Ash would immediately know what was wrong.

"Where's Ash?" He asked Carter.

"Morgue," Carter grunted.

Colt poured a cup of coffee and downed the Advil. After finishing the coffee, he rolled his head around on his shoulders. He poured another cup of coffee and walked to his desk. Maybe the Advil would kick in before Ash returned.

"Layne," Captain Ames bellowed, "where's Denton?"

"Morgue," Colt frowned.

"Get her up here. We have a problem."

Colt called down to Risa's office phone and wasn't surprised when no one answered. She was probably in the autopsy room. He dragged his tall frame from the chair and walked to the elevator. When the elevator door opened, Ash walked out.

"I was coming to get you," Colt said. "Captain wants us in his office."

Ash eyed Colt but didn't comment on his condition.

"I'm glad you two could make time for me," Ames huffed. Colt knew he was disturbed.

"What's up Cap?" Colt asked.

"Looks like our butcher is back," Ames tossed a piece of paper, with an address on it, across the desk. "I notified Risa's team. I want her on this. I want everyone on this. It's bad. The press will have a field day with the real BW killer. Of course, they won't remember they were the ones who tried and convicted Dawson without so much as calling our office."

Colt stopped by his desk and downed two more Advil. It was going to be a long day.

The winding paved road that led from the highway to the Murdock ranch house was lined with red oaks and neatly mowed pastures. The electric gate that usually stopped cars at the property's edge had been set to open.

Colt admired the Quarter horses that grazed in the distance. "The upkeep on this place must cost a fortune," he commented.

"They probably spend more on upkeep than we make in a year," Ash nodded.

Risa's van and two police cars were parked in front of the house. Colt pulled their sedan alongside the cars parked in the circular drive.

They flashed their badges, and an officer pointed upstairs. They could hear Risa giving directions to her team as they approached an open door.

"About time you got here McPretty," Risa scowled as Ash walked through the door. "Colt," she nodded as the detective followed his partner into the room.

Ash walked to the blood-soaked bed. Beverly Murdock was propped up in bed; an open book lay in her lap. Blood drenched the pages and her hands. Her head hung loosely to the side as if hinged at the gaping wound in her neck. A red rose dangled from the hair above her ear.

Ash surveyed the room. The same wine and cheese that had been present at the first three murders were sitting on a table in front of a love seat.

"Whore," was burned across Mrs. Murdock's forehead. Her long blonde hair fell over her collarbone and lay in damp, blood-soaked strands on her breasts.

Risa removed the book to expose multiple stab wounds to her torso. "This is different," she frowned. "I'll have to wait to get the body to the lab, but it looks like ten to twelve stab wounds instead of our usual single stab wound to the stomach. The nipples are gone."

"Your killer was angry or frustrated," Lana said as she entered the room. "He took his fury out on her. He is getting more and more deranged."

"Honey," Ash walked to her wife and brushed her lips with hers. "I'm glad you're here. We need all the help we can get on this."

Colt hugged Lana then left the room to gather information.

Lana walked around the bedroom, taking in the wine bottle and cheese. Two empty glasses sat on the coffee table. A small amount of wine was in the bottom of each glass.

"He usually washes the glasses," Lana noted. "Maybe we will get lucky and get his fingerprints."

"You have a TOD?" she asked Risa.

"Around midnight, Tuesday night," Risa said. "Out here in the middle of Bum Hump Egypt, there won't be any witnesses."

"There is an elaborate security system," Colt reentered the room. "Unfortunately, it was disengaged around seven yesterday evening, so all the cameras were turned off. Apparently, the killer knew the entrance-gate code."

"Let me guess," Ash grimaced, "her husband is out of town."

"Left yesterday morning," Colt nodded.

"This is definitely the work of our serial killer," Risa stated the obvious. "This is identical to the first three murders."

The ME turned to the detectives, "Colt, there is no way Lee Dawson is the BW killer."

"What's that supposed to mean," Colt growled.

"My guess is your ex-wife murdered Dawson in cold blood and tried to make it look like self-defense." Risa didn't pull any punches. She was tired of Colt's little pity parties and wanted to shock him into reality.

"Why don't you do your job and leave the police work to us," Colt glared at the woman. He stomped from the room.

"That was pretty brutal," Ash said.

"I know," Risa grimaced. "I just wanted him to see what is as plain as the nose on his face. She uses him and then throws him out like last night's leftover fish."

Ash nodded in agreement. "I'm going back to the station. Can you give me a ride, honey? I'll leave Colt the take home unit."

"Will you be able to do the autopsy on her today?" Ash asked Risa. "I'm curious if she is pregnant and if the baby has the same father as the other three."

"Just for you McPretty," Risa winked at her friend.

"Can we go to your office," Ash asked her wife as they drove away from the crime scene.

"Yes, but why my office?"

"I need you to put on your profiler's hat, and I don't want us to be interrupted. I'll call Ames and let him know what we're doing.

"When we finish, hopefully, Risa will have information for us."

"I don't suppose you would buy a girl lunch first," Lana smiled.

"I would buy you the world," Ash leaned over and kissed her on the cheek. "You're driving; you select the restaurant."

##

Lana didn't see clients on Monday, keeping the day free to make notes on her observations and review videos of client sessions. Her secretary had Mondays off.

She unlocked the door and led Ash into her office. She locked the door and switched on her light. She sat on one side of her desk, and Ash took the other. Both had a pad and pencil.

"Let's list all the similarities of the women," Lana suggested.

"All wealthy," she started.

"All beautiful," Ash added.

"All active in Fort Worth society," she said.

"All deaths had the same modus operandi," Ash noted.

"Oh, now you're just showing off," Lana laughed.

"All husbands were out of town at the time of the murders," Ash grinned, pleased that she had made her laugh.

"All seemed to know and trust their killer." She pointed out. "They were all in their thirties and beautiful. Our killer had no preference in hair color. Our victims were blondes, brunettes, and redheads."

"Photos of them having sex with another man had been mailed, to their husbands," Ash said. "We don't know for certain if Murdock received photos."

"No one else was aware the women were having an affair," Lana noted.

"Anything else?" Ash frowned

"Something I have noticed," Lana said, "they all worked on the same library fund drive with me. I wonder if they met the killer there and became friends with him."

"That gives me something else to check," Ash nodded. "Thank you, darling."

"From what I see in our killer," Lana closed her eyes as she began profiling the killer, "he has a problem with women. He either hates them or loves them too much.

"He is successful and can move easily among the wealthy. He must be reasonably attractive for the women to have an affair with him.

"He has no ego. He doesn't taunt the police or incite the press, so he isn't doing this for recognition or to show others how smart he is. I think he is almost a recluse or at least very private. He's had some

155

traumatic experience with a woman in his life: a mother, a lover, a wife.

"From the epitaph, he writes on the forehead of each woman he obviously hates cheating wives. He kills them when they become pregnant as if they aren't fit to bear his children."

"I have men canvassing the liquor stores searching for any lead on who buys the wine we find at every scene," Ash said. "It is an expensive wine, so I'm hoping there are not a lot of sales of it.

"I will contact the chairperson of your fundraising committee and get a list of all the volunteers and attendees for the fundraising party.

"Anything else I should be looking for," Ash smiled as Lana walked around her desk and sat on Ash's lap.

"A little time for your wife," Lana whispered in her ear.

"Is now a good time," Ash smiled as she stood and led her to the sofa.

"Now would be perfect," she said her voice husky with desire. "I'm in your arms. That's all that matters."

##

Chapter 14

Christine kicked off her heels as soon as she walked through the door. Her feet were killing her. She'd walked miles today, trying to get Frank Moncrief out of jail. She had finally managed to get him released on his own recognizance. Millie had been thrilled to have her husband back home.

Christine had an early meeting with Ash, Lana, Colt, and Risa in the morning. She poured a glass of wine and melted into the sofa. She was glad Robert was out with his latest tart.

As she relaxed, thoughts of Jessica filled her head. Thoughts she had suppressed for the past two days. *God, I need to hear her voice,* she thought. She never called her from home. She didn't want Robert to overhear her conversation.

She pulled her cell phone from her purse, refilled her wine glass and walked into her bedroom. She closed the door and locked it. *Damn, the phone is completely dead.* She hated it when she did something as stupid as letting her link to the outside world die. She plugged in her phone then entered the ensuite to shower.

The shower had been soothing and invigorating. Christine checked her phone. There was enough charge to call Jessica. There were also nine voice mails and twelve text messages from Jessica

Jessica's phone went directly to voicemail. Christine left a message. "Need to talk to you," she said, stressing the word *need*.

When she hadn't heard from her two hours later, she called again. Jessica always returned her calls immediately. She wondered where she was. Christine fell asleep with the cellphone lying between her breasts.

##

Colt placed five cups of steaming coffee on the conference room table. Ash was rounding up pads and pens. Lana was on the phone talking with her office.

Risa walked in with a stack of papers and report folders. Colt knew the blonde goddess was more than prepared for the meeting.

The only one missing was the woman who had called the meeting, ADA Christine Canton.

A flustered Christine stepped from the elevator, balancing her briefcase, purse, and the cell phone at her ear. "Please, please call me," she said into the phone, leaving her sixth message for Jessica.

"I am sorry to be late," She frowned. "Nothing is going right this morning. I am counting on you to turn my day around." She looked at each person at the table.

"Risa, why don't we start with you," Christine said. "What did you find on Frank?"

"The good news is, nothing," Risa smiled. "I checked him from stem to stern, and he had no gunpowder residue on his body. There was none on his clothes either. There was a little on his hands, but not enough to indicate he fired the gun. There is no way Frank Moncrief fired that gun."

Christine took a deep breath. She knew Frank was no killer.

"Colt," Christine smiled at the handsome detective.

"CSI said his fingerprints are on the gun, but only on the barrel," Colt explained. "That jives with his story of wrestling the gun from the shooter.

"The serial number was filed off the gun, so we are at a dead end there. CSI is running the bullet Risa pulled from Barnes through NIBIN to see if we can get a match with any other crimes committed with that gun. I will let you know as soon as I have an answer for you."

Christine nodded toward Ash.

"I interviewed Frank extensively yesterday," Ash said. "I have the name and address of the John he is suing. His name is Bradford Clemens. I will interview Clemens this afternoon."

"Maybe Lana can accompany you," Christine said.

"I have a patient coming in at eleven," Lana grimaced. "Sorry, honey."

"So, the bottom line is Frank is innocent," Christine reiterated. "Thanks, all of you. I knew I could count on you to be thorough.

"I'd like to put the killer behind bars. I believe he is a hired gun that will lead back to Clemens."

Everyone around the table nodded in agreement with the ADA.

As they filed from the room, Christine hung back. "Dr. Denton, may I have a word with you?"

The use of her title told Lana, Christine wanted to discuss Jessica. She closed the door and turned to face the attorney.

"Jessica told me about her...um...The problem," Christine said slowly. "We talked two days ago then I was tied up with Frank's case. I haven't spoken to her since.

"We left everything hanging in the air. The battery went dead on my cell phone yesterday. When I recharged it, I had several messages from Jessica.

"I've been trying to call her since last night and can't reach her. I'm worried about her."

Christine locked her gaze with Lana's. "How serious is her problem?"

"Christine, I can't discuss her case with you..."

"Dammit, Lana, I'm the one person in the world who loves her more than anything. If she needs help, I need to know what to do. I'm asking you one more time and don't pull that confidential crap on me. How serious is her problem?"

"Nothing meds can't control," Lana said. "If she takes her meds, she is perfectly normal. Without them, she becomes delusional. I consider her one of my success cases. She has been doing great since she met you.

"I believe Jessica has a deep-seated problem. If I can find that, she probably won't even need the meds."

"I love her," Christine declared. "I haven't seen her in two days, and I'm going crazy. I think she may feel I haven't communicated with her because she told me about her condition."

"If I should see her,' Lana smiled knowingly, "I will tell her to call you."

"Yes, please do," Christine almost whispered. "I need to talk to her. Miscommunications can be deadly."

##

"McPretty, are you going to talk to Colt or do I just lay this mess on Captain Ames' desk?" Risa scowled.

"I'll do it soon," Ash groaned. "I know we have to bring Linda in for questioning. Her story has too many holes in it."

##

"You have a visitor in your office," Christine's secretary looked up from her filing.

Christine couldn't hide the smile on her face. Her heart skipped a beat, like a schoolgirl's. She needed to see Jessica even more than she had admitted to herself.

She opened the door, and the smile disappeared from her face. "Robert, what are you doing here?"

"Is that any way to greet your husband?" Robert frowned. "Especially one bearing good tidings."

"I'm sorry. I didn't mean to be rude. I'm extremely busy. What can I do for you?"

"I drew up the papers for our divorce the morning after you asked for it." Robert's smile was smug as he handed her the divorce papers. "Read these over, sign it and presto, you and I will cease being a married couple in sixty days."

"Is this a trick?" Christine eyed him wryly.

"No. No trick. I just want to get on with my bid for the Senate. The sooner we get this behind us, the sooner I can get on with my life."

Christine looked at the papers. "I'll read them over tonight. If everything is as we agreed, I will sign and file them in the morning."

"Could you find a place," Robert said, "I would like you gone."

"I'm certain I can be out by Sunday night," Christine glared at her soon to be ex-husband.

"Thanks. And I assume I'll get your support of my bid for the Senate," he added.

Dr. Lana Denton was getting concerned. She had treated Jessica Barton for over two years, every Wednesday at two o'clock. She had never missed an appointment.

She pushed the button on her intercom and buzzed her secretary. "Did Ms. Barton cancel her appointment today?"

"No. I made the usual reminder call and left a message on her phone."

Lana dialed Jessica's phone. Just as Christine had said, it went directly to voice mail. She called Jessica's secretary, Ana Gates.

"She left Friday morning," Ana informed her. "I haven't heard from her since."

"You're certain she isn't in her penthouse?" Lana asked.

"Pretty sure," Ana sounded concerned. "Give me a few minutes. I'll go to the penthouse and check. I have a key."

In ten minutes, Ana called back. "She's gone, but her meds are scattered on the floor. She told me they were for her heart. That it was imperative, she take them every day."

"It is crucial she take them every day," Lana said. "Where could she be?"

"She has a lake house on Eagle Mountain Lake," Ana gave her the address. "I've never been there, but it should be on your GPS."

Lana was searching her desk drawer for some sample packs of the medication she prescribed for Jessica when the woman walked into her office.

"Jessica," she exhaled, "are you okay?"

Jessica nodded numbly. She looked like hell. Her usually neat hair was disheveled and dirty. Her face was covered in dirt and her eyes had a sunken, haunted look. Her shirttail was out, and her usually perfectly pressed slacks looked like she had slept in them. Blood covered her shirt and blood was under her fingernails.

Lana quickly took a survey of her searching for wounds, slashed wrists, etc. Had she tried to commit suicide?

Jessica collapsed into the chair in front of Lana's desk. She was obviously agitated. "May I just sit here quietly?" Jessica's voice was little more than a whisper.

Lana nodded. "I'll just finish this report. Talk whenever you're ready." She knew better than to push Jessica.

Following a hunch, she typed in her username and password that allowed her entry into the records of the National Crime Investigation Center. She typically accessed NCIC when working with law enforcement on a case.

She typed in Jessica Barton and pushed search. It took the computer less than a minute to search the database and return a file for Jessica Barton.

The Orlando, Florida police department had worked the case. The stamp on the file said, "Closed, Homicide/Suicide." Preston Barton, Jr., shot his wife, then turned the gun on himself while his seventeen-year-old daughter was locked in her bedroom.

Neighbors had called the police. The report said seventeen-year-old Jessica Barton was found huddled in her closet.

The girl was placed with her grandparents, JoAnn and Preston Barton, Sr., who lived in Fort Worth, TX.

"Dear God," Lana mumbled to herself.

Jessica raised her eyes. "Are you okay?"

"Yes," she smiled sweetly, "How are you?"

"Not so good," Jessica stared off into some unknown place Lana hadn't been able to reach. "Not good at all."

"Jessica, are you off your meds?" She asked gently.

She looked at her as if she had sprouted horns.

"Christine is worried about you," Lana tried another approach. "She's been calling you and looking for you."

"Lies," Jessica hissed. "All women lie and cheat."

Lana sat quietly, letting her calm down.

"I've never lied to you, have I?" She watched her eyes for any sign of an outburst. She pulled a needle and sedative from her desk drawer.

Jessica shook her head, no.

"You've been off your meds," Lana kept her voice soft and soothing. "May I give you a shot to get them back into your system?"

Jessica snarled at her, baring her teeth. Lana jumped back surprised at her vicious growl.

"To enable you to talk coherently to Christine." Lana kept her distance to see how she would react.

She looked at her for a long time. Finally, Jessica nodded yes.

She gave her the sedative. She waited until she slumped forward in her chair and called for an ambulance. She called Ash and asked her to meet them at the hospital. While she waited for the ambulance, she printed all the information on the Barton family from the NCIC file.

Lana waited patiently as the nurses attended to Jessica. She had admitted her to the hospital for evaluation and had prescribed the sedatives and medication she needed to return to normal. Her rabid dog act had deeply disturbed Lana. Maybe she was schizophrenic. She was certainly smart enough to hide the disease from her.

"Honey," Ash strode into the waiting room, "are you okay?" She took the seat beside her and placed her wife's hand in hers.

The look in her wife's eyes told Ash she was deeply concerned. Her call for help had frightened the detective.

"I'm fine," Lana sighed. "It's one of my patients. She showed up for her appointment disheveled and covered in blood."

"Blood," Ash exclaimed. "Do you know why she was covered in blood?"

"No. She was like a trapped animal." Lana bowed her head. "I have never seen her like this before."

"Who is it?" Ash asked hoping her wife was concerned enough to share a patient's name.

"Jessica Barton," Lana almost whispered.

"Jessica!" Ash looked at her as if she had uttered a vile curse word. "Our Jessica? Christine's Jessica?"

Lana nodded. "I need you to take her clothes to Risa. I have to know if the blood on her is male or female."

"Are you going to call Christine?" Ash said.

"Yes, but I want to give the medication time to re-enter her system. I don't want her to see Jessica like this."

"Dr. Denton," the nurse walked to Lana, "Ms. Barton is in room 303. She is resting comfortably. I thought you might want to be there when she awakes."

"Thank you, Sonja," Lana stood.

"Do you want me to wait with you?" Ash asked.

"No, I'd much rather know about the blood. I need to know what avenues of discussion I need to pursue."

Ash bent and kissed her gently. "I'll call you as soon as Risa has something. I love you."

She pushed further into Ash's arms. "I love you, too, darling."

##

Chapter 15

Lana settled into the most comfortable chair available in Jessica's hospital room. She opened her briefcase, took out the NCIC file and began to read.

Preston Barton, Jr. and Rosemary or Rosie as she was known to her friends, married their senior year of college.

Preston, Jr. quickly gained recognition in the world of software programming. Like his daughter, he excelled in anything computer related.

Rosie taught grade school until Jessica was born. She was a stay-at-home mom until Jessica started school.

She got her high school certification and taught English in the local high school. The family didn't need her income; she simply was bored at home.

Lana picked up a long newspaper clipping. The heading was *Local Computer Genius Sells Game for Seven Figures.*

A large photo of a young Jessica standing in front of a huge computer screen using a laser pointer was at the top of the story. The story read, *"Jessica Barton has set the gaming community on its ear with the introduction of Armageddon of the Gods.*

"The senior has several major computer giants standing in line to hire her."

The article covered several columns of the front page.

A row of smaller photos across the bottom of the article showed Jessica interacting with her classmates. They were laughing and talking. A handsome young man held Jessica's hand.

Another clipping, dated several months after the article on Jessica, listed the teachers who had not renewed their contracts for the next year. Rosemary Barton was on the list.

"Just tell me you're jerking me around," Ash almost screamed at the custodian. "You threw the bag in the incinerator?"

"I...I...had no way of knowing what was in it," the custodian cringed. "It was sitting outside the room. I thought it was trash for disposal."

"Oh, my God!" Ash wanted to punch something. Lana was going to be upset. She steeled himself and walked back to Jessica's room.

"Honey," she motioned for her wife to step into the hall, as a nurse entered the room.

Lana pulled the door closed behind her. "I thought you would be half way to the station by now," Lana kissed her lightly.

"I'm afraid I have some bad news," Ash frowned. "The hospital custodian tossed Jessica's clothing into the incinerator."

Lana's jaw dropped. She was speechless.

Ash admired the way she remained calm although she suspected she wanted to kick something or someone.

Lana shrugged, "There's nothing we can do about it now."

"I'm sorry, honey," Ash looked stricken.

Lana tiptoed to kiss her. "Not your fault, darling. I appreciate you trying to get her things."

"Dr. Denton," the nurse opened the door, "your patient is awake."

"Should I stay?" Ash whispered.

"No, she won't talk in front of you. I'll see you at home."

"Call me when you leave the hospital." Ash's kiss was chaste and sweet. "Love you."

"Love you, too."

##

Lana waited until the nurse left Jessica's hospital room then entered.

"Doc, I'm glad to see you," she grinned her most disarming grin. "What am I doing here?"

"Don't you remember?" Lana wanted Jessica to tell her what had led to the hospitalization.

"I…," she shook her head no. "I don't remember."

"What is the last thing you do remember," Lana's smile was encouraging.

Jessica seemed to struggle to answer her questions. Lana was glad to see the medication was doing its job. She was trying.

"Friday, I was trying to reach Christine," her voice was barely above a whisper. "She wouldn't take my calls."

"I did what you told me. Thursday night, I told her about my issues. She asked me several questions then her boss called. She said she had to go, and we would talk later. That was the last time I spoke with her.

169

"Friday morning, I was going crazy. I hadn't slept all night. I needed to know how she felt. I went off the deep end. I remember my hands were shaking so hard I spilled coffee on my shoes. I went to the medicine cabinet to get my meds. The pain of Christine rejecting me was too much. I decided I'd rather live in my fantasies than face losing her. I threw my medicine bottle against the wall and left."

Lana nodded encouraging Jessica to continue.

"I drove to my home on the lake and stayed there all weekend. I don't even know how I got to your office. I just seemed to wake up there."

"What did you do at the lake house?"

Jessica scrunched her brows together, trying to recall the things she had done at the lake. "I don't know," she shook her head.

"Christine," Jessica said anxiously. "Is she okay?"

"Yes, she's been trying to contact you," Lana tilted her head. "She's worried sick about you. Where is your cell phone? You didn't have it when you came to my office."

"I think I left it at the penthouse along with my purse," Jessica frowned.

"Would you like to see Christine?" Lana asked, reaching for her phone.

Jessica seemed hesitant. "I…I don't want her to see me like this. But I do want to see her so badly."

"She's worried about you," Lana smiled. "Why don't I call her and let her know you're okay? She can decide whether or not she wants to see you."

Jessica nodded. "I can't talk to her right now."

She watched as Lana pushed the single button to call Christine's phone. The expression on Jessica's face was one of terror.

"ADA Christine Canton," Christine's voice sounded tired.

"Christine, this is Dr. Denton." Lana heard the quick intake of breath from the ADA. "I'm with Jessica, and she's okay."

"Oh, thank God," Christine sobbed. She couldn't stop the tears running down her cheeks. "May I speak with her?"

"She's in Harris Southwest," Lana said. "She's sleeping right now. I will have her call you when she awakens."

"Yes! Yes!" Christine sighed with relief.

Only after Lana ended the call did Christine think *Why is she in the hospital?*

##

It took Christine Canton exactly twenty minutes to get from her office downtown to Harris Southwest Medical Center off Bryant Irving Blvd.

She asked the volunteer for Jessica Barton's room number. She planned to be there when the woman she loved awoke.

Christine stopped outside room 303. She could overhear the conversation between Lana and Jessica.

"Why did you stop taking your meds?" Lana asked.

"I'd rather live in my delusional world than live in the real world without Christine," Jessica said.

Christine eased the door open. "May I come in?"

"Of course," Lana rose to greet her. "I need to leave instructions with the nurses' desk before I leave. I'll be back in a few minutes."

Christine pulled a straight-back chair as close as possible to Jessica's bed. Before sitting down, she leaned over and kissed her. It was a slow, tender kiss. One that allowed Jessica to revel in the softness of Christine's full sensuous lips moving against hers.

"I'm so sorry," she whispered as she pulled her lips from Jessica's. "I love you so much. I wasn't thinking. I thought you were secure in my love for you."

"I reacted like a spoiled child," Jessica smiled slightly. "I need to learn how to act like an adult. I should have had more faith in you, in us."

"Yes, you should have. I'm going to sit with you tonight." Christine's declaration left no room for argument.

Lana knocked on the door and waited for an invitation to enter.

"I'm going to leave now," she informed them. "Jessica is doing very well. I'll check on you in the morning before I sign your release. If you need anything, don't hesitate to call me."

Jessica nodded. "Thank you again, Dr. Denton."

"I'll walk you to the elevator," Christine stood. "I will be right back, darling." She leaned over and kissed Jessica again.

"Is there anything I should know?" Christine asked as they walked to the elevators.

"She became upset when she couldn't get in touch with you," Lana said. "She went to her lake house and can't remember anything that happened this weekend.

"Christine, she showed up at my office in an awful state. She was covered in blood. Not her blood."

"Risa can tell us...?" Christine stopped mid-sentence at Lana's shaking head.

"Some fool pitched her clothes into the hospital incinerator," Lana said. "I thought Ash was going to have a coronary. She came here just to pick up Jessica's clothes and take them to Risa.

"They would have given us some insight into what she has been doing all weekend."

"Perhaps it will come back to her," Christine said.

"We can hope," Lana stepped into the elevator. "Call if you need us."

Christine raised her hand to wave goodbye to her friend then returned to Jessica's room. The food service cart was outside the door. The server was placing the evening meal on Jessica's over-bed table.

Christine waited until the woman left the room, then pulled her chair to the other side of the bed so she could be as close to Jessica as possible.

"Want me to feed you?" she teased as Jessica dropped the fork in her lap.

"No," she laughed. "I think I can feed myself. I'm not incapacitated you know."

"I know," Christine grinned. "I am glad you are okay. I was so worried about you. Please don't ever scare me like that again."

Jessica nodded solemnly. She would feel much better if she knew what she had done all weekend.

Jessica ate the meager meal they served her then pushed the table away.

Christine told her what she had been doing since she last saw her. "Ash and Colt kept my friend from

173

suffering a great injustice. Fortunately, not all officers are as lazy as the one working Frank's case."

She stopped talking when she realized Jessica was asleep. Silently she removed the divorce papers Robert had presented her that morning from her briefcase. The morning seemed like a lifetime ago. The papers were in order, so she signed them. She would file them first thing in the morning. She leaned her head on Jessica's bed and fell asleep.

The night nurse touched Jessica's arm lightly. She opened her eyes and surveyed her surroundings. She smiled when she saw Christine's dark auburn hair falling around her beautiful face.

She placed a finger to her lips, signaling the night nurse to be quiet. She swallowed the medication the nurse handed her and whispered, "Thank you."

After the nurse had left, Jessica was still for a long time; taking in the beauty of the woman, she loved. Her high cheekbones and full, red lips combined with a tiny cleft in her chin made Christine's face the most beautiful she had ever seen.

Jessica couldn't resist stroking her soft auburn hair. Her piercing green eyes opened slowly at her touch. She watched her, a contented smile on her face.

"Chris, may we discuss my issues, now," she frowned slightly.

No one had ever dared shorten her name to Chris. She found she liked it when Jessica did it. On her lips, it sounded like a term of endearment. It was.

"There is nothing to discuss," she caught her hand in hers and kissed her knuckles. "Whatever problems we have; we will face them together. You must trust me. We can make this work."

The divorce papers slid off her lap and landed on the floor. She bent down to retrieve them. She was thankful they were bound together.

"What is that?" Jessica asked.

Without a word, Christine placed the forms in Jessica's hands. Across the top it said, "Joint Complaint, Petition or Declaration for Divorce Decree."

She read the sheet then looked at Christine. "How soon will it be final?"

"Sixty days," Christine beamed.

"I can wait sixty days," Jessica nodded.

"I'll take you home in the morning," Christine said. "Then I must get my things out of the house. Robert wants me gone by the weekend."

"You can move into the penthouse." Excitement filled Jessica's eyes.

"I'm not sure that is a good idea," Christine grimaced. "I don't trust Robert. He'd love to get photos of me in a compromising position. He's not above blackmail."

"You'll be safe in the penthouse," Jessica insisted. "It's built like Fort Knox and the security is state-of-the-art.

"I'll hire security guards to sit in the lobby around the clock.

"I would never put you in a compromising situation. I'll move to the lake house until your divorce is final. You'll be as pure as Snow White," she grinned. "We can make it work, Chris."

Christine nodded; maybe it was a good idea.

##

Chapter 16

Lana sat her tea glass on her home desk. She searched the internet for any information she could find on Jessica's grandparents. If there was a Preston Barton, Jr., there had to be a Preston Barton, Sr.

Bingo, there you are, she grinned as several files containing Preston Barton, Sr. materialized in front of her.

Preston Barton, Sr. was the pastor of a small Baptist Church on the Southside of Fort Worth. He had been very active in setting up food drives for the poor and various other programs for indigent children.

Using her law enforcement privileges, she located an address for Preston Barton, Sr., and sent it to her cellphone.

"Honey," Ash wandered into her study, "Did UPS deliver my advance copies today?"

"I forgot to tell you," she smiled, "they are in the back of my car. They left them at the guardhouse. Vernon loaded them for me when I came home tonight. There are five rather large boxes."

"Um," she hummed as she headed for the garage. She carried the boxes into her study and opened one of them. The boxes contained hardback copies of *Thirty-Six Ways to Die*.

She thumbed through one of the books then wrote on the inside cover. *To my wonderful wife, Lana. You have always been my muse. My reason for living. All my love, Always, Ash.*

She carried her meager offering to her wife and presented it to her. "Thank you for making my life wonderful," she smiled.

Lana read the handwritten inscription and knew the dedication page of the book carried the same sentiments for the world to read, except their real names weren't used. She kept her autographed copies in a closed cabinet in their bedroom, so others would never figure out her wife was author Adrian Austin.

She looked up at her from under perfectly arched brows. "I am trying to think of a way to thank you for such a wonderful gift," she smiled flirtatiously. "Why don't you come with me while I put my cherished book away?"

Ash watched her walk toward their bedroom. *No woman should be that damn sexy*, she thought.

Lana woke early the next morning and snuggled deeper into her wife's arms. *This is what marriage is all about,* she thought. *Waking up next to someone, you love.* She couldn't stop her body from undulating against Ash.

Ash's arms tightened around her. "You better be still unless you want a replay of last night." Her voice was deep with desire and sleep.

"I do," Lana whispered into her ear.

Lana pulled her RX350 into the drive of a neat middle-class brick home in the Wedgewood area of Fort Worth. The home and the yard were immaculate.

An older woman was weeding a flower bed at the corner of the house. She stood as Lana got out of the car.

"May I help you?" Her smile was warm and open.

"I'm looking for the Barton's," Lana returned her friendly smile.

"I'm JoAnn Barton," the woman said as she pulled the glove from her right hand and extended it toward Lana.

"I'm Dr. Lana Denton," she shook the extended hand.

JoAnn Barton's grip was firm and confident. "Is Jessica okay?" she asked immediately.

"Oh, yes, she is fine," Lana nodded. "I just need to speak with someone who can provide me information."

"Please, come inside," JoAnn invited. "I've some sun tea brewing. It should be ready."

Lana followed JoAnn into the kitchen. She noticed every wall in the home had photos of Jessica at various stages of her life. The Barton's were obviously proud of their granddaughter.

JoAnn bustled around the kitchen setting out cups and saucers along with a plate full of chocolate chip cookies. "You must try these," she smiled "they are Jessica's favorite. I bake them from scratch."

She poured tea over ice and placed the glasses on the table. "Dr. Denton. I'm assuming you aren't a medical doctor."

"I am an M.D.," Lana smiled, "my specialty is psychiatry. So yes, I'm a psychiatrist. If that's what you mean."

JoAnn nodded then took a sip of her tea. "How can I help you?" she sighed.

"I've been treating your granddaughter for over two years. I've just recently discovered there was a tragic incident in her life when she was seventeen. Can you tell me anything about it?"

"Yes," JoAnn inhaled as if readying herself for a frontal assault, then charged ahead. "Preston, my son, was a wonderful child. Full of life and laughter. He was witty, thoughtful and brilliant. Then he married Rosie.

"She was beautiful and crazy about my son. Her public display of affection sometimes embarrassed us, but we were glad Preston had found someone who was so in love with him.

"When little Jessica, my granddaughter, was born, she was like a cookie cutter copy of her mother. She adored her mother, and we teasingly called her a mama's girl.

"My granddaughter was good-natured. She adored her mother and idolized her father. She and my son were very close.

"My granddaughter excelled at everything she touched. She was writing computer games and apps by the time she was twelve. She was extremely athletic. She was an incredible basketball player and captain of the debate team. She was popular with the boys and the girls in high school.

"My husband and I often visited Orlando to watch Jessica play ball. Her junior year she led the team to a state championship. We were all very proud.

"I remember her hugging me and saying, 'Not bad for a mama's girl, huh Gram?'"

JoAnn was silent for a long time. She seemed to be trying to make sense of what she was about to say next.

"I don't know what happened. We were watching TV when the call came. Our son had killed his wife and shot himself." Her voice sounded far away. "They were both dead."

"The police found no reason," Lana asked. "No suicide note? Nothing?"

"Nothing," JoAnn repeated. "My husband and I rushed to be with Jessica. She was in shock, traumatized.

"We settled the affairs of our son and brought Jessica home with us. It was heartbreaking to see how she changed. She became sullen. Never rude or disrespectful, but withdrawn.

"The local high school basketball coach was ecstatic that Jessica was going to his school. Jessica didn't even go out for the team. She buried herself in her computers and studies.

"She graduated valedictorian from both high school and college. Companies from all over the world were making her offers. By the time she finished her doctorate, she had single-handedly built a cyberspace empire.

"You know she's incredibly wealthy?" JoAnn looked up at Lana. "She takes such good care of me and always visits me and takes me out to dinner and the movies. She's a good girl."

"But..." Lana prompted.

"But she's different," JoAnn continued. "She's been so much better the last three months. So much like her old self. Happy!"

"Has she ever had long periods of time she can't recall?" Lana asked. "Blackouts."

"No."

"What about delusions?" she didn't want to distress JoAnn but needed answers.

"No. Not that I am aware of."

"How about friends? Did she make new friends after she moved here?" Lana asked.

"No, she seemed hesitant to get close to anyone. She just hung around my husband and me."

"Where's your husband?" Lana asked.

"We lost him last year," JoAnn bowed her head.

"I'm sorry for your loss," Lana said the meaningless words. Someone really should be able to come up with adequate words to describe one's sorrow for those who have lost loved ones.

"Jessica was sweet and protective," JoAnn smiled. "She took care of everything, the funeral and talking with the preacher."

Lana nodded. Although she had learned a lot about Jessica, JoAnn had shed no light on why her father had murdered her mother and killed himself. She stood to leave.

"Would you like to see Jessica's room?" JoAnn offered as if sensing she hadn't been much help to the doctor.

"Why, yes," Lana smiled.

"I haven't changed much about it." JoAnn gestured toward the bed. "Just replaced her Minecraft bedspread with a burgundy comforter. She spends the night here sometimes."

"What's that?" Lana walked toward a dark blue chest in the corner.

"That was my son's," JoAnn cringed. "Neither Jessica nor I could bring ourselves to go through it. I suppose we really should."

"Do you mind if I look in it?" Lana asked hoping to find something—anything that would give her direction on treatment for her patient.

"I don't..." JoAnn hesitated. "I'll just leave you with it." She left the room.

Lana opened the old trunk slowly, painfully aware she was about to go through the belongings of a tortured soul.

There were dozens of scrapbooks containing photos of the little family. Apparently, Rosie loved to scrapbook. Little messages, written in the neat, flowing style of a woman.

As Jessica aged; the photo albums contained mostly photos of her. There were pictures of her in a basketball uniform. Photos of her going to the Junior-Senior prom, sitting with a beautiful blonde girl that Lana had seen in other pictures.

Jessica always had a smile on her face. Obviously, her life was a happy one. Lana wondered what had caused the tragedy that had changed that.

She found Jessica's letter jacket, her letter sweaters, and letters from colleges offering scholarships. All the things a father would cherish from a daughter of which he was extremely proud.

Lana started to replace the items when she noticed a book in the back corner of the trunk. She picked it up. It was a diary.

The first page contained one entry that filled the page. "Today is the most wonderful day of my life. Rosie Morgan has agreed to be my wife."

Lana caught her breath. She knew she was holding the diary of Preston Barton, Jr., Jessica's father. She wondered if it would provide the answer to the catastrophe that had affected so many lives.

She closed the book and walked into the kitchen where JoAnn set drinking a second glass of tea.

"May I take this?" Lana asked. "I will return it as soon as possible."

"Keep it. I don't want it," JoAnn said morosely. "I don't want to know what is in it. I probably should have read it long ago. I just couldn't bring myself to open it."

"Nana," a toddler ran into the kitchen, "I awake."

Lana stared. The little boy was the spitting image of Jessica. He had a cast on his tiny arm. "Is he Jessica's?"

"Oh, heavens no," JoAnn laughed. "I keep him for his mother while she works."

For the first time, the youngster noticed Lana. "You pretty lady." He smiled, Jessica's smile.

"Thank you," Lana squatted down to his level. "What's your name?"

"Presley," the tot smiled. "I hungry, Nana."

"What happened to your arm?" Lana touched the cast.

"Big shelve of cans fell on me," he giggled as he ran into JoAnn's arms. "I in the hospital for a long time. Now I well. I hungry, Nana."

Lana gave JoAnn a business card. "Please call me, if I can ever be of help."

Thoughts were whirling ninety miles a minute through her mind. Jessica had a son! She was certain of it. How had she not known that? How could one counsel a woman for over two years and have no clue she had a son?

Jessica Barton was beginning to make her doubt her abilities as a psychiatrist. What had Jessica said, "I was afraid you would tell Christine I was a delusional schizophrenic."

Lana had never diagnosed Jessica as schizophrenic. That was her own diagnosis. She was certainly an enigma. She had spent two years bragging about her sexual conquests. Now she was vowing she had never had relations with anyone. Presley certainly disproved that.

Lana drove to her office. She hoped the diary would help her dispel the shadows that had slipped into Jessica Barton's life. Where 820 split from I-35, Lana changed her mind about going to the office and took the Abilene exit. *I think I will go home and read this,* she thought.

Lana called her secretary and asked her to move her appointments to tomorrow.

It was early, but Lana felt she would need a big glass of wine to make it through the diary.

Today is the most wonderful day of my life. Rosie Morgan has agreed to be my wife. Lana re-read the first page. Her phone rang.

##

Chapter 17

"You guys are such wusses," Jessica laughed as she followed Ash and Colt onto the elevator. Each carried a large box of Christine's belongings.

"Is she moving her entire household," Colt whined. "This must be the refrigerator."

Lana and Christine followed the three, laughing at their antics.

"I can't tell you how much I appreciate this," Christine shook her head as if she couldn't believe her friends had shown up to help her move.

"Thank Jessica," Ash's voice came from behind a box that was almost as tall as she was. "I hope you're a strong woman, Chris because she begs so pitifully she's irresistible."

"Ash," Lana slapped her wife's arm indignantly.

Laughter filled the elevator again. *It was good to have friends*, Jessica thought.

"Wow," Colt whistled as he set down his box. "This is your place, Jessica?"

"It's Chris' for as long as she wants it," Jessica smiled. "Honey, where do you want this box? It has personal items, written on it."

"The ensuite," Christine directed.

By early afternoon, they had moved all the things Christine was taking from her house.

Jessica made a phone call, and Colt collapsed on the sofa. "I'm starving. You have anything in the fridge to eat?"

As if on cue, Jessica's security guard stepped from the elevator. "The Chinese restaurant just delivered this," he carried a box of aromatic food to the dining table. "Enjoy."

"Having you is even better than having a genie," Christine hugged Jessica and rubbed circles on her back.

"I hope Linda didn't mind us stealing you for the day," Jessica said innocently.

"Nah," Colt huffed. "She'll never miss me."

Christine looked around the table. "How did the four of you meet," she asked as she speared an eggroll.

"Ash and I have been joined at the hip since my folks moved in next door to hers when we were five," Colt explained.

"The four of us attended a summer course on the campus of the University of Texas," Lana added. "It was about crime scene investigation."

"Colt and I were sitting on the window sill, checking out the coeds as they entered the lecture hall," Ash smiled at the memory. "When the two most beautiful girls in the world walked in."

"I was still trying to catch my breath when Ash said, 'I've got dibs on the brunette.'" Colt laughed. "So, she lucked out and got Lana, and I got Linda."

"Dibs on me, hum," Lana smiled suggestively at her wife.

"Yes, you never stood a chance," Ash grinned.

"Just for your information," Lana blushed slightly, "When Linda and I walked into the room, I said 'the

186

blonde one is mine.'" She hugged her wife's arm between her breasts. "You were the one that didn't stand a chance."

Ash caught her breath. "Well, if we can be of no further help to you, we'll head home." She was ready for some alone time with her beautiful wife.

Everyone stood and walked toward the elevator doors. Jessica bent down and kissed Christine lightly. "I will pick you up at seven. Wear jeans. We'll go somewhere casual. I am too tired to dress up."

"You always say just the right thing." Christine tiptoed to kiss her again.

Jessica stepped into the elevator as the doors closed.

"You're not staying?" Colt raised his eyebrows.

"No," Jessica smiled shyly, "Chris' divorce isn't final for sixty days. We aren't taking any chances on providing Robert any reason to stop it."

"Bastard that he is," Colt said, "he definitely would try to cause her trouble if he thought she was in love with someone else."

"Where are you staying," Ash asked.

"My place on the lake," Jessica said. "It's not that far."

Jessica bid her friends goodbye when they reached the lobby. She was glad to see her security guard was on duty.

On his way home, Colt called Robert Canton from his burner phone. "I've been following your wife for several weeks. She's not sleeping around."

"Damn," Canton hissed, "I was afraid of that."

"Want me to continue my surveillance," Colt asked. "I don't mind. I have the time if you have the money. Personally. I think you're wasting your dough. All she does is work."

"No," Canton said. "Our business is concluded."

##

Chapter 18

Colt called Linda and left another message. It had been over a week since she'd moved out. He could find no way to contact her. She had changed the entry code on the estate gate.

Yeah, Ash lucked out when she got Lana, Colt thought.

##

Lana lay beside her wife, trying to slow the beat of her heart. Ash always left her breathless. She was certain Ash was the best lover in the world. She turned onto her side and threw her arm and leg across her. "You just keep getting better and better," she smiled.

"I do get a lot of practice," Ash chuckled. "Thank, God!"

"Um," Lana hummed.

Ash raised herself on her elbow and kissed Lana gently. "Now that we have satisfied our lust, why don't I grill a couple of steaks? Unless you would rather go out."

"I'd love a quiet evening at home alone with you," Lana murmured.

After dinner, they settled in their respective offices. Ash had to autograph the five-hundred advance-sales books, and Lana wanted to read the diary kept by Preston, Sr.

Today is the most wonderful day of my life. Rosie Morgan has agreed to be my wife. Lana re-read the first page.

The diary was mostly about how happy he was with Rosie.

She is insatiable, he wrote. He drew a little smiley face beside the sentence.

She skimmed through the diary.

I was exhausted today. I thought Rosie would be too. It is the first day of school. School seems to energize her. She is so excited and aroused. I may be the first man to die from making love to his wife.

If I don't get some rest soon, I am going to be ill. I can hardly keep my eyes open at work. Dear Lord, I love her.

Then a page with hearts and stars, drawn on it. He had written, "Happy," in big block letters across the page.

Rosie is pregnant. I am the luckiest man alive. I am married to the woman of my dreams and will soon be a father.

There were nine months of entries about his pending fatherhood. The first three months bemoaned his disappointment in himself.

God, I can't keep this up. Rosie is hormonal and even more demanding than ever. I know other men would kill for a wife willing to go at it three or four times a day. I just can't keep doing this.

Finally, Rosie has settled down. In a couple of months, we can abstain altogether until after the baby is born. Maybe I can build up my strength.

It's a girl! We named her Jessica. She is perfect. She is beautiful. She has Rosie's eyes and cute little nose. She has my hair and lips. We are indescribably happy. Our lives are perfect.

The next five years were filled with Jessica stories and Preston, Jr. wishing for a break from his wife's constant demands.

Today is Jessica's first day of school. She looks like a little doll in her school uniform. She is such a good little girl.

Rosie went back to school and received her certification to teach high school. She makes more money teaching HS. Not that we need it. She finds it more challenging and enjoys it. She seems happier.

Around Christmas, the writings changed.

I know Rosie is having an affair. Part of me is furious. Another part of me is relieved. Maybe I can rest. Her incessant demands for sex are more than I can stand, but I can't live without her.

Preston Jr., was torn between wondering if something was wrong with him and his sex drive or if the problem lay with his wife. He visited a psychiatrist and his family doctor. Both had assured him there was nothing wrong with him.

The writings returned solely to Jessica. It was obvious his daughter was more important to him than anything in the world.

I'm proud of my daughter. She is very smart—a child prodigy. She is also a gifted athlete.

The writings told of Jessica and her accomplishment on the basketball court and in the field of computers. There were occasional mentions of Rosie's new lovers, but he seemed to be okay with her infidelities.

She led the team to the division championship. She is beautiful. So tall and strong. She is brilliant. She has patents on apps and games. She is making almost as much money as me. She has his mother's beauty and my brains.

Then a year later.

I am popping my buttons today. Jessica led the team to win the state championship. Colleges are recruiting her. She has such a level head on her shoulders. She is a fine, Christian girl, with a very bright future. My daughter would make any father very proud.

Everyone constantly tells me how lucky I am. Gorgeous wife and incredible daughter. Rosie is gorgeous but very promiscuous. I love her too much to walk away from her.

Today is indescribable. My heart has been ripped out, and my soul seared. How could she do that to Jessica and me? How can I still love her so much?

Rosie has been having sexual relations with students in her senior English class. I met with the school board. I was stunned when they told me both boys and girls were involved. They have agreed to let her go quietly. They won't press charges. Of course, some of the student's parents may still file indecency with a minor charges against her. I pray to God Jessica doesn't hear the rumors. It would kill her. She worships her mother. School will be out in a few weeks. Maybe this will all blow over.

I looked up nymphomania on the internet today. Nymphomania is a mental disorder marked by compulsive sexual behavior. Women act out their compulsions by engaging in risky behaviors such as promiscuity. I begged Rosie to see a psychiatrist. She laughed at me.

She said just because I was inadequate didn't mean she had a problem.

I spoke with an attorney today. He said I would have no problem getting a divorce, but Rosie would probably get custody of Jessica. I can't allow that. She has shattered all my dreams. I can't allow her to tarnish Jessica, too.

The last entry was the most distressing. It was dated the day before Preston, Jr. killed his wife and himself.

Today she crossed the line. I hit her. I've never hit her before. For Jessica's sake, I must put an end to this insanity. Rosie has destroyed my life. I can't let her destroy Jessica, too.

"Dear God," Lana mumbled as she read the last entry in the diary. This must be what Colt is going through. She wondered if she could get Linda to see her for counseling.

"Are you okay, Honey?" Ash frowned at the stricken look on her wife's face.

"No," she exhaled realizing she had been holding her breath.

"Anything you can talk about?" Ash sat down beside her on the sofa.

"Patient..."

"...confidentiality," Ash grinned. "I know. How about a glass of wine? I have writer's cramp."

##

Chapter 19

"Come on, McChicken. I am going to buy your lunch." Risa had made up her mind to place all the evidence in front of Captain Ames today. She wanted Ash to know what she was doing.

"This will kill Colt," Ash said as she squeezed lemon into her iced tea. "It's probably for the best. I'm sorry Risa. I tried to talk with him, but he got angry."

"It's a pretty heinous accusation," Risa nodded. "It would take a cold, heartless woman to plan something like that.

"Honestly, I had pegged Linda for all the murders just to frame Dawson. Then Beverly Murdock was butchered."

"I was leaning in that direction, too," Ash admitted. "It will cost me Colt's friendship, but I'll go with you to talk to Ames."

Captain Andrew Ames cursed under his breath as he ushered Ash and Risa from his office. He shut and locked his door. He closed the blinds that hid his office from the rest of the world. Ash and Risa had just confirmed his suspicions.

He scrolled through the contacts on his iPhone until he reached Trinity Jewett. Jewett was a long-time friend, and owed Ames a favor.

"Agent Jewett," Trinity answered.

"Trinity," Ames greeted his friend. "I need a favor."

Trinity laughed. "Of course, you do, Andy. Why else would you be calling me?"

"Sorry, buddy, I…"

"Just jerking your string, Andy." Trinity laughed. "I haven't called you either. What can I do for you?"

"Have you been following our Branded Wives Club case?" the captain asked.

"Yeah, that's a doozy. Have you gotten any breaks in it?"

"Sort of. That is where you come in." Ames gave his friend the rundown on the case.

"So, are you inviting me in to help?" Trinity asked. "You want the FBI involved in your case?"

"Yes," Ames said flatly. "I think my guys are too close to it."

"I have a few things to wrap up, but I can be there Monday," Trinity said. "How do you want to play this? You know your people won't like the FBI getting involved in a hometown case."

Dr. Risa Mercer was in no way prepared for the tall, dark goddess that sauntered into her lab at seven-thirty in the morning. She caught her breath. She didn't even know her name or reason for being there, but she knew she wanted to sleep with her.

"May I help you?" Risa scanned her from head to toe and liked everything about her: the long, wavy black hair; the sparkling blue eyes; the little smile that played on her full lips. Then the smile broke revealing perfect, white teeth. Risa knew from that smile she was used to women reacting to her the same way Risa had.

She held out here hand, "I'm FBI agent Trinity Jewett," she smiled again.

"I need to see some ID," Risa demanded. She didn't want to be a complete pushover.

The goddess reached inside her fitted jacket and withdrew an ID case, flipped it open and held it up so Risa could read it. Just to touch her, Risa wrapped her fingers around Trinity's and pulled the ID closer, pretending to read it thoroughly.

She nodded. "What brings you to my lab?"

"The Branded Wives Club," Trinity grinned. "Is there any place I can get a good cup of coffee? I'm not supposed to be here until ten, but I wanted to get the lay of the land."

"There's a coffee shop across the street," Risa finally smiled. "Good coffee and Danish."

"Could you join me?" She ducked her head slightly as if she expected Risa to turn her down then looked up at her through the longest lashes Risa had ever seen. "Please?"

Risa doubted anyone ever turned her down. "Yes," she smiled, removing her lab coat.

##

"Why is the FBI getting involved in our case?" Risa sipped her black coffee.

"Your top brass called us in," Trinity frowned. She wasn't lying. Ames was top brass to his squad.

"Look I don't want to step on anyone's toes," Trinity smiled, "So I would like to get your take on the case. I've heard about you, and I know you're good at what you do." *Actually, I've heard that you're hot and that's an understatement,* Trinity thought.

"So, you think I will open my mouth to sing and drop the bread?" Risa laughed at her reference to the Aesop's Fable. "Flattery doesn't work on me, Agent Jewett."

"Then you won't think I'm trying to flatter you if I tell you that you are definitely on my list of the top ten most beautiful women I have ever met," Trinity said seriously, "and I'd like to date you. Now that we have that out of the way, can we talk?"

"So, you're just going to ride in here and slay all of our dragons, Sir Lancelot," Risa half teased.

"I would appreciate your take on the case," Trinity said. "Not the official version, but your gut feeling."

Risa gave her the run down on each case, pausing at the death of Lee Dawson. "I don't believe Dawson is the BW killer. Obviously, the BW killer has struck again with the death of Beverly Murdock, although there are a few differences in her case.

"What was different?" Trinity asked.

"Beverly Murdock was raped," Risa huffed. She wasn't pregnant. She was stabbed repeatedly. I thought I'd have only her DNA, but the killer left his on a wine glass. It matches the DNA from the babies in the first three cases.

"Everything else is identical. The red rose, wine, and cheese. The throat and stomach wounds and the removal of the nipples."

"You have a theory?" Trinity asked.

"I believe the killer was someone Mrs. Murdock knew and trusted. I believe he showed up with the wine and cheese and attempted to woo her. It was probably intended to be the photo session he always stages then sends to the husband. When she refused his advances, he raped and murdered her. Her tox screen showed drugs.

"I believe Linda Dawson murdered her husband and staged it to look as if he was the BW killer. She didn't count on the killer continuing his murder spree.

"At first, I toyed with the idea that Linda had murdered the other women to make it look like Dawson was the killer so that we would accept her story. Then Beverly Murdock died."

"Who do you think the BW killer is?" Trinity asked.

"I honestly have no idea. All the women were pregnant by the same man, and their husbands had received sexually explicit photos of their wives. They hired the anonymous photographer to get additional photos to strengthen their case in a divorce suit.

"I have run the fetus' DNA against every database in existence. I haven't found a match.

"I'm not even sure the father of the babies is the killer. Honestly, Trinity, the number of theories we have floated in this case make me dizzy."

Trinity suppressed the tremor that threatened to run through her body when she heard the way Risa said her name.

Trinity and Risa discussed the case until time for her to report to Ames. Trinity paid the check and walked Risa back to the lab.

"Thank you for being so open with me," Trinity smiled. "I already have a few positive actions I need to take."

Risa nodded and turned to walk into her lab.

"Seven," Trinity called to her.

Risa turned frowning, "Seven what?"

"That is the time I will pick you up for dinner." She disappeared through the double doors.

Trinity Jewett wasn't a woman to dive blindly into anything. She had conducted a thorough search of every member of the BW investigation team.

Risa Mercer was one of the best Chief Medical Examiners in the country. Like Trinity, she was thirty-four and had never been married.

##

Chapter 20

Louis Murdock reminded Ash of a Wild West cowboy, and he was a man on a mission. Wearing jeans and a starched white shirt, Murdock stomped into the bullpen. His boots on the hardwood floor echoed throughout the room.

"I want to see Sgt. Denton," Murdock bellowed.

"Sir, you aren't supposed to be in here," Detective Brandt stepped in front of the man.

Murdock reached out to push Brandt out of his way.

"Don't even think about putting your hand on me," Brandt growled menacingly.

Murdock took a step back. "Denton. I want to talk to Sgt. Denton."

"I'm Sgt. Denton," Ash stepped forward. "I've got this Brandt. Thanks."

"I'm Louis Murdock," the giant said. "My wife has been murdered on your watch."

Ash eyed the man cautiously. He was extremely distraught. At six-foot-five, and two-hundred and fifty pounds, Murdock towered over Ash's five-nine frame. Ash decided Murdock wasn't dangerous.

"Please, follow me." She led the rancher to an interrogation room and pushed the button that turned on the red light above the door, indicating the room was in use. She motioned Murdock to take a seat.

The metal chair creaked under Murdock's weight. To Ash's amazement, the man began crying like a baby.

Ash slid a box of tissues in front of Murdock and waited patiently as the man regained control of his emotions.

They had been trying to locate Murdock for almost a month. The man had been on a hunting trip in Namibia.

Murdock had been the high bid on the Dallas Safari Club's auction of a black rhino-hunting permit, allowing the animal to be killed and taken for a trophy. Murdock's bid had been four-hundred thousand dollars.

Unfortunately, he had been inaccessible by phone and had only learned of his wife's death upon his return home.

"I'm sorry," Murdock exhaled loudly. "I just can't believe my Beverly is gone. I can't believe she was cheating on me. I can't believe you haven't found her killer."

"Sir, I am sorry for your loss," Ash mumbled the empty words. "Have you received any sexually explicit photos of your wife with another man?"

Murdock looked at Ash as if she had levitated in front of him. "What? No!"

Murdock dragged both his large hands down his face as if trying to wipe away the awfulness of the situation.

"I am telling you," he almost whispered, "Beverly was not a cheating wife."

"You're right," Ash nodded. "We found no indication she was having an affair. However, Mrs.

Murdock knew her attacker. She disarmed the alarm and buzzed him thru the gate at seven the night she died.

"Can you think of anyone who would want to harm your wife?" Ash asked.

"No," Murdock shook his head. "Beverly was a saint. She was kind and gracious to everyone. I've never heard anyone say an ill word about her."

Murdock bowed his head, his forehead in his hands. "She was good and lovely."

"Do you have any enemies that would harm Beverly to get at you?"

"No," Murdock frowned. "We pretty much keep to ourselves. We're ranchers. We aren't involved in politics or business operations. We raise and sell cattle."

Murdock jerked his head up to meet Ash's gaze. "Wait, there were, but no…"

"There were what?" Ash gently encouraged the man to continue his thought.

"I did receive horrendous threats because I had the top bid on the rhino hunt." Murdock's words escaped in sobs from his body. "Oh, God! If my Beverly died because I went hunting, I'll never forgive myself."

"Tell me about the threats," Ash encouraged.

"Letters, phone calls," Murdock scowled. "We changed our phone number four times before the calls stopped. I have no idea how they kept getting our new numbers. It had to be someone who could hack into the AT&T database."

"Do you still have the letters?" Ash said. "Did the caller show up on your caller ID?"

"I think Beverly kept the letters," Murdock nodded. "All the numbers on the death-threat calls were blocked. I can bring you the letters."

"That would be helpful," Ash nodded. "We are following all leads. We don't want to leave any stone unturned."

Ash watched Murdock fight to maintain his self-control.

"Sergeant, four women are dead. Do you have any leads on the murders?"

"We do have several persons of interest," Ash said.

Murdock leaned across the table, so he was eye to eye with Ash. "Sgt. Denton, four murdered women, are four murders too many. Do something!"

##

Chapter 21

Captain Ames assembled his investigative team in the conference room. "Ladies and gentlemen, I want to introduce FBI agent Trinity Jewett." He waited until the comments quieted.

"Trinity has been temporarily assigned to the Branded Wives case. Please welcome her and give her your complete cooperation."

Ames introduced each of the members of his team. Dr. Lana Denton, Dr. Risa Mercer, Detective Colt Layne and Sgt. Ash Denton.

Trinity smiled and thanked Ames for the introductions. "I would like to spend today familiarizing myself with the facts of the case.

"Dr. Denton, do you have time to give me your thoughts today?"

Lana nodded and followed Jewett into her temporary office at the corner of the bullpen.

Trinity ran Dr. Denton's history through her mind as she followed her.

Dr. Denton was a top-notch profiler and had helped the FBI on occasion. A highly regarded psychiatrist, she had a thriving practice and specialized in identifying the criminally insane.

She was a prosecutor's dream witness. Beautiful, charismatic and extremely professional, juries seemed to fall in love with her.

After they had exchanged pleasantries, Trinity got to work. "Who do you think the BW killer is?"

Dr. Lana Denton inhaled deeply. "I haven't the faintest idea."

Her hesitation before answering the question caught Trinity's attention. "But you have a theory?" Trinity nudged her to share her thoughts.

"No," she smiled.

She was gorgeous. Ash Denton was one lucky son-of-a-gun. Where Dr. Mercer was among Trinity's list of top ten beautiful women, Dr. Lana Denton was number one.

"You have nothing to add to what I already have?" Trinity raised a skeptical eyebrow.

"Nothing," Lana shrugged. If she were going to share any suspicions, her wife would be the first to know.

"Would you ask your wife to join me in ten minutes?" Trinity smiled as she opened the door for her.

Trinity closed the door and called ADA Christine Canton. She'd had the pleasure of working with Christine and admired her a great deal.

"Christine," Trinity began when she answered the phone.

"Trinity Jewett," Christine smiled into the phone. "I was wondering how long it would take you to call me."

"You know I'm in town on the BW case?" Trinity asked incredulously.

"News travels fast in this town," Christine laughed.

"Well let's try to keep this between you and me," she said seriously. "I need an arrest warrant for someone, and I need it served as soon as possible."

205

Christine hung up the phone. She wished she didn't have to process this warrant.

Trinity Jewett liked Ash Denton. Denton's record was spotless. Thanks to Denton and Layne, Captain Ames' unit had the most solved cases in Texas. Both detectives had been loaned to other departments to help work unsolvable crimes. They always closed their cases. She knew the BW case was truly difficult if the two hadn't been able to catch the culprit.

Denton provided the same information as Lana and Risa. Trinity could see why Lana had fallen for Ash. She was movie star gorgeous, brilliant and fiercely loyal.

Detective Colt Layne was her last interview. With sandy brown hair and bedroom eyes, Layne was handsome in a bad-boy sort of way. His easy smile and quick wit were refreshing in a world riddled with death and bad guys.

Like his cohorts, Layne had little to add to the information on the BW murders. He had no theories or leads on the killer.

"What about the Lee Dawson murder," Trinity asked. "Any thoughts on that?"

"I'm off that case," Colt narrowed his eyes. "I was married to Linda Dawson before she left me for Lee."

Would have been nice if Risa had given me that bit of information, Trinity thought.

"That is an open and closed case," Colt continued. "Dawson attempted to make Linda's murder look like a BW murder, and Linda shot him. It was self-defense."

"Do you suspect anyone," Trinity asked.

"He has to be someone the women knew," Colt said thoughtfully. "They all disarm their alarms and let him into their homes. They trust him. I'm guessing it is someone who travels in their circles."

Linda Dawson was beyond pissed. Two police officers had handcuffed her and dragged her to the police precinct. *Heads are going to roll for this*, she thought.

Trinity watched the blonde through the one-way glass. She could see why Colt Layne was smitten with her. She was beautiful, and she knew it. Her mane of thick blonde hair was glorious. It framed the face of an angel. Right now, her green eyes were almost sparking with anger. Her lips twisted in fury.

Trinity was considered by many to be one of the finest Neurolinguistics Interviewers in the world. She had a feeling Linda Dawson was going to be a tough nut to crack.

Trinity picked up her file and opened the door. "Mrs. Dawson," she smiled, "I'm FBI agent Trinity Jewett. I am sorry to inconvenience you, but our officers haven't been able to reach you by phone and I need to talk to you about your husband's death."

Linda eyed Trinity Jewett like a hungry lioness. The fury in her eyes was palatable. Trinity knew Linda would rip her from limb to limb if she had the strength to overpower her.

"Why have I been dragged into this hellhole in handcuffs like a common criminal?" she demanded. "Where is Colt? I demand to see Colt."

Trinity smiled her sweetest smile, which only made Linda angrier. "You may demand an attorney, but you can't demand another law enforcement officer."

Linda glared at her, confident Trinity was no match for her. "Ask me your questions, FBI Agent Trinity Jewett, then have one of your underling's take me home." She tossed her long blonde hair back in that way gorgeous women do.

Trinity sat down across from her. She could feel the heat from her body. Linda was furious and gloriously hot in every sense of the word. She tied Lana Denton for first place on her list.

Colt Layne entered the bullpen. "Has anyone seen Jewett? I just thought of something that might be helpful. Where's Ash?"

"Jewett is questioning someone in interrogation four," Carter said. "Denton and her wife are in the observation room."

Colt silently slipped into the observation room. "Hey, Ash, Lana," he nodded. "Who is she sweating? What the hell! What's she doing with Linda?"

Colt reached to open the door, but Ash moved between her partner and the door. With her back against the door, Ash spoke quietly to Colt. "Don't interfere in this, Colt."

"What's going on?" Colt glared at his two friends, his two Judas friends!

"I'm not sure," Ash said. "She just had her brought in. She is just beginning to question her. She asked Lana to observe."

Colt walked to the observation window. He glanced at the cameras in the interrogation room. Both were recording. He pushed the button that would allow them to hear the questioning.

"First, I want to say that I'm so sorry for your loss." Trinity watched Linda closely for any reaction.

"Thank you," Linda never raised her eyes from her hands.

"How long were you married to Lee Dawson?" the agent continued.

"Two years."

"Were you happy?" Trinity wanted to grab her hair and yank her head up, but Linda continued to stare down at her hands.

"Mrs. Dawson, I know this is difficult for you, but could you walk me through that night one more time?"

For the first time, Linda raised her head and locked gazes with Jewett. Trinity rarely saw such arrogance in the face of a killer.

"Of course, FBI Agent Trinity Jewett."

Linda recited her ordeal as if she had memorized it word for word. She did not deviate from the story she had told the night she shot Lee Dawson. Her facial expression never changed.

"Obviously, your husband is not the BW killer," Trinity smiled patiently. "Another murder has occurred that fits the exact MO of the BW killer. There are things, at the scene of your husband's murder, that do not match the BW killer's mode of operation."

"You mean like the wrong wine label and wrong brand of cheese. The knife to remove the nipples wasn't an X-Acto knife. It was a utility knife. No branding iron found. Those sorts of discrepancies?" Linda raised her perfect eyebrows and her smile morphed into a snarl.

Trinity nodded. She was fascinated. She felt as if Linda was leading her down the rabbit hole.

"That is because I didn't tell him the wine or cheese brand, or the exact type of knife used to remove the women's nipples. I certainly didn't tell him about the banding iron." Linda's smug grin was infuriating. "I did tell him all those things in generalities, just not in detail.

"I've never believed my husband was the BW killer. He wouldn't murder innocent women." She leaned forward revealing too much cleavage for Trinity to ignore. "Eyes up here FBI Agent Trinity Jewett," she hissed.

"However, he was certainly capable of murdering me and trying to make it look like the work of the BW killer."

"Why would he want to kill you?" Jewett said. "How did you know the details? None of those details were released to the public."

She smiled slowly, clearly enjoying the little cat and mouse game they were playing. Jewett could feel it coming. Somehow, Linda had gained control of the interrogation and was about to blindside her.

"I can answer both your questions with six words." Her grin was evil. "I sleep with Detective Colt Layne."

"Detective Layne told you the details?" Trinity gasped.

"Yes, and my husband knew I was sleeping with Colt." She shrugged as if proud of the coup she had pulled off. "He wanted me dead. A divorce would have cost him a fortune. The whole thing was simply a coincidence that worked in my favor."

"There is no such thing as a coincidence," Trinity said. Her calm exterior gave no indication of the seething rage going on inside her. She would have Layne's badge.

"FBI Agent Trinity Jewett," Linda looked up at her through long lashes, "I did kill my husband, but I can assure you, it was in self-defense. I have done nothing wrong.

"May I go, or do I need to call my lawyer?"

"You're free to go," Trinity mumbled. "Oh, one more thing, Mrs. Dawson. Whose baby are you carrying?"

Linda looked as if Trinity had slapped her. It took her a few seconds to regain her composure. "If you're asking me if I'm pregnant," she smirked. "The answer is no!"

"Does Evan Trask know you have aborted his baby?" Trinity wanted to do a little happy dance at the look of horror on Linda Dawson's face. The blonde picked up her purse and stomped from the room.

Colt Layne went berserk. It was all Ash and Lana could do to keep the detective from going after his ex-wife.

As soon as they were certain Linda had left the building, they opened the door to the observation room. Colt immediately went after Trinity.

"What the hell kind of interrogation was that?" he stormed as he grabbed the FBI agent.

Trinity shoved Colt away from her. "Necessary interrogation," Jewett growled. "Questions you didn't have the balls to ask her because you're sleeping with her. You shouldn't be working this case at all."

Colt made a dive for Trinity, but Ash and Ames caught him and dragged him into one of the interrogation rooms.

"You need to calm down," Ames commanded. "Stay here until I send for you."

"In my office," Ames directed Trinity.

Captain Ames closed the door, "Well?"

"It was self-defense," Trinity huffed. "She didn't plan to kill Dawson; it just worked out that way."

Trinity shook her head, "She's one cold bitch."

"Yeah," Ames nodded.

"Colt," Ames called his detective as Trinity left the office.

"I'm taking you off the BW case," Ames informed Colt. "I'm putting you on the Candy Barnes case. We let it slide to the back burner when Beverly Murdock died. Now Christine is riding my butt. She needs some answers."

Colt nodded. "I'm sorry, Captain. I shouldn't have gone off like that on Jewett. I'll apologize to her."

Ames nodded. "Please, do. However, I'm serious. Stay away from the Branded Wives case."

##

Chapter 22

ADA Christine Canton took the elevator down to the parking garage of the Flatiron Building. She was a little disappointed to find Colt Layne assigned to the Barnes case. Christine liked Layne but felt that Denton was the superior investigator. Besides, she enjoyed doing things with Lana and Ash socially.

Colt was waiting for her when she emerged from the elevator. She greeted the security guard Jessica had stationed in the lobby then made her way to Colt's sedan.

"You didn't have to come with me tonight," Colt smiled as he leaned over and pushed open the door for Christine.

"I thought it might be a nice break. Jessica is trying to run down a hacker that is doing his best to get into our criminal history database. You know Jessica. She is like a dog with a bone when someone dares to attack her security systems."

Colt nodded. The Cyber Chief was certainly dedicated. "I have been setting at that house for a week. I haven't seen a sign of Jody Swift. I think he must be lying low. Maybe he made me."

Christine looked around the inside of the city-issued car. A gray Taurus, it disappeared into the pavement. She had never seen a more nondescript car. Unless one were truly searching for the car, they would never be aware of it.

"I doubt anyone made you in this car," she chuckled.

Colt pulled the sedan into a different position from the night before as he set up surveillance on the suspect's house

"So, you and Jessica," Colt smiled. "How is that going?"

"Good," Christine smiled as she thought of how protective and thoughtful Jessica was of her.

"How much longer on the divorce?"

"Ten, long awful days," Christine frowned.

"I guess you and Jessica will be celebrating when it's final," Colt mused. "Got any special plans?"

"I don't know what Jessica has planned," Christine said, her voice dropping to that low sexy sound women use to drive men crazy, "but I know what I have planned for her."

Colt threw back his head and laughed. "Lucky, Jessica," he laughed again.

"Christine, see that car approaching with its headlights turned off?" Colt immediately un-holstered his Glock. "Don't move. Let's see if he goes into the house."

As the pair watched, a dark figure emerged from the vehicle and entered the front door of the house.

"Please wait here," Colt instructed. "This could get dangerous."

He shoved a piece of paper into her hand. "Wait until I get into his car then call this number. Tell him who you are and that you have a warrant for his arrest. That should spook him."

Colt quickly moved to Jody's car and climbed into the back seat. He loved how stupid low lives could be. They rarely locked their car doors.

He settled in the car's back seat just before the man ran from the house and jumped into the front seat. Before Swift could get the keys into the ignition, Colt had the barrel of his Glock in the man's ear.

"Put your hands on the steering wheel where I can see them," he growled into Jody Swift's ear. "Put your left hand behind your neck."

Colt snapped the handcuffs on the man's wrist. "Now, nice and slow, put your right hand behind your back."

Swift complied

Colt snapped the cuffs onto the pimp's right wrist then stepped from the car.

"Now get out of the car," Colt pulled open Swift's door and dragged the man from the car. He shoved the perp against the car, frisked him and shoved him toward his sedan.

"Are you a cop, dude?" Swift stumbled as Colt gave him another shove.

"Oh, did I forget to say that," Colt growled as he opened the back door of the sedan and shoved Swift into the back seat behind Christine.

The bullpen was almost deserted when Colt and Christine brought Jody Swift into the interrogation room. At ten at night, most of the detectives were either following up on cases or eating dinner.

"No one knows I have you," Colt maliciously grinned as he cuffed Swift to the table and shoved a chair under him. "You can give me some straight answers and walk out of here tonight, or I can book you and hold you for forty-eight hours in the general population. I will even be nice and let you wear your fancy duds."

He looked Jody Swift up and down. "Do you know what happens to slender, blonde, fancy pants in general lockup?" Colt grinned. "And, they won't even pay you. You'll be putting out for free, Jody."

"Hey man, just tell me what you want?" the pimp was almost hyperventilating. "I ain't done nothing. What you need?"

"I need the name of your girl that is servicing this man." Colt slid a photo of Bradford Clemens in front of Jody.

"That would be my Miss. Goody," Jody exhaled.

"Miss. Goody, have a first name and location," Colt asked.

"Goody," Jody said.

"First name," Colt barked.

"That's her name," Jody looked like he was about to cry. "Goody Goody."

"Seriously," Christine frowned.

"You know, Mama, I could make you some good money," Jody grinned. "I got clients that would throw down some big bucks for a looker like you."

Colt grabbed Jody's spiked hair and yanked his head back. "Don't you dare address her again," he snarled in Swift's face. "I'll tear off your bal…"

"Colt," Christine cautioned.

"Where can I find her?" Colt still had Jody's hair firmly in his grasp.

"Paradise Motel on Lancaster," Jody croaked as Colt pulled his head further back. "She works out of room 101."

"Let's go," Colt said to Christine.

"Hey, man, what about me?" Swift squealed. "You can't leave me here, like this."

"We'll be back," Colt grinned. "Make yourself at home."

It was almost midnight when Goody's trick left room 101. Colt knocked on the door. A young white girl opened the door. Colt grabbed her wrist and yanked her outside. He had her hands cuffed behind her and headed toward the car before she knew what was happening.

"Wait, wait," she wailed. "Don't leave my door unlocked with my purse in there. Someone will steal it. Man, I've tricked all week for that money."

Colt shoved her into the back seat of his car and returned for her purse. He turned on the light. The room stunk of cheap perfume, booze, and sex. He spotted her purse. After overcoming his revulsion, he gingerly picked it up by the strap and pushed the button to lock the door behind him.

"You got no right to be busting me," Goody whined.

"We just want to ask you a few questions, Miss. Goody," Christine smiled. "You want to talk here?"

"Hell no," Goody snapped. "Jody will see me and beat the hell out of me for talking to the cops."

"We have Jody at the precinct," Colt said. "He gave you up to us."

"That sniveling little son-of-a-bitch. He's supposed to protect us. Watch out for us. Sorry little…"

Colt checked her out. She looked decent enough for public consumption: jeans, a pullover shirt, and flip-flops.

"How about we drive to a better area of town and buy you breakfast," he offered.

"You sure Jody's locked up," she double-checked.

Christine and Colt nodded.

"Yeah, I could use something to eat," she agreed. "Did you lock the door? Everything I own is in that room. If it ain't locked, the low life will steal everything. I got it paid for until the end of the month."

The law enforcement officers watched Goody finish off a full order of Ol' South Pancake House blueberry pancakes and an order of steak and eggs. "Gotta get it while I can," she grinned. "I don't get free food very often."

Christine was surprised at how pretty her teeth were. She wasn't a drug user. That was unusual. Most hookers were heavy users.

They all sat quietly as the server refilled their coffee cups.

"Would you like anything else?" Colt smiled.

"Nah. Don't know where I'd put it."

"Do you know this man?" Christine slid the photo of Bradford Clemens in front of her.

"Sure, that's Mr. Smith," Goody snorted.

"How long have you been on the streets?" Christine asked.

Goody looked Christine over as if sizing her up. "Too long," the girl frowned.

"Is Goody your real name?" the ADA asked.

"It's real enough," the girl nodded.

"How old are you?" Christine said.

"Twenty-two," Goody scowled. "Why?"

"Just curious," Christine smiled slightly.

"How old are you?" Goody smiled.

"That's none of your business," Colt interrupted their Kum Ba Yah moment. "Christine?" He cautioned the ADA. In the past, he had seen his peers try to help these women. It never turned out well.

"Mr. Smith. That's not his real name, right?" Colt continued his questioning.

"No," Goody smiled. "I saw his driver's license once. His name is Brandon or Brad, Bradford. Yeah, Bradford. Like the Bradford Pear."

"Bradford Clemens, he's president of Clemens Motors," Colt said.

"Yeah, Clemens Motors!" Goody exclaimed. "His automobile dealerships are all over the metroplex?"

"Yes," Christine nodded.

Goody pushed the brown hair back from her face. "Teresa," she murmured. "My name is Teresa. Teresa Long"

"Teresa we're going to put you in protective custody," Christine declared. "Is that okay with you?"

"Hell, yes," Goody grinned. "That means a clean place to sleep with no bedbugs. Three meals a day and hot running water. No Johns, Right?"

"Right," Christine grimaced.

##

Christine arranged Teresa's stay at the Omni Hotel in downtown Fort Worth. She felt the girl had little chance of encountering anyone associated with her current employer.

Frank Moncrief was suing Bradford Clemens because his repair policies had resulted in the death of two men who had brought their vehicles in for warranty service.

Three of Clemens mechanics had testified that their repair directives had resulted in the death of the two men. They said they weren't allowed to replace defective parts. Clemens claimed the mechanics had done shoddy work and were now lying about it.

Christine had made certain that Teresa had gotten an attractive haircut and a manicure. New clothes and makeup had topped off the young woman's new look. No one would recognize her as the hooker from the Paradise Motel.

Colt and Christine were having breakfast with Teresa in the hotel restaurant when Jessica joined them.

Christine frowned as she saw a look of recognition cross Teresa's face.

Jessica spotted them and walked to their table. Christine made the introductions. *Cleaning her up has gone a long way,* she thought. *Jessica doesn't recognize her.*

"Your office said I would find you here. I have the information you need," Jessica smiled at Christine. "I think this will seal the case."

They hadn't questioned Teresa any further, preferring to win her confidence first.

Teresa could see how pleased Christine was with Jessica's declaration. Not wanting to be outdone, she volunteered her information.

"Mr. Smith, uh, Bradford told me he made a lot of money on recalls," Teresa said. She paused as she realized she had the total attention of the other three at her table. "He said he made the repairs with used parts and pocketed the money from the auto manufacturers."

"Will you testify to that?" Christine asked, pleased with the breakthrough.

"Yes, ma'am," Teresa smiled broadly. "That's the least I can do after all you've done for me."

Christine nodded and watched the girl closely as Teresa looked up shyly at Jessica and smiled. Jessica was completely oblivious to her. She only had eyes for Christine.

Christine was surprised at how much Teresa looked like a younger Jessica.

"Teresa, I need you to do something crucial for me," Christine said seriously. "I need you to wear a wire and meet Clemens one more time. Here is the list of questions. Try to get him to answer them. We will be standing by at all times and will make certain he doesn't lay a hand on you."

Colt had to admit Goody was a very attractive young woman. He wondered if she knew she would be returned to the streets as soon as the trial was over.

##

Chapter 23

Risa Mercer smiled when her doorbell rang. She had gone the extra mile to look ravishing tonight and had been wondering if Trinity Jewett would be detective enough to get her address. Obviously, she had.

"Agent Jewett," she smiled as she opened the door. "You're right on time."

"And you're breathtaking," Trinity's look of admiration told Risa the extra effort had paid off.

"How did you know I love Japanese food," Risa smiled as Trinity pulled her car into the parking lot of the Japanese Palace.

"You have friends in high places," Trinity laughed. "I asked them."

They sipped sake and talked as the Hibachi chef prepared their dinner and entertained them with his cooking skills.

Dinner was a two-hour affair served in courses. By the time it was over, they knew the high points of each other's careers and their reasons for selecting their fields in law enforcement.

"Do you know where we might go for an after-dinner drink and some slow dancing?" Trinity suggested. She didn't want the evening to end yet.

"I do," Risa nodded.

The club Risa took them to was perfect. Low-level lighting, a combo playing easy listening music—quiet enough they could talk—and excellent service.

"I heard about the altercation between you and Colt today," Risa said as she sipped her Dubonnet.

"I didn't expect that reaction from him," Trinity swirled the ice in her Scotch. "It would have helped if you had warned me he was sleeping with Linda Dawson."

"Linda Dawson is his ex-wife," Risa frowned. "They divorced over three years ago. Poor devil, he can't seem to move on with his life. I have never met a man so obsessed with a woman."

"I imagine that could happen if one met the right woman," Trinity smiled. "Of course, it would be disastrous if she didn't reciprocate the feelings."

"Yes, it would," Risa nodded. "Please, cut Colt some slack. He's going through hell right now."

"At least, he can rest easy knowing Linda didn't plan to kill Lee Dawson," Trinity grimaced. "I believe her story. She may be a cold-blooded bitch, but she is not a cold-blooded killer."

The combo began playing *Unchained Melody*. They both stopped talking to listen to the excellent male tenor sing the song made popular in the sixties by Bobby Hatfield of the Righteous Brothers.

Trinity took Risa's hand and led her to the dance floor. Finally, they were both where they had wanted to be all evening—in each other's arms.

Trinity Jewett stood looking at the door Risa had just closed. More than anything, she wanted to pound on her door and beg Risa to let her hold her. Jewett smiled as she controlled her impulse. She had a feeling she would spend the rest of her life begging Risa Mercer.

Dancing with Risa had driven her slowly insane. She could still feel how soft and warm she had been in her arms. Her chest still burned where she had pressed Risa's softness tight against her.

As the dance progressed, she had let her hand slip from her slender waist, down to the small of her back and pressed her hard against her. Risa had moaned softly before pulling out of her arms when the song ended.

Although she looked like a player, Trinity had always played it safe. Women threw themselves at her, but she wasn't interested in easy women. She wanted a woman who would be there every night at the end of the day. Something told her Risa Mercer was that kind of woman.

##

Risa was still leaning against her door when Trinity's car left the driveway. It had taken all the self-control she had to say goodnight without inviting her in. She knew she would be in her bed in the morning if she let her in. The ME didn't want Trinity to think she was easy.

God, it felt good in her arms, she thought as she recalled their dancing. Trinity was an excellent dancer. She led easily. Her strong arm had encircled Risa's waist, gently moving her around the dance floor. When her hand slid to the small of Risa's back and splayed across her hips, she had stopped breathing. She couldn't recall anyone affecting her as Trinity had.

She made a mental note to call her friend in the FBI's forensic department in the morning. She wanted to know more about FBI Agent Trinity Jewett.

"I'm so glad you have the morning free and can go with me," Ash slid her arms around her wife's waist as Lana fixed her collar.

"There," she patted the front of Ash's blouse and tilted her head for a kiss. "I never miss an opportunity to spend time with my beautiful wife."

"Your beautiful wife truly appreciates that." Ash slowly pulled Lana into her arms and kissed her gently. Their tongues danced a slow dance of desire. "Whoa," Ash said hoarsely, "If you keep that up we won't get out of the house all day."

"Promises! Promises!" Lana said seductively.

Both their phones rang simultaneously. Ames informed Ash that Mrs. Barnes had called to postpone their meeting an hour.

Jackie called Lana to tell her that her early afternoon appointment had rescheduled for the next day.

"It seems we have an extra hour to kill," Lana smiled a predatory smile, as she slipped Ash's vest down her arms.

Ash gave into the charge of excitement as she yielded to her wife's whims. "I love you so much," Lana murmured as she kissed the cleavage she had exposed. "So much."

##

Lana exhaled slowly as her wife pulled from her. "I could do that all day," she said, her soft lips against Ash's ear.

"I could let you," Ash whispered as she pulled Lana on top of her. "You know you make my life worth living." She kissed her again, a long, deep kiss, thrilling to the feel of her full, firm lips moving against hers. Nothing in the world was as wonderful as kissing her wife. Well, almost nothing.

It had taken them almost a month to track down the real name of Candy Barnes and her parents. Lana inhaled deeply. How does one tell parents their twenty-one-year-old daughter was a drug addict and a prostitute who was murdered by one of her tricks? No parent should ever have to hear that!

"It's the house on the corner." Lana referenced a sprawling, red brick colonial with massive columns.

"Candy's parents live here?" Ash raised a questioning eyebrow.

Lana double checked the address and nodded yes.

"This doesn't look like a home that would produce a hooker," Ash noted, as they approached the steps leading up to the porch that spread across the front of the house.

Ash rang the doorbell. A petite woman in her late forties opened the door.

"I'm Sergeant Ash Denton with the Ft. Worth police department and this is Forensic Psychiatrist, Dr. Lana Denton."

"Oh, dear Lord," the woman almost crumbled to the floor before Ash caught her. Holding her up, she led her to the sofa.

"Has something happened to Nicole?" Her eyes begged them to say no.

"Is your husband here?" Ash asked. She wanted to break the bad news to both at the same time.

"Yes, I'm here," a handsome man wearing the clerical collar of an Episcopalian priest entered the room.

"Martha, what's wrong?" He sat down beside his wife and put a protective arm around her.

"Reverend and Mrs. Barnes," Ash began, "I am so sorry to tell you that your daughter is dead."

Mrs. Barnes collapsed against her husband, sobbing into the front of his jacket. Rev. Timothy Barnes bent his head as silent tears streaked his face.

"How?" Barnes finally asked.

"She was shot." Ash delivered her message as sympathetically as possible.

"Who would shoot our baby?" Martha sobbed quietly.

"That's what we're trying to find out," Ash said. "Are you up to answering a few questions?"

The reverend nodded yes.

"Where are my manners," Martha Barnes stood as if sleep walking and started toward the kitchen. "I have fresh-squeezed lemonade. Let me get everyone a glass."

Ash raised her hand to stop her, but her husband placed a firm hand on Ash's arm. "Let her," the reverend encouraged, "It will give her something to do."

"I'll help her," Lana followed Martha into the kitchen.

"Sir, when was the last time you saw your daughter?" Ash asked.

"It's been over two years. She dropped out of college. She always carried a three point five or above, on the Dean's list then it was as if she had gone brain dead. She started skipping classes. She failed all her courses.

"Martha and I tried to talk to her, find out what was wrong. She became increasingly antagonistic. I suspected drugs and searched her room one night while she was out. I found marijuana along with a bag containing a needle and a baggie of white powder hidden in her closet. I flushed it down the commode.

"I confronted her when she came home. She told me she was holding it for a friend. When I told her, I had flushed it down the commode, she went berserk. She screamed the most horrible things I've ever heard come out of a human mouth."

Barnes stopped and shook his head as if trying to erase the image of his rampaging daughter.

"I tried to calm her down," he continued. "I begged her to get help. She just continued to scream and hiss, like a trapped animal. I...I..." he searched for words. "I've never seen anything like that. How could my baby girl turn into that monster? How did we let that happen?"

Lana and Mrs. Barnes retuned carrying a tray of lemonade and cookies. They set down beside their respective spouses.

"It was truly atrocious," Martha agreed with her husband. "I have never heard anything as vile."

"When we awoke the next morning, she was gone," Rev. Barnes said. "We haven't heard from her since."

"Have you seen her at all?" Lana asked gently.

"No," Martha said. "We called her cellphone for a while and left messages, begging her to come home. She never called us back. Then our phone bill showed her service removed. After that, we just received the 'you've dialed a non-working number recording'."

"What about you, reverend?" Lana watched Barnes. He cast his eyes to the right then met her gaze.

"No, I never talked to her," he choked.

"Do you know anyone she might have been running around with?" Ash asked.

"We never met any of her friends after she dropped out of college," Martha grimaced.

"I saw her at the Denny's on I-35," Barnes frowned. "She was with some punk looking guy. He was all dressed up in fancy clothes. Blonde, spiked hair; skinny, sleazy-looking character."

"Did you try to talk to her?" Lana asked.

"No, I couldn't bear to look at her." Tears ran down the reverend's cheeks.

##

Chapter 24

Ash filled out the report on their visit to Reverend and Martha Barnes. "Is Christine filing criminal charges against Bradford Clemons?" She asked Colt.

"We don't have enough evidence to charge him with murder," Colt shrugged. "Shagging a prostitute is a class B misdemeanor. We'd spend more time doing the paperwork than Clemons would spend in jail."

"She does have an ace up her sleeve. She's hiding a prostitute named Goody, who will testify in Frank Moncrief's civil case. If Frank wins that case, Christine is going to file criminal homicide charges against Clemons."

"We have her pimp in lockup. I think he will do anything to stay out of general population. I have him in isolation right now. He's a blonde, pretty-boy."

"Skinny blonde, spiked hair," Ash asked.

"Yeah, slimy little bastard," Colt nodded.

"Get him up here," Ash said. "I am betting he was also Candy Barnes' pimp."

"The whore Frank was accused of killing?" Colt frowned.

Ash nodded yes.

##

"Hey Jody," Colt said menacingly, "I've been missing you. Are you enjoying our accommodations?"

"I want out of this dump," Jody Swift whined. "I want to make bail."

Colt was grinning at Jody maliciously. Ash knew her partner was intimidating the pimp.

"Hello, Jody," Ash smiled as she slid a Sprite to the man. "I'm Sgt. Ash Denton."

"Are you his boss?" Jody glared at Colt.

"Not really," Ash continued smiling. "He pretty much does as he pleases. He is very effective."

Jody opened the canned drink and took several long gulps of the cold liquid. *That is the best thing I've ever tasted,* he thought.

"Do you know this girl?" Ash slid the morgue shot of Nicole Barnes—aka Candy Barnes—in front of Jody.

Jody took another long drink, trying to decide whether he should lie or tell the truth. "No," he lied.

"I think you knew her as Candy Barnes," Ash continued patiently. "She was Bradford Clemons' favorite prostitute."

Jody watched Colt as he moved about the room. He didn't trust the detective, even with his sergeant in the cubicle.

"She wasn't one of my ladies," Jody said.

"I told you she wasn't one of his," Colt snorted. "She had too much class. Jody only runs skanks."

"Take a good look at her, Jody," Ash said.

"Don't know her," Jody shook his head.

"He's no use to us, Sarg," Colt grinned as he wrote on the paper in his file folder. "If you will just sign this form, I am putting him into the general population cells."

Ash reached for the pen in her inside jacket pocket.

"No! Wait," Jody squealed. "She was mine. What do you want to know?"

"What happened to her?" Ash's narrowed eyes bore into the pimp.

"From your morgue shot, I'd say she was murdered," Jody smirked.

"By whom?" Ash asked.

"I don't know." Jody's eyes darted around the room, looking for Colt. "She serviced several customers that night. Clemons was her last trick. He had left before the killer shot her."

"How do you know?" Ash asked.

"She called me to see if she could quit for the night. Said she had a bitching headache." Jody's eyes darted to the right, then back to Colt.

"I drove by and picked up my money. I told her to lock the door and get some sleep." Jody continued. "No one was there."

"So, you were the last one to see her alive?" Colt said.

"Yeah, but man I didn't kill her. She was my best earner. She hadn't been in the business long. She still looked good. Most days she'd bring in a thousand bucks. I felt awful about losing her."

"Before you could use her up," Colt snarled.

"Hey, look, man, I didn't get her hooked on drugs," Jody whined. "She did that all by herself. She came to me for a job."

"Did she have any other steady customers?" Ash said. "Guys who were obsessed with her?"

"There was one guy," Jody recalled. "He would pay for her all day. A Thousand bucks a day, he paid it once a week."

"I need a name," Ash said.

"I got no idea," Jody frowned. "She just called him Big Daddy. You know like in *Cat on a Hot Tin Roof*."

"What did he look like?"

"Don't know," Jody smirked. "Never met him. His money was good that is all I cared about."

"Has he switched to any of the other girls?" Ash asked.

"Nah, I called him. Tried to interest him in Goody, but he wasn't interested. I tried to call him once more, but his phone just went into voicemail."

"You still have his number?" Ash was getting excited. This was the closest thing she had to a lead.

"It's on my cell phone," Jody snorted. "The one you took away from me."

##

Ash and Colt walked into the bullpen. Colt called the property division and had them send up Jody Swift's property bag.

"What does Christine have planned for him," Ash asked.

"She has enough on him to put him away for ten years. It is his fourth arrest for pimping. He was out on parole when we picked him up."

The property clerk dropped the bag on Ash's desk and handed Ash the clipboard to sign for Jody's things.

"Wait just a minute," Ash said, as she pulled the cell phone from the bag. "All we need is this phone. You can return everything else to the property room."

"Sure thing, Sarg."

"Phone's dead," Ash frowned.

"I have a block," Colt grinned.

"Aren't you mister gadget," Ash teased as her partner produced the black power block.

The phone dinged, then came on when Colt plugged it into the block. Of course, it was password protected.

The two detectives carried the phone back into the interrogation room.

"What's your password," Colt demanded.

"I'll type it in," Jody snorted.

"You can either give me your password or go back to a community cell," Colt threatened.

"Zero, two, fourteen," Jody huffed.

"Aww, Valentine's Day," Colt shook his head. "Aren't you just an old softy, you little piss ant."

The phone began to ding and played ringtones like the battle of the bands. It vibrated as if it were alive. Message after message loaded into the phone.

"Jessica is going to have a field day with this," Ash smiled.

"How do I find his number," Ash asked.

"Duh, in contacts, under Big Daddy," Jody snorted as if the detectives were stupid.

Ash found the number but didn't want to call it. "Let's take this to Jessica and see what she thinks."

"Good idea," Colt called the jailer. "Please return Mr. Swift to his private quarters."

He couldn't resist grinning evilly at Jody. "Till next time, Jody."

#

"Christine's divorce is final today," Colt informed Ash as they drove to Jessica's office.

"You're becoming quite the office gossip," Ash chuckled. "How did you find that out?"

"On stake out," Colt grinned. "Christine and I had plenty of time to talk. She's crazy about the woman."

"I never thought Christine played on my team," Ash said. "My gaydar must be on the fritz. I'll call Lana. We should take them out to dinner tonight to celebrate."

"I don't think that is the celebration Christine has in mind," Colt laughed.

"Oooh," Ash exhaled and nodded her head. "Lucky Jessica."

"Yeah." Colt agreed.

##

Colt was surprised to see Teresa Long at the receptionist's desk in the lobby of the Flatiron Building.

"Hey Teresa," he smiled. "How is the world treating you?" He couldn't believe the stunning young woman was Miss Goody they had picked up for prostitution.

"Wonderful, Detective Layne," she beamed. "Ms. Barton gave me this awesome job. Her personal secretary took the time to train me, and I love it."

"Would you let Jessica know we're here?" Colt winked at the young woman. "She's expecting us."

"She is in the computer room. The one she calls her War Room," Teresa informed them. "Go on up: the second floor, room 210. I'll let her know you're on your way."

Jessica stood and shook hands with both detectives as they entered her computer room.

Ash never ceased to be amazed by all the screens and information Jessica seemed to control. *So, this is Jessica's War Room.*

"What can I do for you?" Jessica motioned for them to sit down.

Ash explained their mission.

"No problem," Jessica nodded. "I can have this ready for you by tomorrow afternoon."

"Are you sure?" Colt asked.

"All you need me to do is run these phone numbers and cross reference them with the phone company's database to provide you a list of names and addresses that correlate with the nicknames in Jody's phone. Right?"

"Yes," both detectives nodded.

"I will have it for you tomorrow," Jessica smiled.

There was a soft knock at the door then Christine walked in. She looked weary.

"Are you okay, honey," Jessica rushed to her side. "I am so sorry you had to go through that alone."

She bent down and kissed her gently. "Sit down. We were just discussing Jody Swift." Jessica sat beside her.

Christine brightened at the mention of the pimp's name. "I hope you have something that will let me put him away for life," she huffed.

"No," Ash said. "I think the best we will be able to do with Jody is ten years without parole."

"That's better than two or three years," Christine frowned. "By the time he gets out of jail, I want him to be so bowlegged one could drive a car between his legs."

"Whoa, someone is in a foul mood today," Colt teased. "Was divorce court that hard?"

"Robert didn't show up, and Judge Crane wanted to postpone the ruling until it would be convenient for Robert." Christine scowled.

"So, you're not divorced, Chris," Jessica said pitifully.

For the first time since she entered the room, a smile lighted Christine's beautiful face. "I'm a free woman, darling," she laughed. "It just took some convincing of the judge."

She caught Jessica's face between her hands and kissed her as if her life depended on it. "I love you," she whispered.

Jessica blushed and whispered back, "I love you too."

"We should celebrate," Colt teased them devilishly.

"I am sure you mean well, Colt Layne," Christine stood. "But, get the hell out of here."

Colt and Ash left the room laughing.

"I need to talk to Goody," Ash told Colt as they rode down the elevator.

"Help yourself," Colt grinned. "That's her in the lobby."

Ash looked questioningly, "The receptionist? She was a hooker?"

"Also, Frank's star witness," Colt grinned. "It was Christine's idea to hide her in plain sight."

"Yeah," Ash said. "I'd bet a month's pay she doesn't look anything like Goody, the hooker you picked up."

"You'd win that bet," Colt laughed.

"Let's go back to the office," Ash said. "I want to pick up those pictures of Candy Barnes."

"I have a few things I need to take care of at the office," Christine smiled sweetly at Jessica. "I do hope you will move your things back to your apartment tonight."

"Of course," Jessica smiled weakly. "I have appointments this afternoon, too. I'll see you around five."

Christine kissed her again and left.

"How're you doing?" Christine greeted Teresa Long.

"I am doing great, Mrs. Canton," the girl said exuberantly. "Thank you so much for all you have done for me."

"I'm glad you are turning your life around," Christine eyed the girl. "How did you ever end up on the streets?"

"It's a long story," Teresa bowed her head. "One I'd rather not tell."

"I can respect that," the ADA smiled. "How did you know Jessica?"

Teresa's eyes darted around the room like a trapped animal looking for a place to hide.

"Did Ms. Barton say she knew me?"

"No," Christine smirked, "But I know you do."

Teresa stared into the ADA's eyes. "I never saw her before that day in the Omni restaurant. I thought I knew her, but that was someone else.

"Ms. Barton is a lady," Teresa smiled slightly. "She's always a perfect lady."

Christine had interrogated enough criminals to know when someone was lying to her. She would leave it for now, but she knew Teresa was keeping something from her.

Teresa didn't notice the look Christine gave her. The girl was too busy trying to figure out a way to get her belongings out of the Paradise Motel.

She didn't own much in this world: a few CDs; a bracelet and watch; her iPhone and an evening bag that had belonged to Candy Barnes. Barnes had told her Big Daddy gave it to her. Candy had called it her bag of tricks.

She felt bad about keeping Candy's purse, but Candy had left it in Teresa's room the night they had partied with the two TCU fellows. Besides, Candy had no use for it now.

##

"I don't have an appointment," Jessica Barton was almost hyperventilating. "But, I have to see Dr. Denton."

"Hold your horses," Jackie stepped between Jessica and the door to Lana's office. "Dr. Denton is with another patient right now. Take a seat. It shouldn't be more than ten minutes."

Jackie led Jessica to another waiting room and closed the door. Dr. Lana Denton was always careful to protect the identity of her patients.

Jessica paced the floor. She was on her meds, but she was scared to death. The door opened, and Lana walked in. "Jessica, it's good to see you, but your appointment isn't until Friday."

Jessica inhaled deeply, trying to slow the pounding of her heart. Her breaths came in short, shallow pants. Lana recognized an anxiety attack when she saw one.

She placed her hand lightly on Jessica's arm. "Come with me." She led her into her office and closed the door.

"Please sit down," she motioned toward the sofa and gathered her pad and pen. "Are you on your meds?"

"Yes," Jessica nodded. Her mouth felt as if it was full of cotton. "May I have some water?"

Lana walked to the small refrigerator in her office and returned with two bottles of cold water. She considered increasing her dosage.

Jessica drank half the bottle before she closed her eyes and seemed to steady herself.

"You seem agitated," Lana said.

"I...Dr. Denton...I..." Jessica stammered for another minute.

"Christine's divorce was final today," she blurted out.

"I thought you would be happy about that," Lana smiled.

"I am, but," Jessica inhaled deeply, again. "I'm scared."

"Of what?" Lana suppressed her smile. She had a pretty, good idea what was agitating her patient.

"She has made it clear to me that she intends to consummate our relationship tonight." Jessica looked as if she would throw up.

"And you don't want that," Lana furrowed her brow.

"Oh, I do," Jessica exhaled, "More than anything. I love her, so much, but…"

"But, what," Lana nudged her to continue.

"What if…," she swallowed loudly and drank the rest of the water. "What if I disappoint her? What if I am unable to please her? What if…"

"Jessica, calm down," Lana said soothingly. "Do you believe Christine loves you?"

"Yes," she smiled hesitantly, "and I love her more than anything in my life."

"Two people in love, working together, can work out anything," Lana assured her.

"But I…She," Jessica was beginning to hyperventilate again. She looked wildly around the room.

"Jessica, look at me," Lana commanded.

Jessica seemed to snap out or her panic attack and stared at the doctor.

"She was married," Jessica mumbled. "She has been with other men. She will compare me…"

"Won't you compare her to other women?" Lana asked. "It's human nature. The bottom line is Christine is in love with you."

"I would never compare her to another woman," Jessica wailed. "I've never been with a woman!"

Seriously, Lana thought. *After all the bragging, I've had to listen to for the past two years. None of it was true!*

"Jessica, just talk to Christine," Lana smiled. "Tell her how you feel. It isn't something that has to happen tonight. Don't force anything, just let it happen."

Jessica seemed to consider her advice. She nodded. "You're right. That's what I'll do." She shrugged her shoulders as if a great weight had been lifted from them.

"Jessica," Lana said casually, "do you want children?"

"I...I haven't given that any thought," Jessica furrowed her brow. "Honestly, Dr. Denton, I never thought anyone would want to have a family with me."

Lana recalled the toddler, Presley. She was certain the boy was Jessica's son. "Would you like a son?"

"Of course," Jessica smiled tentatively, "but I think we are getting the cart before the horse. I'm hyperventilating over having relations with the woman I love." Her eyes grew huge. "I can't even imagine us having a baby."

Lana sat at her desk for a long time after Jessica left. She knew she would be upset when she found out Lana had visited her grandmother.

Her thoughts went to his father's diary. She knew Jessica hadn't read it. It was probably good she hadn't. Obviously, Preston Barton, Jr., had killed his wife to save his daughter from the humiliation her mother was bound to bring to the family.

Children always blamed themselves for their parents' actions. Most children blamed themselves for their parents' divorcing. Knowing Jessica, Lana was certain the seventeen-year-old had blamed herself for her parents' deaths. If she read her father's diary, she would definitely blame herself.

Lana needed Jessica to recall what had happened. She didn't want to be the one to tell her.

She felt a little guilty for having read the diary, but it had given her such insight into her patient, she would do it again in a heartbeat.

Chapter 25

"There is something creepy about making out in a morgue," Risa laughed as she pulled from Trinity Jewett's arms. "Why don't we take this to my place?"

"My thoughts exactly," Jewett kissed her again. They had been dating over a month, and Trinity was certain Risa was the one for her.

Jamie, Risa's assistant, shoved the heavy morgue doors open. "Dr. Mercer, there's a couple here to make a positive ID on Candy Barnes uh...Nicole Barnes."

"Get Ash down here," Risa hissed. "How did they get here alone?"

"Don't know," Jamie shrugged.

"Well, that's a mood killer," Trinity grinned sheepishly.

Risa patted her on the arm then moved toward the human file cabinet. The doors opened again, and Ash Denton led the couple into the morgue. Risa wondered how the detective had gotten there so quickly, but thanked God for her speed.

"Are you sure you are up to this?" Ash asked Mrs. Barnes as she and her husband followed her into the cold room.

Martha Barnes stopped to collect herself for a moment then walked toward the drawer Risa was pulling out.

"Are you ready?" Risa gently asked.

Both parents nodded and steeled themselves for the inevitable.

"Oh, no," Martha sagged against her husband. "Oh, Timothy, how could this happen to our baby?"

Trinity and Ash moved to catch Martha as she fainted. Trinity easily lifted the petite woman in her arms and carried her to a waiting room.

Risa cracked an ampoule of ammonia inhalant and waved the smelling salts under Martha's nose. The woman roused and looked around as if trying to ascertain her location. The look of mental anguish on her face told Risa, the full impact of her situation had hit Martha.

"Here, Mrs. Barnes," Ash held a bottle of water toward Martha. "Drink a few sips of this. It will make you feel better."

Reverend Timothy Barnes was still staring at his daughter's body. Risa walked to him.

"Is this Nicole Barnes?" she asked.

He nodded. "She's skeletal. Are these needle tracks? How did she become this? She was beautiful and smart. What happened? She was such a good Christian girl. Where did I go wrong?"

"You can't blame yourself, sir," Risa consoled him. "I'm sure you did everything you could do."

Reverend Barnes stared through her as if she weren't there then silently walked away.

##

Ash and Colt walked into the Flatiron Building.

"Ms. Barton is out," Teresa smiled.

"We need to ask you something," Ash said, as she pulled the morgue photo of Nicole Barnes from the envelope. She placed it on the desk in front of Teresa.

"Do you know her?" She asked.

Teresa gasped and silently nodded.

"Who is she," Ash asked as if she didn't know.

"Her name is Candy," Teresa looked as if she might cry. "Jody worked her off I-35. What happened to her?"

"I was hoping you might give me some help with that question," Ash smiled. "She was Bradford Clemons' lady of choice before someone shot her. We theorized that Clemons had hired a hitman to kill her, but we can't connect him to anyone.

"Apparently, Clemons pillow talked with her just like he did you. She knew all about his crooked dealings."

"I didn't know her very well." Teresa's hands shook as she picked up a pen just to have something to do with her hands. "I didn't know she was dead. Jody told me to take over Clemens because Candy had moved on.

"I used to see her sometimes at the Denny's on thirty-five. We talked. She was a hard drug user, a mainliner."

"Do you have any idea who her supplier was?" Colt asked.

"No. I know she had a John she called Big Daddy, but I don't think he was a dealer. He was weird, though. Candy said he paid Jody a thousand dollars for twenty-four hours of her time, one day a week.

"He would take her to breakfast and dinner. Other than that, he made her sleep. Just rest."

"Did you ever see him?" Colt said.

"Once, but not very close." Teresa cast her eyes to the right, trying to recall how the man had looked. "He was just average. Average height. Average weight. He always wore sunglasses. He always wore a ball cap. He might have been bald. I don't know." She shook her head. "I'm sorry. I'm not much help."

"You were great, Teresa," Colt smiled and patted her shoulder. "Just great."

##

"Who's going to be there," Lana called to Ash. She stepped out of her jeans and pulled her polo over her head. Wearing only her bra and panties, she walked toward the shower.

"Everyone," Ash said as she entered the bedroom.

"Oh, wow! You will be the hit of the party," she teased as she slowly ran her eyes over her wife's perfect body.

"I do need some help with these hooks," Lana invitingly smiled as she turned her back to Ash so she could unfasten her bra.

She slowly unhooked the bra and kissed her shoulders and the nape of her neck as she slid the straps down her arms. Her hands gently caressed Lana's breasts as she pulled her back against her.

Lana turned in her arms and kissed her. Lightly at first, then harder as she moved her soft, full lips against hers. Her breasts against Ash's chest set her on fire.

"We're going to be late," Ash murmured against her lips.

"Ask me if I care," Lana giggled as she pulled Ash down onto the bed. "God, I love you, Ash Denton."

##

Just as Ash forecast, they were late. Risa and Trinity were hosting an anniversary party for Captain Ames and his wife, Debbie.

"About time you showed up," Risa opened the door. She laughed at the goofy smiles on both their faces. "And I see why."

"How does she do that," Ash hugged her wife's shoulders.

"Some women can tell these things," Lana leaned into her as they walked. "For instance, I'm pretty sure Trinity hasn't hit a home run yet. From the look on Christine's face, neither has Jessica."

Ash leaned down and kissed her chastely. "You are right," she smiled. "I never stood a chance."

Carter and Brandt were there with their wives. Colt had convinced Linda to come.

"Help me get dinner on the table?" Risa asked Lana. "Trinity, why don't you make sure everyone has a drink."

"Yes, my queen," Trinity's eyes sparkled as she bent down and kissed her lips. "We will be in the game room. Just let me know when you're ready for us to move to the dining room." She kissed her a quick kiss and disappeared.

"You and Trinity," Lana raised a perfectly arched eyebrow. "Seems to be working out pretty good."

"She is wonderful," Risa smiled. "I think I'm in love with her."

"But you're keeping her at arm's length," Lana's quizzical look made Risa laugh.

"Look at her" Risa exhaled. "She is so damn gorgeous; like your Ash. She could be a player. I don't want a month or two, and then she's gone."

"Talk to her," Lana advised.

"That's your solution to everything," Risa laughed. "What about Ash. Weren't you hesitant to sleep with her?"

"Honestly, I couldn't get in bed with her fast enough," Lana grinned. "She's every bit as good as I knew she would be.

"Everything just happened so fast. We'd only known each other a week, when she showed up with a ring, asking me to marry her.

"Our engagement lasted ten days then we married. It was the fastest and best decision I've ever made.

"I've worked with the Dallas FBI on some serial murder cases. Everyone thinks very highly of Trinity. Of course, all the single women—and some of the married women—have the hots for her. From what I have heard, she doesn't partake of the goodies."

"Yeah, that's what Evelyn in Dallas CSI said," Risa smiled. "She's almost too good to be true."

"That's everything," Risa surveyed her dining table. "Let's turn the gang loose on it."

Lana watched her best friends as they interacted with each other in the game room. Trinity and Ash were shooting pool.

"This is our championship game," Trinity laughed. "I need a kiss for good luck." She grinned at Risa. "That would be your cue, honey."

Risa walked to her, slipped her arms around her neck, and pressed the entire length of her body firmly against Trinity. "For good luck," she said against her lips. As their kiss deepened, Trinity dropped her cue stick and wrapped her arms around Risa. The rest of the world slipped away as she lost himself in Risa's lips and the feel of her luscious body pressed hard against her.

"Let me catch my breath," Risa smiled as she broke the kiss.

Loud applause erupted in the room as Lana led their friends in clapping for the lovers.

"That's a little too much PDA for my heart," Ames teased.

"Try it, you'll like it," his wife laughed.

"Dinner is served," Risa called out. She was still in Trinity's arms. "You have to let me go, darling," she grinned, as their guests headed for the dining room.

"Was that a promise of things to come," Trinity whispered her plea.

"Lana says we should talk," Risa smiled.

"I can talk," the FBI agent knew she was putty in Risa's hands. That was okay as long as she didn't take those soft hands away. "I can dance. I can sing. I can be whatever you want me to be, Risa."

"Right now, you need to be the hostess," Risa smiled, gently pushing her away.

Jessica found herself seated between Christine and Linda. Everyone was laughing and talking.

Christine could understand why Colt loved Linda. The woman was delightful. She was charming and funny. Linda and Lana kept the guests in stitches with stories of their first crime scene experiences.

Colt was almost overly possessive of Linda, trying to anticipate her every need. She didn't seem to mind and was very attentive to him.

"Do you miss police work?" Christine asked Linda.

"You know, I do," Linda smiled a crooked little smile. "I always thought I should be in the CIA or some other clandestine agency. I think I'd be great undercover, don't you, honey?"

Colt nodded and blushed, wondering if she had intentionally used a play on words to drive him crazy.

Everyone laughed and began teasing Colt.

Jessica reached for Christine's hand under the table and pulled it onto her thigh. She just wanted to touch her. Christine smiled up at her. She understood her. She loved her.

A shadow crossed the ADA's face as Jessica stiffened with a jerk. She looked around the table to see what had made her react so violently.

Linda was telling a couples' story about Colt, Ash, Lana and herself. Everyone was laughing except Jessica, who continued to sit ramrod straight.

Rage swept over Christine as she realized the source of Jessica's anxiety. Linda was slowly moving her hand up and down the inside of Jessica's thigh.

Christine stood and began clearing the table. Jessica immediately followed her example.

As everyone carried dishes into the kitchen, Christine held Linda back in the dining room. She leaned close to the woman's ear and hissed. "Touch her again and I will find a way to put you away for a very long time. What the hell is wrong with you? Colt adores you."

Jessica stopped in the doorway as she realized Christine was angrily talking to Linda.

Risa put on some background music. Trinity and Ash continued their pool game. Risa, Lana, Linda, and Colt were playing a rousing game of air hockey.

Jessica sat in an overstuffed armchair and Christine sat on the arm of the chair. Jessica slyly slipped her arm around Christine's waist and slid her onto her lap.

"Are you okay?" She asked softly.

Christine nodded then kissed her sweetly.

"What did you say to Linda? You looked angry," she said.

"I told her if she touched you again, I would put her away for a very long time."

Jessica smiled. "My protector," she teased. "She's a piece of work. What an awful thing to do to poor Colt."

"Did he see her stroking your leg," Christine asked.

"I hope not," Jessica grimaced. "I hate cheaters."

Ash made a toast to Captain Ames and his wife applauding their fifteen-year marriage.

Risa and Trinity served black forest cake and coffee to their guest.

"Risa made this herself," Trinity announced proudly. Groans of delight echoed from their guests, as they tasted the dessert.

Ames pulled Debbie onto the patio and began to dance when *Don't Know Much* by Linda Ronstadt and Aaron Neville began to play. The other couples followed their lead and joined in the anniversary dance.

Christine closed her eyes and reveled in the feel of Jessica's strong arms around her. She held her tightly. "I love you, Chris," she whispered.

"I know you do, baby" her breath on Jessica's ear sent a shiver through her body. "We'll work this out."

"You're coming home with me tonight, sweetie," Linda whispered in Colt's ear. He nodded and pulled her closer.

The music ended, and everyone began talking. Obviously, Risa was a Linda Ronstadt fan. The singer's hit song *Long Long Time* started playing.

Linda moved into Ash's arms. "I believe they are playing our song," she grinned devilishly.

Ash cast a "save me," look at her wife. Lana shrugged as Colt swept her into his arms.

"Other than Captain Ames," Ash said, "is there anyone here you haven't rubbed all over tonight?" She intentionally held Linda at arm's length as they danced.

##

Chapter 26

Trinity Jewett looked at her list. The BW killer was as baffling to Trinity as the monster was to the Fort Worth team.

She needed to discuss a theory with Dr. Denton. She looked around the bullpen for Ash then walked into Ames office.

"Morning, Captain," Jewett grinned. "I enjoyed celebrating your anniversary with you."

"It was nice of Risa and you to put that together," Ames grinned. "It's always good to celebrate special occasions with friends."

Trinity nodded. "Have you seen Ash this morning?"

"She and Colt are collaborating with Jessica," Ames said. "They're working on the dead prostitute case."

"Speaking of collaborating," Trinity grinned, "I need to collaborate with Dr. Denton. Is that okay?"

"Just give her a call," Ames nodded. "Hang on a second and I'll give you her office phone number."

Trinity called Lana and made a date for lunch at the Texan, a small restaurant, famous for its home-style cooking. She entered the morgue to invite Risa to join them. She was sitting in her office typing furiously.

"Hey, pretty lady," Trinity leaned down to kiss her. "How are you this morning?"

"Better, now," Risa smiled.

"I'm meeting Lana at the Texan for lunch at one today. Want to join us?" She sat on the corner of Risa's desk

"I would love to," Risa nodded, "but I can't get there until one-thirty. Is that okay?"

"Any time with you is okay," she grinned. "What have you got going today?"

"A tour for the seniors from Tech High School. They think they want to be forensic scientists." She grimaced as she recalled how they always streaked to the closest bathroom to vomit right after she made the Y incision.

"It only takes about fifteen minutes to change their minds," she grinned, "so I may be able to get there sooner."

Jessica leaned back and double-checked her handiwork. Everything was working correctly. She had always taken great pride in the fact that she could hack anything: iPhones, computers, alarm systems, security keypads, anything anyone was stupid enough to connect to the internet. If it was an algorithm, paradigm or contained even a byte of code, it spoke to Jessica, and she understood it. FORTRAN, COBOL, C++, HTML or Javascript, they were all as clear as day to Jessica Barton. Source codes were like poetry to her. She could remotely deactivate, reactivate or observe any alarm system that was being monitored by a service. If it connected to the internet or electricity, it was fair game for the computer savant.

Jessica stretched and rolled her head, trying to work the crick out of her neck. Her stomach growled reminding her she hadn't eaten in twenty-four hours. The Cyber Chief called Christine to see if she wanted to catch a late lunch with her but received her recording. She left a message ending with "I love you," and walked to the small restaurant closest to her office.

Jessica ordered a club sandwich and took a sip of her tea before she noticed the couple in the back booth of the restaurant. The laughter had caught her attention. She would know that laugh anywhere. She loved that laugh.

Dr. Denton and FBI Agent Trinity Jewett huddled in the booth, furthest from other diners. Their heads were together. Their foreheads were almost touching. Jewett was holding her hand, palm up and tracing a sign in it. They both laughed as Jewett leaned down and kissed her fingertips.

Jessica felt faint. *Dear God, not Dr. Denton. Dr. Denton isn't the cheating kind. She loves her wife, doesn't she?*

Jessica threw a twenty on the table and scurried from the restaurant.

"And that is how I plan to propose to her," Trinity sighed as she released Lana's hand. "Only with a ring, of course. For the first time in my life, I want commitment, and I'm ready to make it!"

Both started talking about the case as Risa entered the restaurant.

"Was Jessica with y'all," Risa said in her best southern drawl. She slid against Trinity and kissed her.

"No," Lana frowned. "I didn't see her in here, but we were pretty deep in discussion."

##

"What if we are looking at this all wrong," Lana asked her wife as she handed her a glass of lemonade.

Ash turned the chicken, basted it then closed the lid on the grill. "I sense an epiphany," she smiled.

"Or just a woman's intuition," Lana grinned.

"We have assumed that Nicole Barnes aka Candy Barnes died because she knew too much about Bradford Clemens and his shady business dealings.

"What if, her murder had nothing to do with Clemens? Maybe her death is tied to drugs or this Big Daddy character."

"I've chased Big Daddy to a dead end," Ash shrugged. "I questioned everyone at Denny's. Several of the servers remembered Candy and Jody because he slapped her around. None of them could recall a man fitting the description of Big Daddy."

"Did Jessica find anything on Jody's phone?" Lana placed the plates beside the grill and checked on the roasting potatoes.

"She did trace a burner phone to the hotel the night Candy died, but it's off now. Probably in the bottom of a lake somewhere." Ash frowned. "If you will bring out the salad, the chicken is ready."

They served their plates then settled on the patio. "Jody swears he doesn't know where Candy was getting her drugs," Ash continued. "I believe he would tell us if he knew. The little prick would do anything to stay out of general population. I pray we will get a break on the dealer. I think that is where we will find a killer."

"What has happened to the prostitutes Jody was running?" Lana frowned.

"Another pimp probably took them over," Ash said.

"Have you questioned any of the other women?" Lana asked. "Maybe Jody can give us a list of his girls who were users and we can question them to run down their supplier."

"That's a great idea. And here I thought you were just another pretty face," Ash grinned. "Beauty and brains. I'm a lucky woman."

"Sometimes we can't see the forest for the trees," Lana smiled. "I think we have all been on edge about the BW killer. I know that is on my mind night and day."

"You're the only thing on my mind night and day," Ash smiled.

"You want the day or night shift," Ash asked Colt.

"Nights," Colt frowned. "It will give me something to occupy my mind. You've got someone to go home to."

"Are you and Linda having trouble," Ash raised an eyebrow.

"Honestly, Ash," Colt inhaled. "I have got to find a way to get over her. I know she just jerks me around, but I can't stay away from her."

"I'm sorry, buddy," Ash nodded. "Have you ever thought about transferring to another state? Just get away from her. Ames posted a bulletin this morning that Hawaii has some openings."

"And leave you?" Colt looked horrified.

"Just a thought," Ash laughed and slapped her partner on the back.

Jody had given them a list of the prostitutes that used drugs. They planned to run stakeouts on them until one led them to their supplier.

Christine jumped when her phone rang. "ADA Christine Canton," she answered.

"ADA Canton, this is Willie Shy. I run the Paradise Motel," a gravelly voice said.

"Yes, Mr. Shy, what can I do for you?" Christine rolled her eyes.

"The hooker you arrested in room 101," Shy said. "She had the room reserved thru the first. Tomorrow's the first."

"And…" Christine encouraged him to go on.

"She left some things in the room. After tomorrow, I'll either sell them or trash them."

Christine looked at her watch. It was three in the afternoon. She was cooking dinner for Jessica, and she still needed to grocery shop.

"May I pick up her things in the morning?" Christine said.

"Sure, that'll be okay," Shy agreed. "I just wanted to let you know. I don't want to get crossways with your office."

"Thank you, Mr. Shy. I appreciate your call. I'll be there by eight in the morning."

Jessica smiled at Jackie, as she entered Lana's office. "I know I'm a little early. Do you want me to wait in the other room?"

"No. I think Dr. Denton is just finishing some paperwork. I'll let her know you're here."

"Please, send her in," Lana told Jackie.

"Jessica, it's so good to see you," Lana smiled sincerely. "You look wonderful."

"The love of a good woman," Jessica ducked her head shyly. "You were right. Christine has been so understanding and loving."

"So, no big step yet?" Lana asked.

"Not yet," Jessica sat down in the chair in front of Lana's desk. "But I'm more at ease with her every day, and I love sharing my life with her. She's brilliant. It's so interesting to exchange ideas with her. We're really from two different worlds. It's fascinating to learn about her world. We share many of the same passions."

Lana laughed. She couldn't recall hearing Jessica talk so positively or so long.

"I just...Every time we get close to intimacy," Jessica almost whispered, "I freeze."

"What seems to be holding you back?" Lana frowned as she watched her patient struggle for an answer.

"I don't know." She exhaled.

"Jessica, are you familiar with hypnotherapy?" Lana watched her eyes ascertaining how receptive she was to the suggestion.

"Yes," Jessica nodded. "I know that some people are more susceptible to hypnosis than others. Do you use hypnotherapy in your practice?"

"I have used it with many of my patients who seem to have a block or even want to stop smoking," Lana shrugged. She didn't want Jessica to see her excitement.

"Do you think it would help me overcome my fears of inadequacy?" She looked around the room, avoiding the doctor's eyes.

"It might," Lana said tactfully. "Want to give it a try?"

Jessica nodded. "Should I lie down on the sofa?"

"That will be best. Let me tell Jackie not to interrupt under any circumstances." Lana walked into the waiting room and spoke with her secretary.

Jessica was lying on the sofa, staring at the ceiling. Lana lowered the lights and turned on the video cameras.

"Jessica, do you see the silver ball hanging from my ceiling?

"Yes," she said.

"Just concentrate on that ball and relax. Begin by relaxing your feet, then your legs. Now let the relaxation move up your body, through your torso. Relax your shoulders and neck. Just concentrate on the ball and the sound of my voice.

"Your eyelids are getting heavier. If your eyelids are getting heavier, blink twice."

Jessica blinked twice. Lana could see the woman was almost asleep. "If your eyelids are too heavy, just close your eyes and drift."

She could tell Jessica was hypnotized. "Can you hear me, Jessica?"

"Yes, Mommy, I hear you."

"How old are you, Jessica?"

"Six." A huge smile crossed Jessica's face.

"What are you doing?"

"Mommy is giving me a bath," she frowned. "She is lathering me with soap. No! No! Mommy, I wash there. I a big girl. Daddy says big girls wash their own…" She lay silently.

"Jessica, can you go to your seventeenth birthday?"

Jessica described her birthday party and all her friends. Her parents gave her a car for her birthday. "My birthday is wonderful.

"Today we won the state championship," Jessica grinned. "My mother wants me to take her for a ride in my new car. Dad says it's late we should go to bed. My mother is crying. She wants to ride in my new car. I'll take her, Dad."

"We should return now, Mom. Dad will be worried. I pulled the car into the driveway. Mother grasps my hand and pulls it into her lap. 'My brilliant, gorgeous daughter,' she giggles. She kisses me. It doesn't feel right. I push her away. She jumps from the car and runs into the house." Jessica laid still for a long time.

"School is almost out," Jessica started talking. "So many colleges want me to play for them. My parents are jubilant.

"I asked Mary Lou to go steady with me. She said yes.

"My mother keeps hugging me and rubbing my back. For some reason, it makes me uncomfortable.

"I'm exhausted. I take a bath and fall into bed naked. I am dreaming. Soft hands are touching me— dreaming about Mary Lou.

"No, there is someone in bed with me. Someone is stroking me, fondling me. It's, no, God, it's my mother. She's straddling me. I scream out. She puts her hand over my mouth to silence me.

"She's yanked off me. Dad has her by the hair. He's dragging her from my room. He's screaming at her. Whore. He calls her a whore and hits her. My door slams.

"It's bad enough you screwed everyone in your English class, but… Oh, my God, Rosie, not your own daughter. I try to talk to them, but my door is locked. I can't get out.

"What was that? A gunshot then another. My world is turning black."

Jessica jerked spasmodically.

"Jessica, wake up," Lana said.

Jessica opened his eyes and looked wildly around the room. She sat up then fell back against the back of the sofa. She dragged her hands down her face. "My mother," she choked. "I was raped by my mother."

Lana couldn't move fast enough to keep her from throwing up on the carpet. She shoved the wastepaper basket toward her. She threw up in it. Lana retrieved a cold, wet cloth from her restroom and gave it to Jessica to wipe her face.

She sat with her head hanging almost to her knees. She had stopped vomiting and simply looked at her hands. Slowly, she raised her eyes to meet Lana's eyes.

Her eyes shone with disbelief, pain and something else Lana couldn't decipher.

"My mother," she gasped. "That's why my Dad killed her then turned the gun on himself. He was trying to protect me from my own mother.

"All these years, I never knew…" she started to cry. Lana let her grieve until she could cry no more.

"I had no idea," Lana said, dazed. "Jessica, I'm sorry."

"I need to go," Jessica grimaced. "I'm fatigued."

"Should I call Christine to pick you up?" Lana asked.

Jessica shook her head no and left the room. The wild look in her eyes concerned Lana, but she knew they could work through Jessica's recent discoveries.

##

Christine showered and slipped into a pair of jeans and one of Jessica's Henleys. She loved the softness of the shirt. Most of all, she loved the scent of Jessica that wafted up from it.

They had been living together for five wonderful weeks. Jessica took her dancing and to the latest musicals at Bass Hall. They walked hand-in-hand through the water gardens or ducked down the stairs to Simply Fondue for dessert and coffee. They watched Fox News and discussed politics. They often shared the same book. Jessica would hold her on her lap and read to her, or she would lay her head on Christine's lap, and the ADA would read to her. They had already done more together than she had ever done with Robert. What they hadn't done was make love.

"Just be patient and keep the communication lines open," Lana had advised her. "Jessica is worth waiting for."

The elevator dinged, and Jessica strode into the penthouse. Her heartbeat quickened as she observed the woman she loved filling their glasses with ice.

"Dinner in about thirty minutes," Christine smiled.

"Shower," Jessica grunted like a caveman and left the room.

Now she goes articulate on me; Christine smiled to herself as she placed the salads on the table.

Jessica rejoined her at the breakfast bar and took her usual place on a stool. Christine sharply inhaled as she looked at her. She was so gorgeous, dark, wavy hair, Caribbean-blue eyes. She had donned jeans and a light-blue Henley the same color as her eyes. Like Christine, she was barefoot.

Christine moved to stand between her knees. "Don't I even get a hello kiss," she teased.

Jessica pulled her into her arms. Her eyes never left Christine's until their lips met. Her kiss was hesitant at first but became more demanding. She ran her tongue along her full, bottom lip. Christine parted her lips more, and Jessica slid her tongue between her teeth, searching for her tongue. Their tongues languidly fanned the flame of desire. Christine moaned, and Jessica pulled her tighter against her.

"Christine, I love you more than you can ever imagine," Jessica whispered as she nibbled at her ear.

"Prove it," she murmured.

Christine gasped as Jessica swept her into her arms and shoved their bedroom door open with her foot. She placed Christine on the bed and kissed her again.

Jessica moved her warm hands under Christine's shirt, caressing her breasts. "You have on no bra," she mumbled against her lips. The vibration sent fire shooting throughout Christine's body as she imagined those lips on her nipples.

"Don't tease me, Jessica, please."

Jessica pulled Christine's shirt over her head and paid homage to her lips, her neck, her shoulders, and her perfect breasts. Jessica groaned as she pulled a nipple into her mouth. Christine buried her hands in Jessica's hair and pulled her hard against her.

Christine whimpered as Jessica sat up on her knees and pulled off her shirt then deftly unfastened her jeans.

"Believe me, darling," she breathed. "I'm not teasing."

...and she wasn't. She was perfect, just perfect. She was everything a lover should be: slow and easy, hard and demanding. Jessica smiled when Christine begged and screamed her name.

"Jessica, Jessica, Jessica..." It was like a delirious, pagan chant and she loved it.

##

Colt had been on the stakeout for three hours. He wondered how many men could go in and out of one room in three hours. He hoped there was more than one woman in that room.

He downed his last swallow of coffee to stay awake. He was debating driving down the block to Sonic for another coffee when a black Cadillac—that had pimp written all over it—pulled onto the parking lot. The burgundy carpet on the rear deck matched the steering wheel cover.

Colt made a note of the license plate. The Caddy turned off its lights and waited. A John left the room, and a tall, black woman walked to the car. She exchanged money for a baggie.

Colt followed the Cadillac to a nicer part of town—not exactly Westover Hills—but nice. A garage door went up; the car entered, and the door closed.

Colt wondered how often the man delivered drugs to the hooker. He drove back to his stake out, stopping by his favorite Sonic on the way. He wanted to sit on this for a couple of days.

"Dr. Denton," Lana answered her phone.

"Oh, my God," Christine whispered into the phone. "Lana, you were right. My God, she is incredible."

Lana laughed. "I take it some fantasies came true last night."

"I have no words to describe…gotta go; she's coming out of the shower. We'll talk later."

Jessica walked into the bedroom wearing only a towel wrapped around her waist. She grinned as if she had just won the Texas Lottery. She sat on the edge of the bed and picked up her phone.

"What are you doing?" Christine frowned.

"Oh, I thought I'd call Ash and tell her how great you are in bed," she teased.

"You wouldn't dare," Christine said aghast.

"Isn't that what you just did, darling?" she laughed.

Christine's mouth worked, but no words came out.

"That will be the topic of my next meeting with Dr. Denton." Jessica grinned even broader. "Why is it okay for some women to brag about their lover's prowess, but you don't want us to share with one another how terrific our wives are in bed?"

"You wouldn't dare," she huffed, again.

"You're right," Jessica smiled. "I would never brag about how wonderful you are because I don't want other's lining up to find out for themselves. Something you might think about."

Christine pulled her back into her arms. "Let me just go on record as saying, you make all my fantasies come true."

"Christine, I couldn't even imagine how wonderful making love with you would be. There are no words."

"Then stop talking and start doing," Christine grinned as she straddled her. "I don't seem to be able to get enough of you."

Christine slid her hand to Jessica's side of the bed. She was gone. She sat up and looked around then heard her humming in the kitchen. She slipped on a gown and joined her.

"I made coffee," Jessica smiled as she slid a cup in front of her. "Did you sleep well?"

Christine looked up at her through dark lashes. "I didn't sleep much, as I recall."

Jessica chuckled. "Me either. We do need to get moving. It's almost one in the afternoon."

"Oh, my, gosh," Christine slid off the stool and carried her coffee to the bedroom. "I had a meeting at eight this morning. I need to see if I can salvage it."

She showered then dressed as Jessica showered. She was adjusting her shoulder holster when she entered the room.

"Do you wear that all the time," Jessica asked, staring at Christine's Ruger.

"Yes, except when I'm in court. No guns are allowed in the courtroom." She pulled the gun from the holster, kicked out the magazine and held it out to Jessica. "Would you like to see it?"

"No, I don't know anything about guns. They're dangerous." Jessica laughed. "I will just have to trust you to protect me."

She kissed Jessica goodbye as she was zipping her slacks. "I will never hurt you, Jessica. I promise."

##

Chapter 27

"Damn," Trinity cursed as she slammed down the phone. "Ash, it looks like we have another BW murder."

Ash joined the FBI agent in turning the air blue with a string of expletives. Trinity called Risa and gave her the address. "Better get your coach rolling, baby," she said. "The first responder says it looks like a BW case."

Ames stepped from his office. He had received a similar phone call. "I want every one of you on this. Ash, call Lana. I don't care what she is doing. Get her over there. Trinity, call Christine and give her a heads up. Where's Colt?"

"Right here," Colt responded as he walked through the door. "Just coming in off an all-night stakeout, Captain."

"We have another BW case," Ames growled. "I want you to stay here and man the phones."

"Why?" Colt demanded. "This is my case, too."

"The murder is at the Dawson Estate," Ames said flatly.

Colt's knees buckled. Ash caught him and shoved a chair beneath him. Colt bent over and put his head between his knees. He couldn't faint. They would certainly leave him behind if he fainted.

"Captain, please," Colt begged, as he regained his composure.

"No, you stay here. That's an order," Ames barked.

Trinity never understood how she did it, but Risa was at the scene and barking orders when she and Ash arrived. Lana pulled in front of the house as they left their cars.

"Ash," Lana caught her wife's arm, "is it, Linda?"

"We don't know yet, honey. Why don't you catch up with Risa? Trinity and I need to help disperse the looky-loos and set up perimeters until the black and whites get here. We'll be there as soon as we can."

##

"Everything's the same, Ash," Risa shrugged, "except for a few things I want to double check when I get back to the lab. One thing that is clearly different is the word 'whore' is carved into her forehead, not branded."

Both Ash and Trinity cringed as they examined Linda's forehead.

"My biggest problem is temperature. The place was like a freezer when the first responder arrived. He said the air-conditioning was as low as it would go. Unfortunately, he turned it up as high as it would go. Therefore, the body has been cooled down and then heated up. It's going to be hell to set a precise time of death. I'd rather not call it right now."

CSI collected the usual wine bottle, glasses, cheese, hair, and liquids.

Risa had a bitching headache. The BW murders were beginning to get to her. She'd been so sure Linda was a killer, and now she was dead.

Colt would go ballistic when he found out his ex-wife had been cruelly murdered. Lana was right; the killer was getting more and more violent.

Colt was in the morgue when they rolled in the gurney. The look in Risa's eyes told him all he needed to know.

"I'll help lift her to the lab table," he choked. Tears began streaming down his cheeks.

"Let us do this," Risa placed a comforting hand on Colt's arm. "Get some coffee. I'll call you when she's ready."

"No. I want her handled gently," Colt choked. "I'll lift her head. You get her feet."

He unzipped the body bag and gasped at the carving on Linda's forehead. "Risa, this…this is the work of a butcher."

"I know, baby," Risa put her arm around him, and he cried into her shoulder. "This was done by a monster."

Ash entered the morgue and took in what was happening. She wrapped her arms around both her friends. "Colt, I'm sorry, buddy."

"You lift her feet," Colt straightened and wiped his eyes with his shirt sleeve. "Be gentle with her, Ash."

The two moved Linda's body to the morgue table. Colt gently removed the red rose from behind Linda's ear

"Come on, Colt. Let's get a cup of coffee." Ash put an arm around her friend's waist. "You've been on stakeout all night. You must be exhausted."

##

Christine pulled her car up to the front door of the Paradise Motel. After the wonderful night she'd had with Jessica, she doubted anything could ruin her good mood.

"I'm looking for Mr. Shy," she announced to the skeletal man at the front desk.

"That would be me."

Christine was certain nothing could make the man look worse than he did, then he smiled. Decaying teeth seemed to be racing to see which one could rot to the gum line first.

"I'm ADA Christine Canton." She flipped open her ID case and showed Shy her credentials. The slight bulge under her suit jacket told him she was packing a gun. "I am here to pick up the items from room 101."

"You were supposed to be here at eight," Shy whined. "I told you if you weren't here by eight, I was throwing everything away."

"Did you?" Christine glared at the man. She had spotted the box marked 101 when she entered the office.

"I might've." Shy grinned, again. "I'm not sure."

She pulled a twenty from her pocket. "Does this help your memory?"

Shy hesitated.

"Or maybe I should just have my office send over a dozen officers with a search warrant. Maybe they will find it."

Shy reached for the twenty, shoved it into his pocket and pushed the box across the counter to her.

"Thanks," she called over her shoulder as she left the lobby.

##

The four friends gathered around the dining table in the Denton home. Ash, Lana, Risa and Trinity were pooling their thoughts and gut feelings to solve the BW cases.

Trinity unrolled a calendar. An X marked the dates of each BW murder. "I asked all of you to bring your personal calendars, so we can see if anything social or work related was going on at the time of the murders."

They discussed each murder and could find nothing that linked them.

"Something happened that changed the Beverly Murdock murder," Trinity frowned.

Lana thumbed through her Franklin Day Planner. She always made notes on her sessions in the planner.

She sucked in her breath as she realized that the morning after Beverly Murdock's murder; Jessica had been covered in blood when she showed up late for her appointment.

"What's wrong, honey?" Ash laid her hand on her wife's.

"Nothing, I just realized I have an appointment tomorrow. I thought I had a free day."

Risa shuffled the papers in her file and handed each of them a copy of her final report. Both Lana and Ash gasped as they read it.

The killer didn't just kill Linda Dawson. He tortured her first.

"As you already know," Risa began, 'the word 'whore' wasn't a brand. He engraved it into her forehead with the X-Acto knife.

"Just like all the others, her nipples were cut off. What you didn't know until now is that these things were done to her while she was alive.

"He didn't drug her. There were no signs of anything used to quiet her. No tape across her mouth. Nothing stuffed into her mouth. Whoever killed her wanted to hear her cry out and beg for mercy.

"She was strategically stabbed so she would die a slow, painful death. He slit her throat after she died."

"The BW killer is getting more vicious and sadistic," Lana grimaced. "He must truly hate women."

"One more thing," Risa grimaced, "She'd had two abortions. From the scar tissue, I'd say one about three years ago and one just recently. The recent one would be Trask's baby. I don't know about the first one."

"What? Who?" Ash choked. "I know she had a miscarriage when she and Colt were married."

Risa shook her head no. "I saw no sign of miscarriage, only two abortions."

"Oh, my, God," Ash inhaled deeply. "Has Colt seen this report? It will kill him."

"It's my official report," Risa scowled. "As soon as I file it, it will be available for anyone to see. I must file my findings, Ash. I can't jeopardize my career by leaving something out."

"Of course," Ash hung her head. "I would never ask you to do that, Risa."

After Risa and Trinity had left, Ash turned to her wife. "What did you discover?"

"The morning we took Jessica to the hospital was the morning after the Beverly Murdock murder," Lana frowned.

"Surely, you don't think Jessica would kill a woman, do you?"

"I'm not sure what to think, at this point," Lana frowned.

"There is something you aren't telling me," Ash said. "Is Christine in danger?"

"I…I don't know."

"Lana, doctor-patient privilege be damned," Ash scowled. "If Jessica is dangerous, you can legally notify the authorities. I am the authorities, so give."

"I think the best thing to do is let you watch the video of her last three sessions." She walked to her study, her wife followed.

Ash sat down on the sofa while Lana slipped the CD into the player and turned on the TV.

"This will start with the visit when her clothes were covered with blood. You start watching," she said. "I'll get us a glass of wine. You'll need it."

Ash sat silently in the dim light of the room. "First, let me say, that was the most disturbing thing I have ever seen. How could a mother do that to her own child?

"Second, I don't like you dealing with dangerous patients like Jessica.

"Third, what is your diagnosis?"

"I diagnosed Jessica as delusional," Lana said. "She keeps referring to herself as schizophrenic. The two diagnoses are completely different. I don't know why she thinks she's schizophrenic. I don't see it. Schizophrenia is incurable. It's somewhat controllable, but not curable.

"A severe delusional, like Jessica, lives in a world of her fantasies. Sometimes they are sexual fantasies.

They often see themselves as omnipotent, or God-like. They believe they have unlimited powers and are capable of anything. Both delusions are usually the opposite of what the individual is.

"In Jessica's case, she had unbelievable sexual fantasies that entailed women crawling all over her throwing themselves at her and performing unbelievable sex acts with her.

"A schizophrenic often has a dual personality. A good side and a bad side. A Dr. Jekyll and Mr. Hyde, so to speak.

"I have never seen any sign of split personality in Jessica, but her parent's death was something that would cause a psychotic break in a seventeen-year-old girl.

"Symptoms of psychotic breaks can range from harmless delusions to violent outbursts. Delusions of sexual conquests are all I have ever seen in Jessica.

"What does disturb me is that she now has black-out periods. That is unusual in delusional personalities."

"Should we warn Christine?" Ash frowned.

"She knows," Lana said.

"I think you should also read the diary kept by Jessica's father." She walked to her desk and withdrew the thick book. "It will provide you great insight into the woman Jessica was before the death of her parents."

##

Ash shook her wife gently. She had fallen asleep on the sofa. "Honey."

Her dark eyes opened, and a smile touched her lovely lips as she realized Ash was leaning over her. "I didn't mean to go to sleep." She yawned and stretched before sitting up.

"My reading certainly didn't put me to sleep," Ash frowned. "That diary is the most disconcerting thing I have ever read. I may steal from it for my next book. Names changed to protect the innocent, of course. Poor Jessica. What an awful thing to live with."

"That is just it," Lana shook her head. "She didn't live with it. She withdrew into a web of fantasies and delusions."

"I'm amazed she was functional enough to create a software empire," Ash noted.

"Computers speak to Jessica the way the written word speaks to you," Lana explained. "Computers are an extension of Jessica. She is a savant in the field of computers."

"She is your patient," Ash frowned. "How should we handle this?"

"Can we simply keep an eye on her? I have a hard time believing Jessica is capable of murder. As you saw in the last video, we had a tremendous breakthrough.

"She and Christine have finally had intimate relations," Lana smiled slightly. "That is a tremendous step forward for her."

"How do you know that?" Ash frowned as she watched her wife's eyes darken.

"Christine called me while Jessica was in the shower." Lana wrinkled her nose. "She said Jessica was awesome."

"I don't believe you two," Ash grinned, "do you discuss everything with one another? I mean do you discuss our love life with Christine?"

"No," Lana smiled. "I don't need to. Everyone can tell by how happy we are."

"That's good to know," Ash nodded her head as she processed the information.

"I don't want to cast suspicion on Jessica," Lana continued. "She and Christine deserve to be happy. Let's not steal that from them unless we are certain."

"Only you and Christine know Jessica is my patient. I'd like to keep it that way for now."

Ash nodded and kissed her wife.

##

ADA Christine Canton took a deep breath and prepared to face a demanding day. *At least, I was able to start the day in Jessica's arms*; she smiled to herself.

She gathered the things from her home office she would need in court and called Teresa Long. "I'm on my way down," she informed the girl.

Christine glanced at the box, marked 101. She debated whether she should take the box to Teresa or leave it for later. *Later*, she decided.

##

Teresa Long was nervous. This was her first time in a courtroom. Although Christine had coached her in her testimony, she was still uneasy.

She was sworn in then took her seat.

"Thank you for taking the time to be here today." Attorney Frank Moncrief tried to put his witness at ease. "Ms. Long, do you recognize anyone in this courtroom?"

"Yes sir," she nodded.

"Tell us who you recognize," Frank encouraged.

"ADA Christine Canton and you," Teresa said. A titter ran through the courtroom.

"...and that man, Mr. Smith." She pointed to Bradford Clemens.

"You know him as Mr. Smith," Moncrief reiterated.

"Yes, sir." Teresa shifted uneasily in the chair. "I have since learned that he is Bradford Clemens."

"Do you know Mr. Clemens owns automobile dealerships?"

"Yes, sir. He used to brag to me about how he was getting rich by replacing faulty parts with used parts and charging the automobile manufacturers the price for a new part. He said he got rich off recalls."

"Objection," Clemens attorney jumped to his feet. "Pure hearsay, your honor. I move to strike this witness' statements from the record."

"Overruled," Judge Paul Clay frowned. "Proceed Mr. Moncrief."

"Did Mr. Clemons tell you just once that he was participating in criminal activity?" Moncrief continued.

"No sir, he told me many times." Teresa seemed to think about her statement. "At least six times."

A rumble went through the crowded courtroom.

"That is all the questions I have for this witness, at this time," Frank said. "I reserve the right to recall her."

Clemens leaned over and whispered in his attorney's ear.

Attorney Randolph Shyster pulled at the lapels of his expensive suit as he marched back and forth in front of the jury.

"How did you know my client as Mr. Smith," Shyster grinned maliciously at Teresa.

"I...I was..." Teresa's eyes darted around the courtroom looking for a port in the storm she was about to create. "I was Mr. Smith's call girl," she said cautiously.

Clemens' wife fainted, and his grown children shook their heads as they escorted their mother from the courtroom. Muttered comments swept thru the courtroom observers.

"I'm sorry," Shyster bellowed. "Could you speak up? I didn't hear what you said."

"I was Mr. Clemens' call girl," Teresa said clearly.

"How often did Mr. Clemens call you," Shyster asked.

"Once or twice a week," Teresa answered.

"Once or twice a week," Shyster stroked his chin as if thinking. "Did you provide your services for anyone else?"

"What the hell is wrong with you, Frank," Christine hissed. "He is badgering your witness. Object!"

"This is a civil court," Frank whispered. "Things work a little differently than criminal court."

"Yes," Teresa answered Shyster's question.

"So, you aren't honestly a call girl," Shyster continued. "You're a low-class hooker that works out of the Paradise Motel. I believe you go by the name of Goody Goody."

A loud murmur and some stifled laughter came from the courtroom observers.

"Ask for a recess," Christine hissed into Frank's ear.

"Your honor, we request a recess."

"Fifteen minutes," Judge Clay barked. "I'd like to wrap up this trial today, Mr. Moncrief."

"Tell Shyster you'd like to discuss a settlement," Christine whispered.

Frank spoke with the lawyer and his client. Both men nodded and followed Frank to a small meeting room off the courtroom. Christine followed.

"Do you know who I am," Christine addressed both Shyster and Clemens.

"You are the hot-shot ADA," Shyster snickered. "You have no jurisdiction in this case."

"Not in a civil case," Christine smirked, "but I will be Mr. Clemens' worst nightmare in a murder case.

"If I may suggest a compromise. If Mr. Clemens agrees to pay the damages asked by the families of the two dead men, I will give you my word my office will not prosecute you for criminal activities."

Shyster turned to his client. "What do you think? Do you want to settle or continue this trial?"

"Hell no, I won't settle," Clemens snorted. "That little whore didn't do us any damage. We will win this case."

"If you lose it," Christine pointed out, "It will go against you in criminal court."

"We won't lose it," Clemens sneered as he pushed his face toward Christine's face. "You saw the look on the jury's face. You and your little whore can go back to where you came. We have this case won." He jerked his head for Shyster to follow and left the room.

"I gave him a chance," Christine shrugged. "When we return to the courtroom, call me to the witness stand, Frank."

"But…"

"Just do it, Frank. I won't have Teresa demeaned anymore by those two lowlifes."

As the court reconvened, Jessica, Ash and Lana walked into the courtroom and sat down behind Frank Moncrief.

"I would like to call ADA Christine Canton to the stand," Moncrief said.

A low roar spread thru the crowd as the gorgeous ADA took the witness stand. There was complete silence as she was sworn in.

"Ms. Canton do you know Teresa Long?" Moncrief asked.

"Yes, I do," Christine smiled at Teresa. "Ms. Long is a confidential informant for my office and works closely with the police department."

"Can you tell us how you became involved with this witness," Moncrief asked because he—sure as hell— didn't know.

Christine nodded. "Another young woman who had kept company with Mr. Clemens was murdered by a man."

"Objection," Shyster jumped to his feet.

"Please, Mr. Shyster," Judge Clay waved the man back to his seat. "If the assistant district attorney has taken time from her busy schedule to be in my courtroom, I want to hear what she has to say."

Christine smiled sweetly at the judge and turned back to the jury. "In the course of investigating that murder, we questioned Ms. Long. In questioning her, we discovered that Mr. Clemens had admitted to her that he had committed criminal practices in his repair facilities. She agreed to testify in this case."

Christine surveyed the jury, smiling sadly. "She knew she would be ridiculed and that Mr. Shyster would try to paint her as something less than human, but she chose to appear here today to make certain justice was done for the families who have lost their loved ones because of Mr. Clemens' greed."

"Your honor," Shyster tried again.

The judge held up his hand and addressed Frank Moncrief. "Counselor, do you have any further questions for this witness?"

"No, your honor," Frank said.

"I have questions," Shyster's voice was two octaves higher than before.

"Do you think we're just going to take your word for this," Shyster strutted. He was desperately trying to think of a way to discredit the ADA.

"No, I don't," Christine's smile lit up the courtroom. "That is why I have asked Sgt. Ash Denton, Criminal Psychiatrist Dr. Lana Denton and our Chief of Cyber Operations Dr. Jessica Barton to come here to testify. Please feel free to question them."

"Your Honor," Shyster squealed, "We request a recess."

"Would both attorneys approach the bench," the judge motioned for Frank and Shyster to approach him.

"Why do you want another recess," the judge asked.

"My client wishes to settle," Shyster said.

"With all due respect, your honor" Frank said. "We offered a settlement thirty minutes ago. At this time, we would like to give our closing arguments and let the jury decide the merits of this case."

It took the jury less than an hour to award the families millions of dollars. The judge ordered Clemens to make certain the payment was made within ten days or be in contempt.

At Christine's nod, a bailiff slapped handcuffs on Clemens and led him away to be booked for manslaughter.

"Oh, my, God, you were so hot," Jessica whispered as she held Christine in her arms.

"Do you like seeing me in action," Christine teased as the elevator door opened into their penthouse.

"It was the most arousing thing I've ever witnessed," Jessica grinned as she caught Christine's hand and pulled her to their bedroom. "You are very exciting and incredibly sexy."

"Show me how much you liked it," Christine giggled as she slid off her jacket.

##

Chapter 28

Detective Colt Layne sat on the patio of his home. He sipped his coffee and cried. He cried for a baby son he never knew and a wife he never really knew. *How could she abort our son?*

If Colt were honest with himself, he would admit he had always suspected that Linda had aborted their son. He just couldn't bring himself to admit that the woman he worshipped was capable of such evil.

Two hours later, he had no more tears to cry, and his coffee cup was empty. Ames had insisted he take some time off after Linda's murder. After the funeral he had spent the past week drinking himself into a stupor and popping sleeping pills to keep himself comatose.

It was day seven, and he still hurt. He hurt all over: his head, his heart, his stomach but most of all his soul.

He would never again wake with Linda beside him. He would never again hold her in his arms. He would never again kiss her lips. He would never again thrill to the sight of her leaning above him in the dark, but neither would any other man.

He showered. His eyes widened as he looked at his reflection in the mirror. He hadn't eaten in days. His eyes were sunken and hollow. His complexion was sallow. He looked like death eating a cracker. He needed to go to work. He needed to be with his friends. He clipped on his badge then spent ten minutes searching for his gun before he remembered Ames had taken it away from him. *Probably afraid I'd commit suicide,* Colt thought.

He caught his breath as he entered his living room. The light coming through the curtains spotlighted the picture of Linda that hung above his fireplace. It looked surreal as if the light was coming from heaven. It was the photo of her in her wedding gown. It had been taken in Fort Worth Botanical Garden. An eight by ten of her in her wedding dress and he in his tuxedo sat below her picture. Colt remembered how happy he had been on their wedding day. He had no idea he was marrying a monster. How could she kill their son?

"You have to get hold of yourself," he said aloud.

They were making love when a series of whistles and beeps filled their bedroom. Jessica hit the floor running.

"I've got the bastard," she yelled triumphantly, as she typed something into her laptop.

"What's going on," Christine pulled on her robe and followed her.

"Colt," Jessica put her cell phone on speaker to free up her hands. "He's on the move. His car is heading north on I-35. He's passing Miller Brewing. Now he's passing under 820."

"I think I can. Give me a second," Jessica responded to Colt's question. "Yes, I have him. The license plate is KC3WWK. Yes, the dark Buick. I see you behind him now."

As Jessica talked to Colt, she ran the plate for ownership. "Oh my, God, Colt," she gasped. "That is…"

"I know who he is," Colt almost screamed. "Tell Christine to meet me at the station."

Jessica watched as Colt pulled over a dark sedan, cuffed the driver and threw him into the back seat of his car.

"I'm heading in with him now," the detective spoke into the phone, again."

"Jessica," Christine grabbed her arm, "tell me what's going on."

"Get dressed, honey. I'll explain on our way to the station."

She began talking as she pulled the car out of the underground garage. "Colt and Ash had me run a check against all the phone numbers in Jody's cell phone. We were trying to identify the phones that were near Candy Barnes' room the night she died.

"There were only two phone signatures, Frank's and a burner phone. There were dozens of calls between Candy's phone and the burner. The burner phone has been turned off since her death.

"I wrote a program to notify me if the phone turned on again. It is very complicated, so I will spare you the boring details. The end of the story is, the phone turned on tonight and Colt has the perp."

##

"He's in interrogation room three," Colt directed the ADA. "I have the cameras running. You ready?"

Christine nodded and followed Colt into the room. Jessica watched from the observation room.

287

"You," Christine gasped as she realized who the man was. "You killed her, but why?"

"I couldn't stand what she had become," the man laid his cheek on the table and began to cry. "She was the whore of Babylon. My daughter was the whore of Babylon."

"Reverend, I..." Christine was at a loss for words.

"I tried so hard." He continued to cry. "I begged her to come home, to get help. I even bought her for twenty-four hours every week so that she could rest. Do you have any idea how it hurts to pay a pimp for your daughter's time?

"She didn't even care. She laughed at me and said she loved the life she was living. She loved taking drugs, and she loved screwing strange men every night.

"I finally realized she was like a rabid dog. I couldn't help her, so I put her out of her misery. I ended her pathetic life."

Christine slid a yellow legal pad in front of Reverend Timothy Barnes. "Please write down your confession," she sighed.

##

Risa Mercer smiled as she opened the door for Trinity Jewett.

"I brought a movie and wine—no cheese," she grinned, as she leaned down to kiss the woman that haunted her every waking hour and filled her dreams each night.

She followed her into the TV room. "I just happen to have hors d'oeuvres," Risa chuckled, "and you brought the perfect wine."

288

They sipped wine and ate the snacks Risa had prepared as they watched the movie. Mid-way through the video, Trinity paused the DVD player.

"Risa, we need to talk."

Risa sat very still. Her stomach threatened to do a flip, and her heart stopped beating. She recalled Ash's comment on "we need to talk," *Nothing good has ever come from that lead-in.*

"I don't know where to begin," Trinity said. "I have been trying to find the right time and the right way to tell you…"

"It's okay, Trinity," she grimaced. "I knew it was just a matter of time before you would leave."

Trinity nodded. "That's true, but what I'm trying to tell you is that I love you, and I can't imagine my life without you. Will you marry me, Risa Mercer?"

Risa stared at her as if she hadn't understood a word she said.

"A simple yes or no will suffice," Trinity moved uncomfortably. "I know we haven't known each other for very long, but I know you're the only woman I will ever want.

"If you need time to think about it, I…"

"Yes," Risa smiled. "Yes, darling."

"Yes? Yes. You will marry me?" Trinity was overjoyed. "I have a ring and everything." She reached into her pocket and pulled out the most elegant ring Risa had ever seen.

"Oh, Trinity, it's beautiful," she smiled as she held out her left hand.

Trinity slipped the ring on her finger and kissed her as she had never kissed her before.

289

##

Captain Ames looked at the quarterly report. His homicide squad had closed all but two cases on the books. Unfortunately, the BW was one of them. Colt was almost hitting on all cylinders. Colt had taken Linda's death hard. He was still prone to severe bouts of depression but was improving daily.

Except for the Branded Wives murders, they had a stellar record. They had broken up a drug cartel. Arrested and sent to prison an internet pedophile ring. They had arrested the killer of Candy Barnes and the kingpin in a prostitution operation. Overall, Ames was proud of his team.

He was amazed at what a difference Jessica Barton had made. The Cyber Intelligence Chief had become indispensable in their operations. He was glad ADA Christine Canton had taken a liking to Jessica. Christine deserved a good woman after the years she spent with Robert Canton, world-class asshole.

Someone had finally corralled ME Risa Mercer. Of course, it had taken an experienced FBI agent to do it. Trinity Jewett was a good agent. Risa could not have done any better and vice versa.

He wondered how long it would take Jessica to ask Christine to marry her. Maybe there would be a double wedding. The three couples were very close. They always included Colt in everything they did.

It was good to have friends to support you.

He motioned Ash to come into his office. "Our case load is good, except for BW," Ames said. "I have approved the days off next week that you requested. I can't believe you're leaving Lana alone to go Salmon fishing in Alaska."

"I tried to beg off this year, but you know my dad," Ash frowned, "he thinks his children have to brave freezing weather and frostbite to prove how strong we are. My two brothers are also going, so it will be fun.

"As you know, after six years in a northern university, Lana is no fan of cold weather. Texas is her place of choice.

"I tried to talk Colt into going; maybe get his mind off Linda. He is more determined than ever to catch the BW killer. He said he'd feel better if he stayed here and watched over Lana while I'm gone."

Ames nodded. He had observed Colt's dogged determination to apprehend the vicious murderer.

"We're all going for drinks at that place Risa introduced us to. Why don't you and Debbie join us?" Ash invited her captain.

"Let me check and see if we're free tonight," Ames smiled. "I'll get back to you. Maybe Debbie can bring a friend for Colt."

"He needs to get back out there, for sure," Ash nodded.

##

The friends had dinner then moved on to dancing at Risa's favorite club. It was Friday night, and they all had the weekend off unless something ghastly happened in their town.

Debbie Ames had brought a friend who was stunning but paled in comparison to Linda. Colt was polite and danced with her, but it was evident he was distracted.

Ames invited the woman to dance, hoping she wasn't noticing how withdrawn Colt was.

Ash held out her hand to Christine. They talked as they walked onto the dance floor.

"Shall we," Jessica smiled at Lana. She moved effortlessly into her arms.

Trinity and Risa were already on the dance floor. Debbie sat silently at the table, leaving Colt to his thoughts.

Colt sullenly watched the dancers. Jessica was whispering in Lana's ear. She threw back her head and laughed aloud. Jessica chuckled, pleased that she had made her laugh. She tightened her arm around her waist and whirled her around the dance floor.

Colt wondered if Ash was blind to what was going on between her wife and the computer genius.

When the dance ended, Jessica bowed to Lana. They walked hand-in-hand back to the table, still laughing about her bow.

They sat down and snuggled into their respective lovers. Colt wondered if he should say something to Ash, but decided to keep his mouth shut. He would simply talk to Lana.

##

Judge Paul Clay checked his docket for the day. He was delighted to see ADA Christine Canton would be gracing his courtroom today.

At thirty-nine, Clay was one of the youngest judges on the bench in Texas. He had married during law school, but his wife couldn't tolerate the intense dedication required to obtain a law degree from Southern Methodist University. The marriage had lasted less than a year. The truth was, he loved his wife, but he loved the law more. Law was his real mistress.

He had thrown himself into his studies, graduating at the top of his class. He had clerked for a Supreme Court Justice after graduation. He had learned so much while working at the Supreme Court.

Clay was a conservative judge who ran his courtroom by the book. Others in the legal profession highly respected the judge.

He also was enamored with ADA Christine Canton. The excitement he had felt when Robert Canton had informed him that he had divorced his wife was surprising.

Judge Paul Clay felt giddy as he entered the courtroom.

Christine was prosecuting the Clemens case herself. It was no secret she wanted Clemens to spend the rest of his days in prison.

A jury was selected, and Clay had ruled on the usual pretrial motions. All rulings had gone in Christine's favor. Not because he wanted to date her, but because her motions were by the letter of the law.

Everyone rose as Judge Clay entered the courtroom. He couldn't resist a smile at ADA Canton. To his surprise, she blushed slightly and nodded, smiling back at him. She was aware of her beauty.

Each of the attorneys made their opening remarks then Christine began to present her case. By the time she had questioned Clemens' bookkeeper, sales parts manager and three mechanics that had followed his orders, it was evident Clemens was guilty of trading lives for money.

From the ridiculous efforts made by Clemons' defense attorney, Judge Clay wondered if the man had even gone to law school.

The judge called the two lawyers to approach the bench often. His position on the bench gave him a spectacular view of the ADA's ample cleavage. It made the entire trial more enjoyable.

The judge was impressed with the way the other law enforcement officers had attended the trial to lend their support to the ADA.

It had only taken the jury two hours to find Clemons guilty and request the stiffest penalty applicable to the crime.

Clay knew how he was going to sentence Clemons, but he scheduled a hearing on the issue of sentencing, so he could watch Christine in action one more day. She was exciting and dramatic. She had a perfect grasp of the law and wielded it like a razor-sharp saber.

##

"Thank you for meeting me for lunch," Jessica smiled at Lana Denton. "I'm nervous. I need moral support, but most of all the advice of a classy woman."

"Who could say no to flattery like that?" Lana laughed as she slid into the booth beside Jessica. "Do you know her ring size?"

Jessica pulled a ring from her pocket. "This is a dinner ring she wears a lot. I am certain it is a perfect fit. She's in court today, so she won't notice it's missing from her jewelry box, but I have to get it back before tonight.

"I want to have a custom designed ring. One that will let Christine know that I believe she is a one-of-a-kind woman."

She inhaled sharply and looked at Lana. "Dr. Denton, I am incredibly happy, and I owe it all to you. I suspect I would be dead by now, if not for you."

"Oh, Jessica," Lana placed her hand on top of hers. "You are my biggest success story, and honestly, I believe ADA Christine Canton had a great deal to do with you pulling yourself up by your bootstraps.

"You are truly impressive. I'm just glad I was able to help you find the deep-seated cause of your mental anguish."

"I'm still working thru some things," Jessica nodded. "I'm looking forward to our appointment tomorrow."

They finished lunch. Jessica insisted on paying the check. "Let's do this," she smiled.

In the shadowy corner of the restaurant, Colt watched the two cavort. He threw money on the table for his check and followed them.

He watched them thru the window of the shop. It was a successful jewelry store. Colt knew the artisan's work. The man had designed the most recent wedding ring he'd purchased for Linda.

Lana and Jessica studied sketches and selected diamonds. Jessica shook her head no, and the clerk moved from the one-carat diamond case to the two-carat section. Lana pointed to a gem, and all three agreed on it.

Colt scurried to hide in a sunken doorway as the two walked out of the jewelry shop. Lana linked her arm through Jessica's arm. They stopped almost in front of Colt. He could see their joy with one another. They didn't look around.

"When is Ash leaving," Jessica asked.

"I'll take her to the airport in the morning," Lana smiled. "I'll be back in time for you in the afternoon."

"Good," Jessica grinned, "I need you badly this week."

The light changed, and the two walked across the street, deep in conversation.

Colt stood stunned. Of all the women in the world, Lana Denton was the one he knew would never cheat on her spouse, or would she?

Colt shook his head. The realization hurt him almost as much as the first time he'd caught Linda in bed with Lee Dawson.

##

Chapter 29

Judge Paul Clay entered the courtroom. He sat through the defense attorney's pitiful reasons why a man like Clemens should receive a probated sentence.

ADA Canton was quick and to the point. Clemens was a man with few morals. He trafficked in prostitutes and placed a dollar above the lives of his customers.

The sentencing was simple. Judge Clay gave Clemens forty years without parole and dismissed those in his presence.

"ADA Canton, may I see you in my office, please?" Clay smiled.

Christine turned to speak to the beautiful, dark-haired woman the judge knew, was the city's Chief of Cyber Operations. She then followed Clay into his office.

"Please, close the door," Clay smiled as he removed his robe and sat down behind his desk. "I noticed you frowned when I sentenced Mr. Clemens. Is there a problem?"

"With all due respect, your honor, forty years is a light sentence for two men's lives," Christine said. "I was just hoping for life. That's all."

Clay looked thoughtful. "Perhaps you will understand me better if I explain my reasoning. Please sit down, ADA Canton."

Christine sat down in the chair directly across from Judge Clay. *He's very handsome*, she thought.

"After a period, criminals become a burden on the state," Clay said. "Around age eighty, they become sickly and their incarceration becomes extremely expensive for the system.

"They are too old to be dangerous and have nothing to return to upon their release. I try to sentence the maximum amount of time a criminal will need to spend in prison, so his release is on his eightieth birthday. Then he becomes a burden to his family, not the state."

A slow, appreciative smile crept across ADA Canton's lovely face. "You're brilliant," she chuckled. "Absolutely brilliant."

Judge Paul Clay couldn't remember when a woman's smile had made him feel so happy and proud of himself.

He looked at the clock. "It seems our work is concluded just in time for lunch. Do you have lunch plans?"

"Your honor, I do," Christine smiled slightly. "May I have a raincheck?"

"Anytime," the judge nodded. He scribbled something on his personalized notepad along with the word raincheck. "My phone number, please feel free to use it anytime."

##

"What did he want," Jessica asked as she carried Christine's computer and evidence box from the courtroom.

"He wants me to run for district attorney," Christine smiled at her lover. "That way I won't have to appear in his courtroom."

Jessica frowned. "You would make an incredible district attorney." She was certain that wasn't what the judge wanted. It was, however, Christine's solution to whatever was going on.

"He wants to date you. Doesn't he?" Jessica swallowed.

"Take me to lunch and I will tell you what he wanted," she smiled. Jessica was very intuitive. She liked that about her.

After they had ordered, Christine pulled the judge's note from her purse and handed it to Jessica.

"A rain check for what?" Jessica scowled at the note.

"Lunch," Christine smiled teasingly at her. "You're correct. He does want to date me. Unfortunately, I have my eye on someone with whom I happen to be sleeping. Naturally, that would present problems for me in the courtroom.

"The best thing I can do is remove myself from the courtroom. The current district attorney is retiring this year and wants to do everything he can to help me get elected."

"So, you're sleeping with some lucky devil, and you turned down a very handsome judge for her?" Jessica's grin was priceless.

"Yes," Christine smiled. "I just happen to be in love with the lucky devil."

"She is in love with you, too," Jessica leaned down and kissed her.

##

After lunch, Jessica walked to Lana's office. She was walking on air. She hoped the jewelry designer would hurry with the ring.

"She turned down a date with Judge Clay for me," Jessica laughed.

"You seem surprised," Lana laughed with her. "She's in love with you, you know?"

"Yes, that is what she said," Jessica beamed.

"And you believe her," Lana encouraged.

"Yes. Yes, I do." Jessica was happy that she felt completely safe in Christine's love for her. "I truly do."

"Good. What do you want to discuss today?" Lana asked.

"I want to ask Christine to marry me," Jessica hesitated. "But I haven't found a way to tell her what my mother did to me. It is horribly embarrassing."

"Jessica, you are in no way responsible for your mother's actions," Lana said. "I see this often in children who were molested by their parents. They blame themselves because they can't bring themselves to believe their parents can be so deranged.

"Your mother was sick. That is not your fault."

"Could you possibly let Christine see the video of that session where we had the breakthrough? She can see for herself that I was innocent. That I would never..."

"Jessica, have you ever read your father's diary?" Lana watched her face.

"No. I didn't know he kept one."

"I was so worried about you that I did something I have never done with any patient." Lana looked down at her desk. "I visited your grandmother."

The look of horror on Jessica's face was indescribable. "You did what?"

Lana thought she was going to become violent but she slumped back in her chair. She glared at her. Lana opened her desk drawer and withdrew the diary. She slid it toward Jessica.

"You and Christine should read this together then watch the video. It'll explain everything."

Jessica picked up the diary and walked out of the office without a word. *How can my world go from ecstatic happiness to total shit so quickly?* She thought. *I've worked so hard to keep my illness from grandmother. She will be worried to death.*

##

Jessica was glad Christine was home when she arrived. They made love. She hoped this wouldn't be the last time Christine let her make love to her.

Christine lay with her head on Jessica's chest. She smiled at how hard her heart hammered. She knew Jessica had put all she had into making love to her, and she had returned the same to her.

She stroked her hair. "Chris, I want to marry you," she said. "But, there is something we should read together first. I don't know what is in it. It's my father's diary. Lana gave it to me. She got it from my grandmother."

"I didn't know you had a grandmother." Christine raised up on her elbow to look her in the eye.

"I would like very much for you to meet her," Jessica smiled weakly. "First, let's read the book."

##

They sat in silence as the DVD whirled to a stop. Neither moved. The diary slipped from Jessica's lap to the floor.

Jessica stood. "I need to go for a walk. I want to give you; both of us, time to digest this."

Christine nodded. She was shocked.

The refreshing night air hit Jessica's face. She shook her head, trying to decide what to do now. She needed to talk to Dr. Denton. She walked down the stairs to the parking garage and keyed in her passcode.

After watching the video, Jessica was sure Christine would reconsider Judge Clay's offer. There was no doubt in Jessica's mind that the judge would make a wonderful husband for Christine. The thought turned her stomach. She drove for hours, trying to work up the nerve to contact Lana. She knew she needed help.

##

Christine paced the floor. What was taking Jessica so long? What if something happened to her? She dialed her number and was shocked to hear the phone ring in their bedroom.

Christine turned on the light in her office and sat down at her desk. She wished she had just a fraction of Jessica's computer knowledge. She could find her through her GPS system.

The box containing Teresa's things caught her eye. She made a mental note to return the girl's things to her in the morning.

She placed the box on her desk and opened it for the first time. It contained a few CDs, makeup, a beautiful evening bag and a cell phone.

The phone was dead. Christine plugged it into a battery block. It dinged as it came to life. A beautiful, laughing little boy was the wallpaper for Teresa's phone. Just to pass the time, Christine scrolled through the girl's photo album. She gasped as a picture of Jessica holding the little boy on her shoulders scrolled into view. The child was resting his chin on top of Jessica's head. They were mirror images of each other.

Christine jumped when her cell phone rang.

She reached Dr. Denton's gated community and typed in the code she had given her long ago. Jessica never forgot a number.

It was after midnight when she pulled into Lana's drive. She panicked when she realized a strange car was in her driveway. Perhaps another patient needed her advice. She debated leaving then decided to ring her doorbell.

As she approached the home, she could hear muffled sounds from inside. She could identify Lana's voice, but the man's voice was unknown to her.

A cheating wife. Dr. Lana Denton couldn't be a cheating wife. Ash was in Alaska. How could she? Jessica's head felt as if it would burst.

Jessica tried the door. It was locked. She walked to the back of the house. Through the floor to ceiling windows, she would see a man. The man and Dr. Denton were walking toward her bedroom.

Jessica desperately looked for a way to pry open the patio doors. She found a grilling tool and jammed it between the sliding patio doors. It took all her strength to tear the lock loose on the door, but it finally slid open.

A quick glance at the coffee table in front of the sofa revealed two glasses and a bottle of wine. Cheese and crackers were there, too.

She stood silently listening for any sound that would tell her where the man was. She heard nothing but silence. Stealthily she moved down the hall toward the light.

As she reached the bedroom door, she could see Lana handcuffed to the headboard. Her mouth was taped shut with silver duct tape. A red rose tucked behind her ear.

Briefly, Jessica wished she had let Christine teach her how to use a gun.

The man stood over Lana, holding an X-Acto knife. He bent down toward her forehead then stood erect. He grabbed her pajama top and ripped it open, revealing her perfect breasts.

"I think I will start with these first," he growled. The voice was familiar yet unlike anything; Jessica had ever known. "They will be the prized jewels of my collection.

"How thoughtless of me. I bet you want me to make love to you first. I've always wanted to make love to you, you know."

Slowly Jessica moved toward the man. Just as she reached to grab him, he swung around.

"Ah and here is your lover," the man howled like a wild animal and pulled a gun from his shoulder holster. "Did you come sneaking over here tonight to get a little...?"

"No," Jessica lunged for the man's gun. The shot hit Jessica in the shoulder, spinning her around. She landed on the foot of Lana's bed.

"This will do nicely," the man said. "I will just shoot you right now then finish with the cheating wife. I'll be the hero for solving the BWC case.

"It will look like I shot you just as you completed your ritual with the lovely Dr. Denton." He laughed gleefully. "You will go down in history as the Branded Wives Murderer, Jessica Barton."

Jessica slowly inched her way between Lana and the gunman. Her shoulder hurt like hell. She was staring down the barrel of a Glock. Her day couldn't get any worse. She thought she might faint. That definitely would be worse. Jessica glanced down at Lana. She was okay.

The gunman raised his gun toward Jessica's head. Jessica waited for the kill shot she knew, was coming.

A single shot rang out. Jessica didn't feel anything. Was she already dead? She opened her eyes and watched as the gunman's eyes widened, then he lurched forward. The man fired his gun. The bullet only struck the floor.

As the man crumpled to the carpet, ADA Christine Canton came into view. She still had her pistol trained on the gunman. Jessica fainted.

##

Chapter 30

"I never saw this coming," Risa Mercer made the Y incision. "There is no reason to do an autopsy. I just want to cut up the son-of-a-bitch."

Ames gently removed the scalpel from her hand. "Why don't you let your assistant do this one?" The agony in his eyes told Risa he was hurting too.

Risa nodded and followed the Captain from the morgue. "Where is everyone?" she asked as she looked around the bullpen.

"Running the search warrant," Ames handed her a cup of coffee. "I have a feeling what they find will be the things that make nightmares come to life."

Risa nodded.

##

Ash clasped her wife's hand as they prepared to search the house. She had caught the red-eye flight home as soon as Christine called her. Trinity held the door open. CSI was standing by as soon as Ash gave permission to proceed.

"This looks like a shrine," Trinity growled. "What the hell is it?"

Ash flipped the wall switch. It turned on a spotlight mounted on the ceiling. The light showcased a life-size portrait hanging over the fireplace.

An exquisitely engraved jewelry box sat on a small altar in front of the picture. Trinity opened the jewelry box and gagged at the sight. Nipples encased in glass hung from earring posts. The killer had made jewelry out of the nipples. Each pair was different. Some dangled inside large hoops while others just hung from the earring posts.

Each pair of earrings rested within a white velvet square. Each BW victim's name was in red marker above the earrings featuring their nipples.

A branding iron lay on the alter beside the jewelry box. A white leather-bound book lay on the other side of the jewelry box. Candles were on each side of the altar.

A brown leather briefcase containing a million dollars was lying open on the altar.

"But, why," Ash's shoulders sagged. "Why?"

Lana picked up the leather-bound book and opened it. "I believe this will tell us," she grimaced. "It's Colt's diary."

The three couples were sitting in Jessica's penthouse. It had been three weeks since Colt's funeral. They all had attended in remembrance of the man their friend had been once upon a time. They had not discussed the monster he had become. Tonight, was the first time they had gotten together since the funeral.

"You two saved my wife's life," Ash held up her wine glass. "A toast to Jessica and Christine."

"How did you both end up there?" Risa asked.

"Lana called me," Christine said. "She heard a noise at her front door."

"Someone turned the doorknob and pushed against the door," Lana explained. "It frightened me, so I called Christine and Jessica. A short time later, Colt rang the doorbell. I let him in. I thought Christine had sent him. I never had any reason to fear Colt.

"I began to get nervous when he presented me the wine. He went to the kitchen and made the crackers and cheese.

"The more he talked, the crazier he got. He accused me of having an affair with Jessica. He had witnessed me with Jessica at the jewelry store. I was helping Jessica pick out the perfect ring for Christine. Colt thought Jessica was buying jewelry for me."

"I knew Linda leaving him had affected him deeply. Apparently, it drove him insane." Ash said as she pulled her wife's hand into her lap.

"In Colt's darkroom, we found extra prints of all the photos sent to the husbands of the BW victims," Ash continued. "Colt has always moonlighted with his detective agency. Undoubtedly, cheating wives became his obsession."

"He couldn't bring himself to kill Linda," Lana said, "so he murdered other cheating wives. They were women he knew cheated on their husbands. Colt was drop dead handsome, so it wasn't hard for him to gain their trust and affection. He was the man in the photos he sent to the husbands. His DNA was a match for all the babies."

"He had an elaborate video system set up in one of his bedrooms. He took his victims there and videoed their activities. It was easy for him to pull just the right shot from the videos and mail them to the husbands.

"He kept reenacting the same scenes over and over doing to the cheating wives what he couldn't bring himself to do to Linda. When he discovered they had lost their son because Linda aborted him instead of a miscarriage, Colt snapped."

The elevator dinged, and Teresa brought in more wine. She stayed to hear the discussion.

Trinity's eyes narrowed as she processed the information she was getting. "You and Christine were at Lana's in separate cars. Why didn't you both go in one car?"

Silence filled the room.

Jessica cleared her throat. "I am a..."

"Jessica, don't," Christine took her hand.

"I wanted to ask Christine to marry me," Jessica continued. "I was scared she would turn me down, so I went to Lana for advice.

"When I arrived Colt already had her handcuffed to the headboard. I lunged for his gun, and he shot me. Thank heaven Christine showed up right after I did."

Trinity looked at Christine's hand. She wore no ring. "Did you ask Christine to marry you?"

"Yes," Jessica said flatly. "She said she would think about it."

"Oh, that's cold," Trinity grimaced. "Why the reservations, Chris?"

"I..." Christine hesitated. "I have unanswered questions."

"Like what?" Jessica asked.

"Like why you showed up for your appointment with Lana covered in blood?" Christine glared at her lover.

"I can answer that question," Teresa volunteered. All eyes turned toward the receptionist.

"As you all know, I made my living in the oldest profession on earth." Teresa hung her head. "My

309

husband died in Iraq when our son was only two years old. We married right out of high school, so my marketable skills were few. I could only get low paying jobs. I thought I could save enough money tricking to go to college and make a better life for Presley and me.

"One night, Presley and I were at a convenience store when two men robbed the place. My three-year-old thought men with guns were playing and ran to one of them making bang-bang sounds. The man punched him and knocked him out. A display of canned goods fell onto Presley. The cans broke his arm and cut him. He was bleeding everywhere.

"The burglars ran from the store. I put Presley into my car and was driving fast to get him to the hospital. About five blocks from the hospital, a man ran a stop sign and t-boned my car. He backed up and drove away. My car door wouldn't open. I couldn't get out of the car.

"Jessica ran to my car and helped me out. I told her about Presley. She got Presley out of his car seat and sprinted the five blocks to the hospital, carrying my son. By the time we reached the emergency room, Jessica was covered with Presley's blood.

"Jessica called her grandmother. They stayed with me until the doctor said Presley would be okay. Jessica asked her grandmother to take care of us, and she has. Neither of them knew of my profession. Jessica just disappeared. She walked out of the hospital, and I never saw her again until that day in the Omni."

All eyes turned to Jessica. She shrugged. "I honestly don't remember any of that."

"My cell phone," Teresa said, "I can prove it."

Christine gave the girl her phone. Teresa scanned until she found the picture she wanted. "Here," she said, shoving the phone in front of Christine. "I took this the night we were waiting to see the doctor. Jessica held my son and gently rocked him the entire time we waited."

Everyone gathered around for a better look at the cell phone picture. Jessica was holding a small boy in her arms. Blood covered both.

Jessica frowned. "That is the boy my grandmother is now babysitting."

"Yes," Teresa smiled as she swiped to another photo. "Your grandmother took this photo of you and Presley. He's sitting on your shoulders."

"He's not your son?" Christine asked softly.

"Heavens no," Jessica declared.

"I need to go get him," Teresa smiled. "Nana will be worried if I'm late."

Teresa walked to the door then turned to face the group. "All of you have been so wonderful to me. Presley and I have a chance for a great life, thanks to you."

After Teresa left all eyes turned to Christine. Her head was bowed. She raised her eyes to stare into Jessica's glistening eyes. "Yes," she said.

"You'll have to speak up, ADA Canton," Jessica grinned. "I'm not sure everyone heard you."

"Yes," she smiled. "Yes, Jessica Barton, I would love to marry you."

Jessica disappeared into the bedroom. She returned with a ring box. She removed the ring from the box and slipped it onto Christine's finger.

"Just for the record ADA Canton," she grinned, "I wouldn't mind having a son."

"I wouldn't mind giving you one," Christine kissed her lovingly.

Their friends clapped, and wolf whistled. Everyone began hugging Christine and congratulating Jessica.

It was good to have friends.

THE END

Branded Wives by Erin Wade

Learn more about Erin Wade
and her books at www.erinwade.us

**Other #1 Best Selling Books
by Erin Wade**
Too Strong to Die
Death Was Too Easy
Three Times as Deadly

Erin Wade writing as D.J. Jouett
The Destiny Factor

Coming in March 2018
Living Two Lives
Don't Dare the Devil
The Roughneck & the Lady

***Following is a preview of
Living Two Lives***

Chapter 1

The woman pulled the collar of her raincoat tighter around her neck. The drizzling Texas rain was cold for May. She squinted trying to bring into focus the gorgeous brunette that was accepting condolences from everyone. She sincerely regretted that Jules Divine was suffering from the loss of someone she deeply loved.

Hidden in the shadow of the lone oak, the woman watched the pomp and circumstance going on below her as mourners paid their respect to the woman she had murdered.

##

Julie Adair Divine walked to the massive front door of her grandmother's house in Kingston, Texas. She pushed the over-sized key into the lock and turned it. She could hear the deadbolt slide back to allow her admittance into the home where she had grown from a gangly teenager to a responsible adult.

Her mind flashed back to the day she had arrived on her grandmother's doorstep looking for a place to live. On her fourteenth birthday, she had announced that she was a lesbian and her parents had thrown her out of the house. Her grandmother, Nana, was the only one she could turn to.

Nana had taken her in, and christened her "Jules," exclaiming that Julie was too severe a name for her light-hearted granddaughter.

Nana had provided her a home filled with love, mutual respect and laughter. Nana had taken her everywhere she traveled and introduced Jules to so many wonders of the world that Jules had lost track of the locations of the splendors Nana had shown her.

Although Nana would never admit it, Jules suspected that she took great joy in showing up for church on Sunday morning with her granddaughter proudly sitting beside her. She took even greater joy in explaining why Jules' Baptist minister father—Nana's son—had turned his back on his only daughter.

Community leaders and staunch examples for Christians, Warren and Martha Divine refused to acknowledge their daughter saying that "Jules was dead to God and to them."

Nana's response to their ridiculous declaration was less Godlike. "As if God would ever let those two hypocrites know what he thought," Nana had huffed.

Nana—Daphne Adair Divine—made certain that her granddaughter and namesake had all the benefits and opportunities money could buy. Jules worked hard to justify the faith and pride Nana had in her. She had graduated valedictorian from high school and college and earned her Master's Degree in English from Texas Christian University in Fort Worth, Texas. At the age of thirty-four, she was head of the English department at the small high school in Waco, Texas.

Jules' heels clicked on the highly-polished wooden floors of Nana's house as she walked through the foyer into the great room. She slipped off her heels, dropped her purse and jacket onto the sofa then collapsed onto the overstuffed furniture. She buried her face in her hands and cried.

Nana's funeral had been simple with almost everyone in their rural town in attendance. Nana was their most famous local celebrity. A well-known mystery writer, she had been writing for over thirty years and had many best-sellers to her credit. Thanks to a good investment banker and over a hundred books under her name, Nana was very wealthy.

"Money, money, it's a rich man's world," Nana's doorbell jerked Jules from her reverie. She had to chuckle at her eccentric grandmother's choice of chime tones. She wondered who would be ringing the doorbell this late.

Through the opaque glass of the massive door, Jules could make out the figure of a medium-height person. She pushed the intercom. "May I help you?"

The figure held up something to the door and said, "Yes, I am police detective Tanner West. I would like to speak with you, ma'am."

Jules unlocked the door and pulled it open. Although Tanner West was five-eight, she was dwarfed by the massive wrought-iron door. She pretended to take a moment to scrutinize the high ceilings and dazzling chandelier hanging in the foyer, but truthfully, she was trying to stop herself from drooling over the gorgeous brunette standing in the doorway.

"What can I do for you, detective?" Jules tilted her head slightly and acquiesced halfheartedly. She did not move to allow Tanner to enter.

Tanner could tell the woman was weary from the emotional day she had endured and hated to add to it, but the sooner she compiled evidence, the sooner the police would solve their case.

"Are you Jules Divine?" Tanner asked as she still held her badge, so Jules could read it.

"Yes."

"If I may," Tanner said, "I need to ask you a few questions about your grandmother's death?"

Jules stepped back and motioned for Tanner to enter. "Nana died in her sleep," Jules mumbled. "I don't understand why the police need to question me about her death."

As Tanner followed the brunette into the great room, Jules swayed slightly. Tanner caught her elbow, steadying her. "Are you okay?"

"I had a slight dizzy spell," Jules shook her head as if trying to clear the cobwebs. "I haven't eaten all day."

"We have several excellent restaurants," Tanner said, "perhaps we could dine while we visit. Kill two birds with one stone, so to speak."

"That isn't necessary," Jules scowled. "I am sure you won't take long."

"I would consider it a favor." Tanner tried to look pitiful. "I haven't eaten all day either. It would give me an opportunity to sit down and relax."

Jules looked down at her severe black dress and stockinged feet. "Give me a few minutes to change."

Tanner nodded and tried to keep from staring at the brunette's perfect derrière as she left the room. It had been a long time since she'd encountered a woman as beautiful as Jules Divine.

Tanner walked around the room as she waited. A beautiful portrait of Jules hung over the fireplace and a grand piano was nestled inconspicuously into a niche to the left of the mantel. The back wall of the great room was glass overlooking a crystal-clear swimming pool. A waterfall splashed down a ten-foot retaining wall into the pool providing soothing sounds and a delightful ambience.

Tanner jumped when Jules cleared her throat. "I didn't mean to startle you."

"Oh, um, I was just lost in your backyard paradise," Tanner blushed. Try as she might, she couldn't keep her eyes from scanning Jules Divine from the tips of her polished toenails to the top of her gorgeous head.

"Did I pass?" A smile flitted across Jules' lips.

"Pass?" Tanner raised a questioning eyebrow.

"Your intense inspection," Jules smiled.

##

Chapter 2

Tanner placed a comforting hand on the small of Jules' back as she guided her to a booth at the back of the family-owned Italian bistro.

"Nana said this was an excellent place to dine," Jules made small talk as they were seated, "but I haven't eaten here."

"If you like Italian food, you'll love Sabello's." Tanner said.

They placed their orders then silently waited as the waitress placed bread and their drinks on the table. When it was clear they could talk without interruption, Tanner cleared her throat. "What do you know about your grandmother's death?"

"Just that the housekeeper found her in her bed Friday morning. Everyone assumes she had a heart attack." A scowl wrinkled Jules' forehead. "Is there something about Nana's death I should know?"

"I don't know any easy way to say this," Tanner bowed her head then raised her eyes to watch Jules' reaction. "Your grandmother was murdered."

Shock registered on the brunette's face. She seemed to have a problem grasping Tanner's information.

"She was poisoned," Tanner added.

"Poisoned? Nana! Someone poisoned Nana?" She said as if she found the thought incomprehensible. "Why would anyone want to kill Nana?"

Tears rolled down Jules' cheeks as she fought to maintain control of her emotions. "I...I must go," she mumbled.

"No." Tanner placed a firm hand on top of Jules'. "You need to eat something. You'll feel better."

"I need to visit the lady's room," Jules said as she slid from the booth and walked to the back of the restaurant.

"It's good to see you, Tanner," a voluptuous Italian woman placed plates and more bread on the table. "We have been missing you."

"It gets busier every day, Max." Tanner responded to Maxine Sabello, the restaurant owner. "This used to be a sleepy little town, but it is growing too fast."

"Who's the looker?" Maxine nodded in the direction Jules had disappeared.

"Jules Divine."

"Daphne Divine's granddaughter?" Maxine raised a brow.

"Yeah," Tanner exhaled as Jules walked toward them.

"Jules, I'd like to introduce you to Maxine Sabello, the owner of this fine establishment."

"You were at Nana's funeral." Jules shook hands with Max.

"Most of the town was there," Max shrugged. "We all loved her. She was our claim to fame. Daphne Divine was a celebrity."

"Yes, I suppose she was," Jules agreed. "I never think of her that way. She is just…was just Nana to me."

"Eat your dinner before it gets cold," Max chided. "And watch out for Sherry Martin. She's trying to run down Daphne's heirs to see if the house is for sale."

Jules frowned and turned to Tanner for clarification. "Our local real estate agent," Tanner explained.

"Oh," Jules slid into the booth beside Tanner.

"Is it for sale?" Tanner asked eager to learn if the beauty beside her would make her home in their town.

"I…I don't know," Jules stuttered. "I don't know to whom Nana left her estate. I suppose her attorney will contact me sooner or later. I do know Nana had a will."

"Eat," Max commanded. "I'll get you some fresh bread. You've let this get cold."

"How was Nana poisoned?" Jules asked when they were alone.

"Rattlesnake venom," Tanner answered.

"Could she have been bitten by a snake?" Jules asked.

"No, she had too much venom in her system for a snake bite. There was enough snake venom in her system to kill twenty women her size.

"Our pathologist found a needle mark in her arm. She was injected. There was venom around the puncture wound."

They ate in silence for several minutes as each of them contemplated Tanner's revelation.

"Did she live with anyone?" Tanner asked.

"No. She lived alone," Jules shook her head. "I usually traveled with her when she had to make book tours or public appearances. She had several booked for this summer."

"She had a lot of acquaintances, but no close friends. Nana loved writing and that left little time for anything else."

"She had no romantic involvements—no lovers?" Tanner pushed for information.

"Romantic?" Jules looked as if the thought of her grandmother being involved with a lover was the most preposterous idea imaginable.

"She was young," Tanner tried to suppress her mirth at Jules' prudish reaction, "and extremely attractive—an older version of you. I have seen her around town, even talked with her on occasion. I found her to be delightful."

"I noticed her in memoriam stated she was only sixty-seven," Tanner continued. "Most of the sixty-seven-year-old people I know are still sexually active."

"I...she...I must go," Jules blushed a deep red. She reached for the check, but Tanner beat her to it.

"My treat," the detective said.

"Thank you, it was delicious."

##

Jules watched as Detective West's tail lights disappeared at the bottom of the hill. She looked over the lights in the distance. Nana's house had a view of their town. It was a small town; small enough that one could hear the wail of sirens when a firetruck rushed to a burning building anywhere in town.

She wandered into the study and laughed when she spied the high-powered telescope her grandmother had sitting in front of the window that overlooked the town. She fought the urge to look through the instrument and lost.

"Oh, what the hell," Jules mumbled as she pulled a chair up to the telescope and sat down to look through the eyepiece. She wondered what Nana's neighbors would think if they knew she spied on them. She watched her neighbors, Roy and Ashley Craft. Roy was smiling and helping his wife clean up the kitchen.

Jules examined the telescope and discovered there was a device that allowed her to connect her cell phone to the instrument and video through the lens. She attached her cell phone and recorded Roy and Ashley as they settled in front of the television in their den. *This is like being in the room with them*, she thought. She soon tired of her voyeurism and walked through the rest of the house.

Jules was still stunned. She couldn't wrap her mind around the fact that Nana had been murdered. She began to plan. She had four weeks left of school. Her principal had allowed her to use ten personal days to handle Nana's funeral and private affairs. She would return to Waco for the last two weeks of school than be out for the summer.

##

Chapter 3

Jules couldn't sleep. Detective West's revelation that Nana had been murdered deeply disturbed her. She checked her Kindle to see if it had charged while she showered and was relieved to see the hundred percent sign in the corner.

She downloaded the latest book by her favorite lesbian fiction writer Darcy Lake. She secretly harbored a crush on Lake and had even stood in line for several hours to get Darcy's autograph on her book.

Lake was as gorgeous in person as she was in the photos on her book covers and website. She was genuinely nice. Of course, she was also very married. Sometimes Jules' stomach would lurch when Darcy posted on Facebook about how wonderful her gorgeous wife was.

Quickly Jules was immersed in the action of the latest Darcy Lake novel. Lake was a spellbinding story teller. One felt like they were living the action and romance in her novels. Jules could understand why Lake had been the number one lesbian writer for the past ten years. She was incredible. Lake's novels had even crossed over from lesbian fiction to mainstream fiction and helped open the door for acceptance of lesbian fiction writers. Lake wrote murder mysteries, thrillers and suspenseful action with lesbian heroines.

Why can't I find a woman like Darcy Lake? Jules thought.

Sometime after midnight, her Kindle slipped from her hands as Jules succumbed to exhaustion.

##

The sound of a lawn mower outside her window pulled Jules from her dreamless sleep. She lay on her back reliving the last love scene in Darcy's book. She sighed and threw back the covers ready to face the day. Even if her love life sucked, at least she could read arousing stories in Darcy's novels.

Jules put a coffee pod into the Keurig, pushed brew and returned to her room to unpack. It had always been her room or her suite. Jules' freshman year of high school Nana had built the house after signing a multi-million-dollar contract for three books in one year. One side of the house was dedicated to Nana's master bedroom and office. The other side of the house was Jules' master bedroom and office, mirroring Nana's.

She pulled on a pair of jeans and a soft Henley. She had a lot to do today and wanted to be comfortable while she worked.

By the time she had poured her coffee and walked onto the patio, the lawn mower had moved to the back of the house. For the first time, she realized whoever was mowing was doing it in her yard. She watched as a sinewy young woman carefully maneuvered the lawn mower around the corner.

Jules relaxed on a cushioned lounge chair and admired the easy grace of the lawn girl. She wondered where Nana had found her. She was very tall and attractive in a butch sort of way. Collar-length blonde hair curled naturally around her stunning face.

The lawn mower sputtered, warning its operator it was running out of gas. The young woman turned off the mower and softly cursed under her breath. "Damn, fifteen more minutes and I would have finished."

She turned on her heel and noticed Jules watching her. For several seconds, the two checked out each other then Jules realized she was smiling. "I'm Jules Divine," she stood as she introduced herself.

"Chance Howard," the woman flashed a brilliant smile and extended her hand toward Jules, but pulled it back just before their hands met. She removed tight-fitting black leather gloves. "Sorry, my hands are all sweaty," she apologized wiping her hand down the front of her jeans before again offering it to Jules.

Chance's hand was surprisingly soft for one who made a living mowing yards.

"I recognize you from your picture," Chance added.

"My picture?" Jules raised a questioning brow.

"Over the fireplace." Chance gestured toward the great room.

"Oh," Jules nodded. She wondered if the young woman was a frequent visitor to Nana's home.

"I keep Daphne's yard for her," Chance offered information. "I own my own landscaping business. I service most of the single women in this neighborhood and the Crafts."

Service most of the single women, Jules thought. What a strange way of putting it.

"I think they are more at ease with me than with the male lawncare teams," Chance displayed her beautiful smile again.

"How many women do you *service?*" Jules asked.

"In this neighborhood, about twenty," Chance said flashing a grin then turning somber. "I'm sorry that Daphne passed. She was an incredible woman. I saw you at her funeral, but I didn't want to talk business there. I want to make certain you need me to continue taking care of the grounds."

"What does your service include?" Jules asked.

"I mow, weed eat and pull any weeds that dare raise their ugly heads in my yards. I also do all the landscaping, flowerbed maintenance, fertilizing and insect eradication."

Chance Howard was relaxed and easy to be around. Jules chastised herself for thinking the young woman was any more than she appeared.

"Would you like some ice water?" Jules offered. "It's very warm today."

"No, I'm good," Chance's blue eyes seemed to stop short of laughing. "I need to finish here. I have three more yards to do before it gets too hot. It was nice to meet you."

"I want you to," Jules blurted out.

"To what?" Chance slowly raised an eyebrow.

"Continue to take care of the grounds," Jules laughed. "How do I pay you?"

"Oh, Daphne's accountant takes care of all her bills." Chance seemed to know more about Nana's business than Jules. "Unless you make changes, I assume I will continue to invoice her and she will mail me a check."

Jules watched Chance walk away to get gasoline. *I would bet a month's pay you're a lesbian,* she thought.

"How did you meet my grandmother?" Jules asked as Chance filled the mower with gas.

"The police arrested me on a DUI. I used to stay drunk most of the time. I had real anger issues. I didn't figure my life was worth much, being a lesbian and all. That's what my folks said.

"Before they could book me and fingerprint me, Daphne showed up at the jail and talked the arresting officer into releasing me to her. She paid for counseling to help me manage my anger issues.

"She helped me start this business and taught me how to run a small company, so I would succeed. She saved my life."

Jules watched Chance crank the mower. *Nana really was a remarkable woman,* she thought.

Jules finished her coffee then forced herself to enter Nana's world. Nana's office was a large room with floor to ceiling bookcases lining two walls. Another wall was home to Nana's built-in desk and computer with the largest monitor imaginable. Anna's eyesight had started to deteriorate so she had purchased a huge monitor. "I work and tan at the same time she used to tease."

An entire section of the bookshelf was devoted to Daphne Divine's books. Jules inhaled slowly as she recalled proofing every book Nana had ever written.

She hadn't exactly proofed Nana's early books, but Nana had read them out loud to her and Jules had loved Nana's stories.

Sometime during college, Jules had become Nana's official proofreader. She often felt that her desire to be a great proofreader for Nana had led her to major in English. Of course, Nana had beta readers, an editor and an agent who advised her, but she depended on Jules for the final read before releasing a book to print.

Jules pulled the handle on Nana's private bookcase and found it locked. Nana had always kept it locked. "That is where I keep my ideas, so no one can steal them," she used to laugh.

Jules jumped when Nana's cell phone rang. She followed the sound and found the phone on the desk beside Nana's computer. The word Agent flashed on the phone screen. Jules disconnected the cell phone from its charger and sat down in Nana's desk chair.

The phone dinged in her hand as Agent left a message. Jules played back the recording. "I'm getting nervous. Where's the final manuscript? The printer is screaming for it. Just sign off on the damn thing and email it today. I'm serious, today!"

Jules was surprised no one had notified the publisher of Nana's death. She wondered if she could find the manuscript on Nana's computer, but was distracted by the sound of footsteps in the kitchen.

"Hello, is anyone here?" A pleasant voice echoed through the empty house.

"Hello," Jules called back as she walked toward the center of the house. She was surprised to find an attractive, middle-aged woman in the kitchen.

"You must be Jules," the woman smiled.

Jules nodded, "And you are?"

"Daphne's chief cook and bottle washer, Renee Baxter." She extended her hand to shake hands with Jules.

"I thought you might be here," Renee continued. "I saw you at the funeral. You were her favorite, you know?"

Jules nodded and tried to swallow around the knot in her throat. The shock of Nana's death was wearing off and in its place, was a gaping hole of indescribable sadness.

"Why don't I fix you some breakfast?" Renee said.

Jules nodded and refilled her cup before sitting down at the kitchen island. She watched Renee as she moved about the kitchen, easily locating what she needed. It was obvious the housekeeper knew her way around Nana's home.

Jules committed to memory the features of the woman. Renee was short, about five-three and slender. Her mid-length brown hair was streaked with red highlights. Her sparkling hazel eyes fit perfectly in a face that laughed more than it frowned. Jules guessed Renee to be late thirties.

The doorbell rang as Renee pulled bacon and eggs from the refrigerator. "I'll get it," Jules slid from the stool and walked to the front door. Even through the opaque glass, Jules knew the figure on the other side was Detective Tanner West. She licked her lips and opened the door.

"Detective West, what a pleasant surprise," Jules managed to keep her joy from blooming into a huge grin.

"Good morning, Miss Divine," Tanner nodded, stopping short of bowing before the beautiful brunette. "I hope you feel better today and we can continue our talk."

"Oh, yes," Jules said, "of course. I am sorry for abruptly ending the evening."

"It was inconsiderate of me to question you so soon after the funeral. I apologize, but I must move quickly, or any evidence may disappear."

"I understand," Jules nodded. "We're about to have breakfast. Won't you join us?"

Tanner entered the house. *We? Damn!* Tanner thought. *Of course, a woman as gorgeous as Jules Divine would be part of a, "We!"*

"Detective Tanner West, I'd like you to meet Renee Baxter," Jules swept her hand toward the housekeeper. "Renee is—was Nana's housekeeper."

Renee placed a cup of coffee in front of Tanner. "Have you eaten breakfast?"

"No, but I…"

"Then you'll join us," Renee declared as the bacon began to sizzle in the large skillet. "Jules, if you'll set the table and pour the orange juice, breakfast will be ready in two shakes of a lamb's tail."

##

Chapter 4

Tanner enjoyed the conversation with the two attractive women. She had seen Renee around town and was familiar   with her struggle as a single mom raising teenage boys. More than once Tanner had kept the twins from being booked for a DUI.

"Did you find Miss Divine's body?" Tanner asked Renee.

Renee looked down as if overcome by emotion. "Yes," tears filled her eyes.

"Would you mind showing me where you found her?" Tanner turned to Jules, "If that's okay with you?"

"Of course," both women nodded.

Jules stood back as Tanner and Renee entered her grandmother's suite. Nana's latest best seller was stacked on the nightstand along with two other novels by authors unknown to Jules.

"I was told you found her in bed," Tanner frowned.

Renee nodded.

"But her bed is made and…"

"I'm so sorry," Renee mumbled. "I thought Daphne died of natural causes. I gave the house a thorough cleaning to get it ready for Jules.

"I laundered all the bed linens, towels and Daphne's clothes. I also polished all the furniture and waxed the floors."

"That pretty much destroys any evidence that might have been here." Tanner couldn't hide her disappointment. "Are you always this efficient?"

"I…I was just trying…"

"Detective West," Jules cut in, "Renee said she was trying to have the house cleaned for my arrival. None of us knew Nana had been murdered."

Tanner nodded but it still perturbed her that any evidence that would help her catch a killer had been eradicated by the housekeeper. She couldn't even be certain if Daphne's bedroom was the crime scene, or if the mystery writer had been murdered somewhere else then placed in her bed.

Renee had called an ambulance and Daphne had been rushed to the nearest hospital where she was pronounced dead on arrival. Two days later, the medical examiner had declared her death a homicide. Tanner was two days behind the killer and losing ground fast.

"Did she have company the night she died?" Tanner asked. "Was there any evidence of two wine glasses or two dinner plates? Anything like that?"

"There were two glasses of wine," Renee nodded. "But I…"

"Ran them through the dishwasher," Tanner finished her sentence. "Did the glasses have lipstick on them?"

"Yes," Renee confirmed. "Daphne didn't wear lipstick, so it had to belong to her visitor. It was bright red."

"The wine bottle, what happened to the wine bottle?" Excitement colored Tanner's voice. "Maybe we can pull prints from it."

"I put it in recycling," Renee's eyes brightened. "It should still be in the utility room."

The three quickly moved to the small room off the kitchen. "That's it," Renee pointed to an empty Siduri Pinot Noir bottle.

"Dessert wine," Tanner narrowed her eyes as she carefully used her pen to pick up the bottle. "Was there evidence that someone dined with Miss Divine?"

"There were two dinner plates in the sink," Renee nodded as she pulled a gallon zip-lock baggie from the shelf and handed it to Tanner.

"Thank you," the detective mumbled as she placed the bottle into the bag. She was certain the case could have easily been solved if all the evidence hadn't been destroyed.

"Well, I must get to work," Renee hurried back to the kitchen.

"Do you have my phone number in your phone?" Tanner asked Jules.

"No, I haven't entered it into my phone yet."

Tanner pulled her phone from her pocket and pressed the buttons to send her phone number to Jules. Then she sent a photo of her leaning in a doorway. She held out her hand for Jules' phone and synced the photo with her phone number.

"Now you have me at the top of your friends' list," Tanner said with a chuckle. "Please don't hesitate to call me if you need anything. I do mean anything; a friend to talk with or a dinner partner. Anything."

Jules led Tanner to the front door. "Thank you for stopping by, detective," she said as she opened the door.

"Please, call me Tanner."

"Thank you, Tanner."

Only after the door closed behind her did Tanner West realize that she'd been dismissed. *Jules Divine is very smooth,* the detective thought.

##

Jules located Renee in the dining room of the house where she was polishing the magnificent table that filled the room. Jules sighed as she recalled her relatives gathered around the table on holidays.

Nana had always hosted family gatherings in her home. The huge table seated twelve people, just enough room for Jules, her parents and her older brother Lucas, Uncle Buddy—Nana's other son—and his family of seven; Aunt Page, two boys and three girls.

After Jules's parents disowned her, they refused to dine at Nana's because Jules was at the table. Jules recalled being surprised and pleased when her parents didn't show up for Thanksgiving that year, but everyone else did. Even Lucas opted to dine with her and Nana instead of their parents.

"Renee, do you mind telling me your arrangement with Nana?" Jules asked.

"Every morning I cooked her breakfast, then straightened anything that was out of place in the house. I did all the grocery shopping and cooked any other meals Daphne needed."

"Did you cook her last meal?" Jules asked.

"I think I did. She often had me prepare dinner for two and leave it in the refrigerator. That's what I did that day."

"You should've told that to detective West."

"I'll call her and give her that information. Do you want me to continue as your housekeeper?" Renee asked.

"I'm not certain what I'll do. I don't know what will happen to the house. I know nothing about Nana's will."

"Why don't you call her lawyer and find out?" Renee suggested.

"Do you know her lawyer's name?" Jules asked.

"No."

"Neither do I." Jules knew she had a lot to learn about Nana.

"I'm sure you can find it on her computer," Renee said. "She kept her life on that computer."

Jules nodded. "Until everything is settled, let's maintain your regular routine."

"Thank you," Renee bowed her head. "This job makes it possible for me to care for my boys."

Jules left Renee to her chores and wandered into her grandmother's suite. She turned on Nana's computer and watched as the screen requested a password. She uttered a quick prayer that the password hadn't changed and typed in "Jules1410." The computer opened to Nana's emails.

The first email was a complimentary ticket to the awards ceremony for Rainbow Award Winners (RAW). The International Rainbow Literary Society was holding its annual convention and awards banquet in Dallas, Texas. The guest speaker at the banquet was Darcy Lake. Dallas was only an hour's drove from Kingston.

Jules inhaled sharply as she realized that she could use the ticket to see her favorite lesbian author. She quickly checked the date and location of the annual meeting. It was three days away. The convention started Friday morning and ran through Sunday afternoon. Held at Dallas' most elite hotel, Rosewood Mansion on Turtle Creek, the attendance was limited to four hundred people.

Jules printed the ticket and itinerary for the convention. Two of the pages pointed out how popular Darcy Lake was and that she had won every literary award offered to a lesbian writer and several mainstream awards. It touted the fact that Mrs. Lake would be unveiling her latest novel at the convention and would be on hand to autograph her new book for the duration of the convention. Jules was certain that Darcy Lake's appearance was responsible for the sellout of the convention.

An email from Agent dinged into Nana's computer. It had two attachments. One attachment said *manuscript* the other said, *approval*.

Agent's email said, "Sign the damn approval so I can send this to the printer. We're in real danger, here. I must have this today or you can kiss the book release goodbye until next month. We have too much riding on this to wait. You've proofed it a dozen times. Just sign it."

Jules considered proofing the attached manuscript but knew it would take her at least a day to read one of her grandmother's books. Agent's email was frantic. Jules opened the approval form, attached Nana's electronic signature to it and returned it to agent@sbcglobal.us.

I can't believe I have a ticket to attend the awards ceremony where Darcy Lake will be the guest of honor, Jules thought. She turned off Nana's computer as she thought about buying a new dress to wear to the banquet. *I'll need shoes and a matching purse.*

Jules returned to her suite, walked to the table beside her bed and picked up Darcy's last novel. *I will take it and get her to autograph both her newest release and this one, too,* Jules thought.

She walked to her bookshelf and surveyed the many Darcy Lake novels she owned. She left them at Nana's for safe keeping. She had every novel Lake had written.

Nana often teased her about reading "…that lesbian trash. How can you jump from Shakespeare to Darcy Lake?" Nana would laugh as she hugged Jules' slender shoulders.

Jules would argue that Darcy Lake was one of the finest mystery writers of their time. The fact that her heroines were lesbians didn't keep mystery fans from buying her books.

Nana would simply nod and walk away laughing. "Lake certainly out sells me," she would admit.

Jules could almost hear her grandmother's laughter.

"Room reservations," Jules said out loud. "I wonder if Nana made room reservations." She found the hotel's number in the convention information and called the reservation desk. A quick check confirmed Nana didn't have a room reserved.

"The only thing we have available is the executive suite," the reservationist said. "We had a cancellation otherwise we would have nothing."

Jules pulled her credit card from her purse and provided the necessary information to reserve the suite. It was pricy, but how often does one get to spend the weekend with Darcy Lake?

"I have cleaned everything," Renee said as she tapped on Jules' open door. "Do you want me to make you lunch?"

"No," Jules smiled. "I am going shopping. I'll grab something at the mall if I get hungry. Thank you, Renee. I appreciate you taking care of Nana's house."

Jules gathered her purse and car fob then followed Renee from the house.

"See you in the morning," Renee waved.

##

Chapter 5

The porter removed Jules' luggage from the trunk of her Lexus as she turned the car over to the valet. She followed her bags to the registration counter and handed her confirmation to the cashier. The young woman typed information into her computer and looked at Jules.

"I'm sorry Miss Divine," she frowned at her monitor, "but your room isn't quite ready. It will be another hour before you can get into it.

"I'm going to give you the keycard and have the porter hold your luggage until he can deliver it to your room. In the meantime, please accept this chit for free wine and hors d'oeuvres in our private club until your room is ready. The club is through that door." She nodded toward a gold-trimmed mahogany door across from the registration desk.

Jules accepted the items. Hors d'oeuvres sounded good. She had skipped lunch in her eagerness to check into the hotel and possibly catch a glimpse of Darcy Lake.

The private club was spectacularly decorated with plush carpet and secluded booths along the walls. A young bartender beamed as the beautiful woman entered the club. He motioned for Jules to sit at the bar. She slid onto the barstool cognizant of the bartender's admiring glances.

"What may I offer you, madam?" He half bowed pleased with himself for his gallantry.

"A glass of merlot," Jules ordered.

"May I recommend my personal favorite?" The bartender hawked his drinks. "Island Mist Black Raspberry Merlo."

"Sure," Jules laughed. "Why not?" His enthusiasm was contagious.

The young man watched Jules as she took her first sip of the wine. Her pink tongue lightly licked her lips. "This is delicious."

"Everyone has the same reaction." Her compliment pleased him. "It's good, isn't it?"

"Very," Jules agreed.

"Young man. Young man," a woman's voice called from one of the booths. "Can we get some service over here?"

"Duty calls. Don't go away. I'll be right back."

Jules sipped the wine as she thought about her day. Agent had sent a text message to Nana's phone. *We will make this by the hair of our chinny-chin-chin. We must talk when this is over*, the message had read. Jules wondered if Agent had a real name.

Jules had packed her suitcase, loaded her car and driven to Dallas anxious to get a look at Darcy Lake. The convention brochure had also promised that Lake's camera-shy wife would attend the convention with her.

"Excuse me, is this seat taken?" A dark, silky voice spoke softly beside Jules. It sent heat down her spine.

Jules looked at the mirror over the bar and watched in stunned silence as Darcy Lake sat down beside her. She didn't answer the question. She couldn't find her voice.

"Are you okay?" Darcy asked.

"I...I..." Jules licked her lips trying to moisturize them. Everything was desert dry. *Dammit, I'm a thirty-four-year-old adult and this woman has turned me into a stammering idiot,* Jules thought.

"Mrs. Lake," the happy bartender was back. "It is good to have you with us. What would you like?"

"Any wine will be fine," Darcy shrugged.

"This is delightful," Jules managed to find her voice as she held up her wine glass."

"Then I'll have some of that," a beautiful smile slowly spread across Darcy's face.

"There you are," a boisterous voice filled the sedate club as a tall, red-headed, raw-boned woman strode toward them. "And you've finally produced your gorgeous wife. What is your name, dear?"

Darcy smiled and nodded to Jules to answer.

"Jules," Jules squeaked. She cleared her throat and said her name louder. "Jules."

"You really must join us for dinner," the woman insisted. "Everyone will be so thrilled to meet Jules. You know we were beginning to believe that she was a figment of your imagination. You have kept her hidden from us all these years. You are right, she is gorgeous." The woman sexually slid her hand down Jules' arm and flashed a toothy grin.

Darcy grabbed her wrist and pulled her hand away from Jules' arm. "That's why I never bring her with me," her voice was a low growl. "I don't like people touching my wife."

"I'm sorry," the woman stepped back as Darcy stood.

"We've just arrived," Darcy said. "We'll pass on the dinner invitation. I'm certain we'll see you tomorrow."

Darcy's hand cupped Jules' elbow and gently urged her to stand. Jules picked up both wine glasses and allowed the blonde to propel her to one of the secluded booths at the far end of the room.

"I'm very sorry," Darcy said as they settled into the booth. "I didn't want to leave you to the vultures and I didn't want them to know I was alone. Thanks for being a good sport."

Jules nodded. The closeness of the other woman was overwhelming. The touch of her soft hand, her beauty, and the soft fragrance of her perfume combined to send shockwaves through Jules.

"What happens when your wife shows up?" Jules asked.

"She won't," Darcy said.

"The brochure said she would be here," Jules mumbled.

"It's problematic," Darcy shrugged. "The least I can do is buy your dinner." She motioned for the waiter.

"So, are you here for the awards?" Darcy relaxed after they placed their order. "Are you a writer?"

"Oh, no," Jules giggled like a school girl. "I...uh...came to...get your autograph." She rushed out the last three words hoping she didn't sound too star struck.

"So, no one here knows who you are?" Darcy raised a perfectly arched eyebrow.

"No, this is my first time to attend a lesbian literary awards banquet," Jules replied.

"Listen, Jules," Darcy shifted in the booth to face Jules, "I will pay you a thousand dollars a night to be my wife this weekend."

Jules sat in shocked silence. She finally summoned the ability to answer the author. "Mrs. Lake, I may seem like a groupie, but I can assure you I am not a hooker."

"A hooker?" The look of astonishment on Darcy's face was comical. "Oh! No, you think I am offering to buy your services. I didn't mean that. I..."

Jules scooted away from Darcy, but the blonde caught her by the wrist. "Please, I'm in trouble. I need your help. I didn't mean to insult you. I don't want to sleep with you."

Jules stared at Darcy's hand on her arm then slowly raised her gaze to meet the author's sparkling blue eyes. The truth was she'd dreamed of sleeping with Darcy Lake.

"Please let me explain," Darcy pleaded.

Jules nodded, and Darcy pulled her back beside her.

"As you know, I'm the featured speaker this weekend. I am supposed to unveil my latest novel at the convention and let them meet my wife of ten years."

Jules motioned for Darcy to continue.

Darcy took a deep breath. "As of right now, my books haven't arrived, and I have no idea where they are. My wife isn't here and won't be. I'm just generally screwed."

Jules laughed at Darcy's last statement. She was surprised to hear such everyday slang coming from the gorgeous woman sitting beside her.

"Don't they know your wife?" Jules asked

"No, I've been very careful to keep my wife away from these functions and no one has ever seen a photo of her."

"If I agree to help you," Jules frowned, "what do you want me to do?"

"Pretend to be my wife," Darcy sighed, "stay by my side so no one hits on either of us and pray that my books arrive before the convention is over. These women can be vicious when things don't go as planned. Several of my rivals would love to see me with egg on my face.

"Of course, you'll have to dance with me and maybe even steal a kiss for the cameras, but I'll make certain the angle is such that your face won't be visible.

"You can sleep in your own room, just don't let anyone see you going into it or leaving it."

Jules thought of the repercussions of the arrangement Darcy was suggesting. If her plan fell apart the only one that would suffer would be the author. If it worked, it could provide an exciting weekend. The thought of being on Darcy Lake's arm all weekend definitely appealed to her.

"Would you autograph my book?" Jules set the condition of her agreement.

"Of course," Darcy laughed. "I'll sign all the books you want."

The waiter served their dinner as six women from the convention entered the room. Jules recognized four of them as well-known lesbian writers. She didn't know the other two. The women looked around the room then zeroed in on the couple.

"Here we go," Darcy mumbled as she laced her fingers through Jules'.

"Darcy," a woman with green and red streaked hair gushed as she closed in on the two women. "Connie said you were in here and this must be your lovely wife. Oh, my, she is a looker. No wonder you've kept her hidden from us."

"Honey, this is Rita Lafame. Rita, this is my wife, Jules," Darcy made the introductions. "Why don't you all introduce yourselves to Jules?"

The women rattled off their names and Jules graciously acknowledged them.

"We have just gotten our food," Darcy said. "We're going to eat dinner then get some rest before the festivities start in the morning."

"We could drag some tables together and all eat with you," Rita strongly suggested.

"No, not tonight." Darcy's response was firm and final. "I haven't seen Jules all week. I'd like some alone time with her before the convention starts."

Jules snuggled closer to Darcy loving the closeness of the other woman. *I wouldn't mind spending the night in your bed*, she thought before she could stop herself.

Jules stopped listening as Darcy tried to move the women away from them. She watched Darcy's lips as she spoke. They were full and beautifully shaped covering perfect white teeth. Without a doubt, Darcy Lake was the most desirable woman Jules had ever met.

"Don't you think so, honey?" Darcy squeezed Jules' hand pulling her from her reverie.

"Whatever you say, baby," Jules mumbled.

Darcy looked down at her and neither of them spoke as Jules held the blonde's gaze. "I was just saying we were tired and wanted to go to bed early tonight," Darcy said without moving her eyes from Jules'.

"Yes," Jules whispered.

"Registration starts at nine," Rita informed them. "You need to make an appearance sometime before noon. Call me and I'll meet you for brunch."

Darcy nodded as the women moved away filling the club with noise as they pulled enough tables together to accommodate all of them.

"Umm, you're right," Darcy leaned her shoulder against Jules, "this wine is excellent."

Jules couldn't explain the feeling that flooded her body at the other woman's approval of the wine. "I'm glad you like it."

Jules and Darcy talked as they dined. Darcy pointed out the good, the bad and the crazies as the lesbian authors congregated in the club. Jules laughed as the writer used descriptive adjectives to describe her peers.

You have no peers. You are in a class all by yourself, Jules thought as she gazed into the face of the woman she had nursed a crush on for the past ten years.

Darcy ordered one Crème Brûlée and two cups of coffee. "You must taste their Crème Brûlée," she insisted. "It is the best in the world. If we share it, we won't eat too many calories."

Jules flinched when the waiter ignited the dessert with a small blowtorch. Darcy's lovely face through the dancing flames was breathtaking.

"Thank you," Jules said as she finished her half of the dessert. "That was wonderful." She was acutely aware of the glances and nods they were getting from the other diners.

"I think they're talking about us," Jules whispered.

"We should give them something to talk about," Darcy grinned mischievously. She slowly leaned down and placed her lips against Jules'.

Darcy's lips were soft and smooth like...like rose petals. Of its own accord, Jules' tongue lightly traced Darcy's bottom lip. Darcy tasted sweet and dangerous at the same time; like Crème Brûlée and intoxicating wine. The room fell away. The entire world fell away as Darcy increased the pressure on Jules' lips and touched the tip of her tongue with her own.

Jules had no idea how long the kiss lasted. It could have been seconds or a lifetime. The only thing she knew for certain was that no one had ever kissed her the way Darcy Lake had kissed her.

"Now, *that* was wonderful," Darcy murmured against Jules' lips.

Jules bowed her head to hide the turmoil raging in her mind and body. For the first time, she was aware of the total silence that had settled over the room.

Darcy signaled the waiter for the check, then led Jules from the club. Shouts and wolf whistles followed their departure.

"What room are you in?" Darcy asked as the elevator door closed.

"Three-ten," Jules answered as she pulled her card from her purse.

"That's great." Darcy's smile illuminated the elevator. "My room is three-twelve. We are right next to each other. We can pull this off, Jules?"

Jules silently nodded. She was still reliving Darcy's kiss.

"What time do you want to go to breakfast?" Darcy asked as she unlocked her room. "It would be good if we can go down together."

"Is nine, okay?" Jules asked.

"Perfect," Darcy ducked her head into her room "We have adjoining rooms. Unlock your door when you get inside."

Jules inhaled deeply then unlocked the door between her room and Darcy's. Darcy was waiting on the other side.

"This couldn't be any better if we had planned it." Darcy's enthusiasm was overwhelming. "Now, if they will deliver my books, we will have an awesome weekend."

"Yes," Jules agreed. "Right now, I just want to take a shower and get some rest. *Preferably, a very cold shower.*

Goodnight, Darcy." She walked into the bathroom leaving open the door between their rooms.

Jules towel dried her hair as she walked from her bathroom. She was surprised to see the door between their rooms had been closed. She left a wakeup call for seven then slipped between the clean sheets. She hoped sleep would come soon. Reliving Darcy's kiss was pumping adrenaline into her body at an alarming rate.

Jules was no novice when it came to women. College had been a true education for her both academically and sexually. A beautiful woman by anyone's standards, she'd had flings with lesbians and straight women just checking out the "college experience."

After graduation, she had settled down and devoted herself to becoming the best possible in her career field and making Nana proud of her. She jerked as she realized that Nana hadn't crossed her mind all the time she was with Darcy Lake.

Jules fell asleep wondering if making love with Darcy would be like the smoking love scenes the author wrote in her books. If the way she kissed was any indication, it would be.

##

Living Two Lives will be released in March 2018.
We hope you have enjoyed reading this preview.

Printed in Great Britain
by Amazon